Murder among friends

In war-time London, wardens are checking for lights in the blacked-out streets, but inside Cecily Lightwood's flat, behind its thickly curtained windows, a party is in progress. Talented, vibrant Cecily has invited people from the literary and artistic world in which she moves. But somehow, though Cecily is radiant and excited, and though her guests include many old friends, the party is not going well. Everyone is waiting for the arrival of Aubrey Ritter, the handsome and famous playwright who has just moved into the flat upstairs following the suicide of his wife.

Ritter's non-appearance dominates the evening, distressing or annoying guests in differing degrees—until the party is finally shattered by a voice shouting wildly on the stairs, and the discovery of Ritter's savagely murdered body . . .

In the aftermath of questioning, one member of the party stands accused of Ritter's murder, but another, Alice Church, cannot believe that is the answer. As Alice talks desperately to Cecily and her friends, she learns much about Ritter's past, his many affairs, and the complex undercurrent of relationships between the party guests, but night-marishly little that would point to a different murderer, and nothing that could contradict the apparently firm evidence of the outsider who saw the accused on the stairs.

Elizabeth Ferrars has a deservedly high reputation for story-telling, and this superb mystery, first published in 1946, is stamped with the hallmarks of her popular style: acute observation of character, racy dialogue, and a particularly ingenious solution.

Also by Elizabeth Ferrars

The other devil's name
Unreasonable doubt
I met murder
The crime and the crystal
Root of all evil
Something wicked
Death of a minor character
Skeleton in search of a cupboard
Thinner than water
Experiment with death
Frog in the throat
Designs on life
Witness before the fact
In at the kill
Last will and testament
Murders anonymous
The pretty pink shroud
Blood flies upwards
The cup and the lip
Drowned rat
Alive and dead
Hanged man's house
The small world of murder
Foot in the grave
Breath of suspicion
A stranger and afraid
The seven sleepers
The swaying pillars
No peace for the wicked
I, said the fly
Murder moves in
Enough to kill a horse

Furnished for murder
The busy body
Fear the light
Murder in time
The doubly dead
A legal fiction
Ninth life
Zero at the bone
A tale of two murders
With murder in mind
Alibi for a witch
March hare murders
Hunt the tortoise
The lying voices
Milk of human kindness
The clock that wouldn't stop
Enough to kill a horse
Always say die
The sleeping dogs
Seeing double
Count the cost
Depart this life
Rehearsals for murder
Death in botanists bay
Your neck in a noose
Don't monkey with murder
Give a corpse a bad name
Remove the bodies
Skeleton staff
The wandering widows
We haven't seen her lately
Cheat the hangman

Elizabeth Ferrars

Murder among friends

Constable · London

First published 1946
by William Collins Sons & Co. Ltd
Copyright © 1946 by Elizabeth Ferrars
Reprinted 1987
by Constable & Company Ltd
10 Orange Street London WC2H 7EG
Printed in Great Britain by
St Edmundsbury Press Ltd
Bury St Edmunds, Suffolk

ISBN 0 09 466940 6

CHAPTER ONE

ALICE often tried to remember her first impression of Janet Markland. Her very first impression. What had she seen, what had she felt when she entered Cecily Lightwood's sitting-room and saw Janet Markland standing by the fireplace?

But it is never easy to be entirely honest with memory. Particularly if a first impression was not in reality a very strong one, all the knowledge and understanding acquired later tend to colour it with a richness and definiteness that it never possessed by itself. Alice always found it difficult to admit that in that first glimpse she had had no thoughts concerning the viciousness or gentleness of Mrs. Markland's expression. Such an admission suggested that there must be something lacking in her perceptions. Yet all Alice could truthfully say she had noticed on that first evening was a slender woman with a tired droop on her shoulders who was standing looking down into the fire, a woman who was about thirty-five, was wearing a plain, black, woollen dress and had soft light brown hair. Perhaps Alice might also have said that she was conscious of disappointment. From Cecily Lightwood's descriptions she had imagined that Mrs. Markland must possess a far more colourful personality than that of the woman by the fireplace. But later, of course, Alice was able to see that it was precisely Janet's unobtrusiveness and her apparent calm and mildness that had worked so remarkably on Cecily's difficult nerves. If Janet had been more arresting, more commanding, if her strength and her weakness had been less concealed, Cecily would long ago have quarrelled with her and in her jealousy and distrust would never have dreamt of asking Alice Church to meet her.

Cecily took Alice straight across to the fireplace and said: "Janet, Alice—Alice, Janet."

Mrs. Markland smiled and said: "There's an echo of Lewis Carroll about that, isn't there? How do you do, Mrs. Church? I've been so looking forward to meeting you."

As soon as she spoke Alice sensed the professional woman in

her. Controlled, assured and used to dealing with all sorts of people, her friendliness yet seemed a little mechanical, as if it were part of a technique.

Mrs. Markland went on pleasantly: " Have you been here before? I always think Cecily's flat's so beautiful. Mine's just a horrid mess."

" That isn't true, you're a much tidier person than I am," said Cecily fiercely, aggressive as she was in all disagreements and contradictions, even the most trivial.

" Ah, I know that, but that isn't what I meant," said Janet gently. " I meant your things, their arrangement, their colours. . . . There's nothing in my flat I really like, it's just a place I live in. I don't know how to choose things; I lose my nerve and buy the first thing I see. But even I can tell that the result's atrocious—and that this is lovely."

Cecily gave Alice a beaming glance which demanded that Alice should acknowledge at once, immediately, the extraordinary charm of Janet Markland's personality. Cecily seemed proud and possessive as if she were showing off a treasure.

She herself was looking charming that night. She was vivid and brilliant-eyed and excited. She had a splendid figure, which she dressed beautifully except for odd lapses into slovenliness, and her movements were still those of a girl. In a dress of a deep, bright blue and with her grey hair dressed in neat curls close to her head, with a glow in her cheeks and with the whole of her filled with an animation which made all her gestures fluid and graceful, she was really an astonishingly striking woman.

Turning away to a table, she picked up two glasses and as she put them into the hands of her friends, said: " I'm going to leave you two together. I want you to get to know one another. I'm not going to bother introducing you to the others, Alice——" Casually she gestured at the three men in the room. " I want you to talk to Janet, I want you to be friends; the two of you are just made for each other." Then with a warm smile to bless this friendship she had ordained, she moved away. Obediently Alice and Janet regarded, smiled at and tried to talk to one another.

Cecily lived in the ground-floor flat of an old converted house near Parliament Hill Fields. The rooms were high and spacious with big windows and solid marble fireplaces. They were old-fashioned and without any particular grace, but as Janet had just said, Cecily had succeeded in making them very attractive. The furniture was of apple-wood; the walls and carpet were of soft, dull green; there were some nice pieces of old English pottery, and the curtains, of coarse grey silk, heavily embroidered, were beautiful. Before the war Cecily had been a designer of embroideries and these curtains were specimens of her work. To Alice the delicacy and refinement of their colours were surprising. From what she knew of the exaggerations in Cecily's temperament she had expected boldness and crudity. An embroidery-frame with some cream-coloured linen stretched in it and a daylight bulb above it was set up at the far end of the long room. Evidently in the little spare time left over from the censorship department and from the Citizens' Advice Bureau where Alice had made her acquaintance, Cecily was continuing with her own work.

She had crossed the room to talk to a tall, stoop-shouldered man in uniform.

Janet spoke in a low voice: " I think you and I are going to feel rather uncomfortable together, Mrs. Church. We've heard too much about one another and it's difficult to pick up all the threads. You aren't in the least like I expected, you know, and I can see that I don't fit either with what I'm supposed to be. The best thing would be to forget all we've heard."

" I think perhaps I'd better try to do that with everyone in the room," said Alice, though she was wishing that Cecily had told her who the other people were. She wondered if the tall man in uniform with the long, pale face and neat little dark moustache was Frank Lely, the thriller-writer. Cecily, if all that she said of herself was true, had many interesting and talented friends. Her circle at any rate appeared to be very different from that to which Alice herself was accustomed.

" Ah, I know what you mean," said Janet. " You've probably heard all about Frank Lely's women and why they always break off with him, and all about Peter Willing's digestion, and all about Roger Mace's drinking and depressions. I suppose that embarrasses you now because you feel you've got to conceal it, since you realise how uncomfortable each of us would feel if we knew how much you know."

" I don't think I really know so very much," said Alice. " I just know Cecily's view of things."

" But Cecily's descriptions are very vivid," said Janet, " and even if they do tell one more about her than about the people she describes, still they're—" She hesitated. " They're like one stage in a colour process, aren't they? You don't get the whole picture till you've superimposed a few more colours, but still you don't have to discard what you started with. Cecily's very observant and reasonably truthful——" She made another pause. Alice thought she was wondering if she had spoken spitefully, and if so, what Alice was thinking of her for having done so.

After a moment Janet added: " But you know, I don't really mind what Cecily's told you about me—it's only that it puts one out of step, as it were, from the beginning."

Yet she looked uncertain of herself as she spoke and stared down into the fire again. As the glow lit up her pale face it struck Alice how melancholy she seemed and how tired.

At any rate, Alice decided, it would be best to forget everything that Cecily had told her about Janet Markland. That air of listlessness and defeat had had no place in Cecily's portrait of the successful business-woman, who, having married unhappily when she was quite young and soon left her husband, had slowly, after several years of poverty, won a footing for herself, first as a writer of magazine stories, then in publishing, and finally as the partner of Peter Willing, the literary agent.

His partner, Cecily, had stressed with unnecessary emphasis, answering the doubt which it would never have occurred to Alice to feel—his partner, not his mistress.

Janet, Cecily had explained, had been too hurt by her marriage to take much interest in men. Cecily seemed to admire and envy her for this while at the same time somehow resenting it, working herself up into queer, querulous fits of exasperation over what she described as Janet's repressions.

Cecily herself, if her own confessions were to be believed, fled restlessly from one attachment to another, though how deeply she really dared to involve herself Alice had not quite been able to make out. Less, she was on the whole inclined to think, than Cecily had hinted.

" Was it still raining when you got here? " Janet went on, attempting in the midst of some preoccupation to sound interested in what she was saying.

" No," said Alice, " it's cleared up, it's a rather beautiful night at the moment. It's very starry. I found a warden and a policeman discussing astronomy on the doorstep."

" Astronomy? " said Janet. " Really? "

" Yes. That's something good that's come out of the black-out, isn't it? " said Alice. " All sorts of people have suddenly got interested in astronomy."

" I suppose so, though I never could manage to understand anything about it myself," said Janet, " except perhaps its mythology. I find that much easier going than mathematics. In the same way, I've some liking for history, but I can't get anywhere with economics, which is very unfortunate, because one's hardly entitled to have an opinion on anything nowadays without some economics. Tell me, Mrs. Church, you've two children, haven't you? "

" Yes," said Alice.

" Boys or girls? "

" One of each," said Alice.

" How old are they? "

" Fourteen and sixteen."

" You look much too young to have children of that age," said Janet. But it was said automatically without much effort to make her hearer feel that she meant it. Alice, who had a short, stout body and greying hair and who was much too busy to be able to take much trouble with her appearance, felt irritated rather than pleased at having to disclaim the unconvincing compliment.

She was puzzled by Mrs. Markland. To talk appeared a great effort to her and there was a strange emptiness about her glance as if she was hardly aware of the existence of the person beside her.

Across the room Cecily, who seemed to have returned to some discussion that had started before Alice's arrival, was saving to the tall man in uniform: " Well, I tell you, I'm going to write a book myself some day. I've always thought there was a lot I could say if I chose, and I don't see why I shouldn't. I'm quite as clever and well-informed as a lot of people who keep doing it. Aren't I? " She turned suddenly to a small man who stood at her elbow. " Aren't I, Peter? *You* ought to know."

The small man laughed. He was a slender little creature of about forty-five with good-natured, pale blue eyes and with shaggy tufts of sandy hair standing up above a worried-looking, deeply wrinkled forehead. He looked nervy and excitable but had the air of someone who is always certain that he is the only person present who has balance and common sense.

" But then even I keep intending to write a book myself," he said, in a light, affable, tenor voice. " I had a very good idea for one once. I thought I should simply describe all the people I liked and then all the people I didn't. You know, that's as much as a great many writers ever do."

" You'll never write anything," said the tall man, grinning unkindly. " No one who says he means to ever does. It's only the ones who mean never to write another who keep on doing it—bloody fools."

" Come, Frank, that hardly fits you—you haven't let me have anything for three years," said Peter Willing with a sad little giggle. " Oh dear, oh dear, what a pity that is too."

" I made up my mind to write three books and then stop," said Frank Lely. He was sitting in a deep armchair, his long legs in their sharply creased khaki trousers crossed over one another and his long, bony hands, one of which had a large signet ring on one finger, folded over his stomach. His face was long and pale and singularly expressionless, his brown eyes were dull and his skin was heavily lined. " However," he went on, " if the war hadn't come along I'd probably have kept on and made a fool of myself. The war was a stroke of luck for me."

" That's disgusting," said Cecily sharply. " It's always

disgusting, I simply can't bear it, when people say they're glad there's a war. I hate it even when it's supposed to be a joke. And I hate your conceit, Frank. Of course you think you're playing us all a mean trick by depriving us of your wonderful talents, but that's just another bad joke. You've no real feelings about anything, that's what's the matter with you. That's why you have to write the disgusting sort of books you do. Personally, I'm glad you stopped writing. I've always loathed your books. As a matter of fact, I loathe your whole attitude of mind.'' She said it fiercely, extravagantly, and she meant it.

Though Frank Lely's face scarcely changed, he showed that he knew she meant it and that he resented it. Alice, uneasy at the sudden feeling of conflict, thought that he and Cecily must be the sort of old friends who in their hearts have always disliked one another, yet who feel in that very dislike a kind of security with one another.

Alice herself admired the work of Frank Lely. She had read all his three famous thrillers and had seen all the films that had been based upon them. She always said that the films didn't, of course, give you all that there was in the books, though in her heart she preferred the films which had had some of the sex and the violence censored out of them. But she found that the look of Frank Lely himself did not appeal to her. In that dull, unhealthy face and lounging form there was a curious nervous forcefulness, entirely mental, at odds even with the languor of the bony body, which gave her a feeling of acute repulsion. Without her quite realising what it was that she was feeling, she was, in fact, deeply intimidated by him.

The third man in the room, Alice concluded, must be Roger Mace. She knew from Cecily that he was a physicist, working at present in some Admiralty research department. He was a smallish man, thickset and fidgety and apparently far more interested in Cecily's whisky than in anything else in the room. He had wide shoulders, a shock of thick, fair hair, rather large, coarsely shaped features in a brown, leathery-skinned face, and he wore an old tweed coat, flannel trousers and a flannel shirt that was none too clean. Alice noticed that his smile was one of unusual gentleness and that when he did show signs of listening to what was being said, he kept a steady, innocent stare on the speaker.

Jokingly, as if she thought that Roger Mace was being left out of things, Janet suddenly said to him: " When are *you* going to write a book, Roger? Everyone does it sooner or later, you know."

" Give him another five years," said Lely. " By then his sense of scientific authority will have developed sufficiently to overflow into other fields—ethics, perhaps, or politics."

" Why should it? " said Cecily. " He's a scientist. He's interested in truth. You wouldn't understand that, Frank."

" Nobody's primarily interested in truth," said Lely. " They're merely interested in it as scientists, as politicians, as novelists, as parsons, as readers of fortunes in teacups—it's handling the idea of truth with their own particular apparatus that's really of interest to them, not the truth itself."

" Now," said Cecily, " you're simply quoting Rit. That's what he made Tom Robinson say in *Coal Dust.*"

" By the way," Peter Willing piped up in his high voice, " where *is* Rit? "

There was a silence.

Janet Markland turned her head and looked at Peter Willing, Roger Mace gave Janet one of his steady stares.

It was at about that time that Alice realised that Cecily's party was not going to be enjoyable. Unfortunately a group of preoccupied people who happen to know each other sufficiently well for antagonisms, grown dull and uninteresting with time, to be near the surface, is not the best material for a party.

Alice thought it was quite likely that no party given by Cecily would ever be a success. As soon as she was among a number of people some uncertainty of herself always forced her into sharp-tongued contradictoriness. Sitting on the arm of a couch, looking gay and red-cheeked and colourful in her bright blue dress, but with two little hard lines showing between her eyes, she kept on with her argument.

" It's because you haven't any ideas of your own, Frank,"

that you have to write in the way you do. You've got talent, in fact I admit you've probably got an unusual amount of it, but you've never dared to commit yourself to using it honestly. You don't use your mind honestly, you always make it stop short before it gets you anywhere. You seem to think that if only a thing's sordid enough, it's true——"

" Oh, God," said Lely in disgust.

" Do leave him alone, Cecily," said Janet, sitting down on the couch beside Roger Mace. " It seems to me we've heard all this before." The remark could have had a cut in it and perhaps it had, though it sounded good-natured.

Stopping herself at the start of a new sentence, Cecily made a face and said: " Oh well, it's only for his own good—I do think he has talent of a sort."

As if she thought the topic was a soothing one, Janet went on: " Mrs. Church, how d'you manage to have a family and a job? "

As Alice began to explain that the job was only part-time and that most of the family was in Canada, Cecily flung up her hand, struck it against her forehead and exclaimed: " I'd forgotten, I'd absolutely forgotten—Kitty hasn't come yet! Janet, I never told you, Kitty's coming."

" Kitty? " said Janet vaguely, the name obviously meaning nothing to her. Then suddenly, sharply, she added: " Kitty! ""

" Of course, Kitty Roper," said Cecily.

" Good heavens," said Janet, " I don't think I've seen her since——" She thought. " Well, not for ten years at least."

" I met her by accident the other day," said Cecily. " She hasn't changed a bit, but she's got three children, she told me. That's why I suddenly remembered about her when you talked of Alice's family. Kitty with three children—isn't it amusing? " To the others she explained: " Kitty was at school with Janet and me and then at college with us, and of course with Rit too—we used to think she'd marry him at one time, but after running around with half the men in the place she suddenly married a plain, elderly, country doctor and vanished out of sight. I should have thought she'd be miserable with him, still, she's just as beautiful as ever and just as—well, as vital. It was very refreshing to meet her."

" By the way," said Peter Willing again with a friendly pertinacity which seemed to be characteristic of him, " by the way, Cecily, where *is* Rit? "

Alice knew he meant Aubrey Ritter, the dramatist. Cecily had by no means omitted to mention that the author of *Coal Dust* was one of her more intimate friends.

Cecily smiled oddly and said: " He's upstairs."

" Upstairs? " said Willing, puzzled.

Leaning back on the couch, Janet Markland fixed her eyes on Cecily's face. There was no obvious change in her expression, nothing it would be easy to name, yet it did alter. Something in it stiffened and grew watchful. Roger Mace suddenly put his glass down as if he thought he had drunk enough, folded his square, muscular hands and stared down at them.

" Yes," said Cecily casually, " he's upstairs."

" But——" began Willing. He stopped and shot an inquiring glance at Lely.

" Poor old Rit," said Cecily, " it seemed the best thing to do with him. After all, somebody had to do something."

" Yes—yes, indeed," said Willing, " but——"

" But why upstairs? " asked Lely harshly. He did not look at Cecily as he spoke, but at Janet, with a strange, cruel curiosity in the look.

" There was an empty flat," said Cecily. " As a matter of fact, there were two empty flats. Rit's gone into the top one. Hadn't he told you that, Frank? "

" I only came on leave yesterday," Lely answered. " I haven't heard anything from him for about a month."

" Nobody has," said Willing. " Cecily, I'm awfully glad to hear this. I've been damnably worried about him. I tried to do something myself. I tried to take him off to Surrey with me. But he wouldn't let me."

In a quiet voice which brought Lely's glance back to her while a hard little smile appeared on his lips, Janet asked: " How long has he been here, Cecily? "

" Since the day before yesterday." Cecily turned to Alice as if she thought she might not be able to follow what they were all talking about. " You remember I was telling you about Aubrey Ritter, Alice, how his wife killed herself about a month ago, and how he's almost gone out of his mind since it happened? He blames himself, of course; that's why it's broken him up so badly. But it wasn't his fault, it really wasn't, though I suppose people always blame themselves when anything like that happens. But it was bound to happen anyhow, or something like it. I mean, if Rosamund hadn't killed herself, sooner or later she'd have . . . Peter, you know what I mean, don't you? She was always completely unbalanced and it was getting steadily worse. I just knew something would happen; I should think everybody knew it. Of course I didn't actually think of suicide—one doesn't face thoughts like that—but I did sort of expect a mental collapse of some sort. She and Rit—oh, that relationship was always a hopeless tragedy. Both were such wonderful people in their way and yet they always did each other the greatest possible harm. If each had had somebody placid and kind and ordinary to live with it would really have been far better. But of course that sort of person simply won't take an interest in placid, kind, ordinary people. They have a sort of instinct for being fascinated by just the types that are most dangerous to them. Anyway, it wasn't Rit's fault, it was just the way the cards fell. The whole thing was a hopeless tragedy from the start."

"A—hopeless—tragedy," muttered Lely, spacing the words with ironic emphasis.

Janet's eyes narrowed and she turned her face to the fire.

" And you managed to take charge of him and make him move in here so that you could keep an eye on him? " asked Willing, and leaning forward, he patted Cecily on the shoulder. " You really are the soul of goodness," he said gently.

As Cecily shrugged self-consciously, Alice saw that there were tears in her eyes. " It's just that somebody had to do something," she said.

Roger Mace had picked up his glass again. " Why hasn't he come down here this evening?" he asked.

" Oh, he's coming——"

Cecily broke off. A bell had sounded, ringing in the little kitchen that opened out of the sitting-room.

" That'll be Kitty! " she exclaimed. " I was beginning to be afraid she'd forgotten she'd promised to come." She whisked out into the hall, leaving the door open behind her.

Alice later found that she had no difficulty whatever in remembering her first impression of Kitty Roper. Probably few people ever had. It was an impression of colour, warmth and vitality. She came into the room ahead of Cecily, smiling already and full of interest and pleasure. She was a big woman, shaped with a splendid, healthy plumpness, she was rather untidy and more than a bit flashy. Her coat was of a grey Indian lamb, worn over a scarlet woollen dress which was held in round her far from slender waist by a belt of gilded leather. She had a heavy gilt necklace round her throat and chunks of gilt screwed on to the lobes of her ears. With her fair hair, done up in a gaudily striped turban, showing on her forehead in a cluster of dishevelled curls, with her fresh, fair skin, blue eyes and soft, full lips, gaily daubed with a few haphazard strokes of lipstick, she was like some magnificent doll, come to exuberant life.

She went straight up to Janet Markland, holding out both hands. " Janet, my love, isn't this awful, simply awful? " she said. " Ten years if it's a day. Things happen so, don't they? . I always find things keep happening. If one isn't having a baby, it's evacuees or American soldiers or something. If I hadn't happened to meet Cecily and if she hadn't simply insisted on my coming . . . Well, and when I explain that I came up from Hertfordshire just for this evening and the train was three-quarters of an hour late and I've sat for two hours in an unheated train and my fingers and toes are nearly dropping off me, you'll understand that—well, what I actually mean is, things are so difficult, they don't give one time to think, they overtake one, so that ten years pass and . . . But that isn't really what I mean at all. Here I am making excuses, and I don't mean to, I just mean to say I'm awfully glad to have met you again at last, and after all, you could always have looked for me if you'd wanted to. I've lived in the same place all the time, which is more than you've done. Still, you must be glad to see me too, you simply must! Let me look at you—" She had flung an arm round Janet's shoulders. " I want to see if you're glad to see me."

Janet appeared very slender and colourless in Kitty's embrace. Also, although she smiled and said in a good-humoured tone: " Cecily's right, you haven't changed one bit, Kitty," she looked as if, behind some superficial curiosity in her old friend, she was almost completely uninterested in her. There was no more warmth in her greeting than there had been in her greeting of Alice.

Kitty was the kind of woman who has sharp intuitions. After a short scrutiny of Janet, her eyes moved away from her to settle on Roger Mace.

" Who's this? " she asked with a warm, friendly glance at him which suggested that she would like him to understand that he was welcome to help himself to as much of her as he felt he could use. She was obviously a woman who enjoyed her own body and the stir it made in others. As Cecily introduced her to the others there, the same kind, simple, inviting look lighted on each of the men in turn.

As soon as she had smiled at and spoken to everyone, she turned with the air of someone who has recognised what she wants the moment she has seen it towards Frank Lely. His rather dull stare had been on her, moving over her consideringly, from the instant she came into the room. However, what she remarked at that point was: " But where's Rit, Cecily? You promised me Rit!"

" I—I don't know," said Cecily, and sounded worried. " I thought he'd have come down by now."

" I'm longing to see him," said Kitty. " I've kept thinking about him all the way here."

" Perhaps he's taken fright," said Willing. " He's been avoiding people."

" But he did promise he'd come down," said Cecily.

" I'm longing to see him," said Kitty again, her scarlet lips smiling at Frank Lely.

Cecily began uncertainly, " Perhaps I ought to go up and see . . ."

Janet cut in quickly: " Mightn't that annoy him if he doesn't want to come? "

" But he oughtn't to stay by himself so much," said Cecily. " It only makes him worse. It'd do him good to come down."

" Poor Rit," said Kitty, " I felt just awful when I read about Rosamund in the papers. I almost wrote to him but I couldn't think what to say. I couldn't tell him he mustn't worry too much because everyone had always expected it sooner or later anyhow."

" That's just what I've been saying," said Cecily. " Everyone did expect it."

" But really that sounds so terrible," said Peter Willing unhappily. " It makes one feel . . . Well, perhaps between us we could have done something."

" No, no," said Cecily, " you can't do anything with people like Rosamund. There's a sort of psychological pre-destination about it. God knows, I did what I could. I was fond of her, I really liked her. But with people as neurotic as that there's nothing you can do, literally there's nothing. I tried and tried—Janet, you know all the things I tried, don't you? Once I fixed up for her to go and see a psycho-analyst but she simply didn't go. So what could I do? She didn't want to change, that was the trouble. Janet, don't you think that was the point? She didn't *want* to get on top of her difficulties."

Janet seemed not to have heard the question. As Cecily repeated it, it seemed to reach Janet's consciousness suddenly and she nodded briefly.

Kitty repeated: " Anyway, I'm longing to see him." Looking round for somewhere to sit down, she took a chair close to Frank Lely's. " I expect he's changed a great deal, hasn't he? He was wonderfully handsome when he was young, but in that photograph of him with the story of Rosamund's death, he did look as if he'd changed dreadfully, poor Rit."

Janet frowned. " I didn't know you'd ever met Rosamund, Kitty."

"Oh, yes," said Kitty vaguely, "I met them together once."

"Cecily," said Willing, "perhaps someone ought to go up and see why Rit hasn't come down. I'll go if you like."

Cecily did not look as if she liked the suggestion. Perhaps she did not like the idea that anyone should share in her rôle of helper and comforter.

"No," she said, "no, I think not—I'll just telephone first and see what he says. Yes, that's what I'll do, I'll telephone." She crossed to the writing-table, sat down on a corner of it, picked up the telephone and dialled. "I'll tell him Kitty's here," she said. "I'll tell him he must come down. I'll tell him we're all waiting for him."

That indeed was what they were all doing; Cecily's party had turned simply into a business of waiting for Aubrey Ritter to come down. Alice had understood by now that in fact the party had been given only on Ritter's account and that, together with a desire to help the man over some sort of breakdown, Cecily was feeling a good deal of obvious pleasure in being able to demonstrate to her friends her ascendancy over him. But she was apparently expecting resistance from him about coming down to her party, for the moment she started speaking to him on the telephone, she adopted an accusing tone.

"Rit?" she said. "Rit, this is Cecily. Why haven't you come down, Rit? You said you would."

A buzzing sound told that Aubrey Ritter was answering her.

She frowned at whatever he had said and continued: "But you promised. Yes, you promised, Rit! I'm not going to let you off; it's for your own good, you know it is, you even admitted it yourself, you said you'd like to come. I simply insist on your coming . . . What?" The word was spoken sharply. During the next pause her frown deepened.

Meanwhile Janet Markland had begun talking in a low voice to Roger Mace, while Frank Lely was speaking softly to Kitty Roper. Only Peter Willing and Alice were still watching Cecily.

"All right," she said, "all right—I know what you mean,

Rit, you don't have to go into explanations . . . No, of course I'm not offended—as if I should 'be—it's nothing to me what you do, except that I can't help feeling you're being incredibly foolish . . . What? . . . No, Rit, that's something any fool could tell you . . . Oh, be quiet! That's an absurd sort of thing to say! '. . . All right, all right, I won't say any more." She slammed the telephone down, looking furious.

Peter Willing asked quickly: " He isn't coming? "

She gave him a confused look. " Oh, yes, he's coming, but he's been out, wandering around in the black-out and only just got in or something." She sighed sharply.

" Poor Cecily, you sound rather as if he's been putting you through it," said Willing sympathetically. " These nervous wrecks always take it out of other people. I think you're wonderfully good to him."

" You never told him I was here," said Kitty.

" Didn't I? " said Cecily abstractedly.

" No, I wish you had, I'd have liked to know what he said."

" It doesn't matter," said Cecily, " he'll be down soon." But an air of depression had completely quenched her vividness. Alice had seen these changes in her before. Sometimes she had thought that Cecily's youth and vigour must be the result less of real vitality than of some strange immaturity of spirit; her face could suddenly look so ravaged, so lined and peevish, while her handsome body would slump together as clumsily as that of a sulking adolescent, that she became, while the mood lasted, nothing but a bitter and cranky spinster with little emotional development and a grievance against the world.

Going towards the kitchen, she muttered dispiritedly: " I'll go and see about some food."

Kitty at once started to rise. " I'll come and help you, shall I, love? "

" No, no, there's really nothing to do," said Cecily. " You stay there and talk to Frank. And Alice and Janet, don't forget you're supposed to be getting to know one another." She disappeared.

To please her, Alice made an effort to talk to Janet Markland.

But during the last few minutes the preoccupation which had merely taken the liveliness out of Janet before, had developed into a complete inattentiveness. She managed to remember that she and Alice had· been talking of Alice's family, and in a tone of conscientious interest, asked again how many children Alice had. But before Alice could answer, Janet's thoughts had obviously slipped away again to whatever the subject was that was occupying them so grimly. It was something, of course, to do with Aubrey Ritter; Alice could tell that easily enough. Unfortunately she was finding it difficult to feel drawn to Janet. Unhappiness, unless it makes an open demand for sympathy, tends to exclude others and so has an appearance of callousness and self-absorption. As Alice again informed Janet's unlistening ears of the ages and sexes of her children, she realised that she felt rather repelled by her.

That was the time, however, when Alice began to take in Janet's appearance more carefully, so that later her memories of her features were surprisingly sharp. Janet's face was small below a high, straight forehead; her features were delicate but a little too thin; her eyes were grey and large under somewhat indefinite eyebrows; her hair was of the smooth, blonde, brown of oat-straw and very soft and fine so that although she seemed to have dressed it carefully, it kept a slightly limp and unfinished look; her body was slender with pleasing and quite feminine curves, and it was easy to imagine that when she was animated she would seem very attractive. Yet on the whole it was a colourless personality.

Kitty Roper came across after a few minutes and also tried to talk to Janet. But Kitty was not much more successful than Alice had been, though for a little while, as they talked of people they had known and of what had happened to them during the past years, Janet seemed to grow interested, and said some amusing things in a tone of natural friendliness. Kitty, thought Alice, probably had that effect on people. Probably it was largely because she took so little real notice of them; she talked, smiled, stirred and settled her fine body all

entirely for her own pleasure, and never questioned as she did
so that she was causing pleasure to others.

Yet in the middle of it Janet rose abruptly and walked out
of the room. She looked at nobody and said nothing to
anybody. The instant before it happened Alice had seen an
extraordinary thing happen to her face; suddenly, inex-
plicably, every trace of colour had drained out of it. At one
moment she had had pink cheeks, red lips and a smile, and
the next moment there was nothing there but a strained grey
mask with blank eyes burning in dark, hollow sockets. It
was at that moment, Alice always assumed afterwards, that
Janet Markland found the decision to act as she did.

But the decision must have taken her by surprise. It must
have happened suddenly and been a terrific shock to her, so
great a shock that as she rose and left the room she might have
been almost unconscious, with her eyes seeing little but
blackness all around her.

Kitty merely made a face, looked at Alice questioningly,
shrugged her shoulders and went back to the chair beside
Frank Lely. Alice found herself sitting next to Roger Mace.

He waited a moment then, as she found nothing to say,
gave her one of his steady, innocently penetrating stares and
said : " I think I know what you're thinking about."

" Really? " said Alice uncertainly.

" You're probably thinking," he said slowly and gloomily,
" that I drink too much."

Until he said that Alice had not realised that he was in fact
quite drunk.

" Well," she said, still wondering about that tragic trans-
formation of Janet's face, " you should know more about that
than I do. Do you? "

" No, don't—do not—say that sort of thing," he said very
earnestly. " It evades the issue. I am completely tired of, I
am absolutely washed up and finished with all women who
avoid issues. There are situations in which the capacity to
abide by a decision becomes a moral obligation. What do
you think? "

She thought about it, puzzled. In some way, she felt, his
sudden talkativeness and his gloom were connected with

Janet's abrupt departure. " Perhaps if issues have really been avoided, decisions haven't really been taken," she said.

" Unfortunately," he said, " you've got something there, Mrs. Church. Church . . . Any relation of Oliver Church? "

" He's my husband," said Alice.

" Oh," said Roger Mace, " so you're married to *that* Church? "

" Yes," she said. " Do you know him? "

" I used to work under him once. He can drink too."

" Yes," said Alice with a smile, " I know that."

" Ah, so you don't like it, eh? "

" Oh, I don't think I've ever been much disturbed by Oliver's occasional orgies."

Roger Mace eyed her narrowly. " I'm sorry," he said ponderously, " that was probably a much too personal question. I apologise, I oughtn't to have asked it. But I didn't mean it in that sense. It's simply that I'm rather drunk myself at the moment, and I'm sorry to think that it should offend you."

Alice tried to reassure him that anyone who could drink so much and keep their dignity as he was doing, did not offend her in the least.

He brushed that aside.

" But after all, Mrs. Church," he said, " when you consider things—as I hope I always try to consider things—dispassionately—and that, let me tell you, is usually a bloody farce to begin with—but as I was saying, when you consider things, and when you know there's nothing you can do but sit still and look on——"

" At what? " she interrupted.

" At the things which you are, I hope, considering."

" Ah," she said, " yes."

" In that event," he said, " can one really do anything but get drunk, as decently as possible, but fairly often? "

" Perhaps not," said Alice.

Again he looked at her searchingly. At that moment it occurred to Alice that perhaps he was not really drunk at all, that he was one of the people who can never quite succeed in getting drunk and who force a kind of exaggerated pretence of it to deceive themselves.

" No," he said in a deep, solemn voice, " you're avoiding the issue again, Mrs. Church. It's possible you don't recognise it, but you *are* avoiding the issue."

" Very well then," said Alice briskly, " I'll tell you what I think, if you really want to know. I think that there are times when, if people don't drink, something much worse happens to them."

" Ah, yes, that's simple, that's sense, but you don't really think it," he said, shaking his head uneasily. " The truth is, drinking offends you. I'm sorry, for I'm very much enjoying this talk of ours, much more than I expected to enjoy anything at this party. I should really very much like to leave with you and go and drink elsewhere. What d'you think? Does the idea appeal to you? This party's damnable. One just sits looking on . . . You know, I always dislike looking on at things. I dislike looking on at things and being unable to do anything. Take this war, for instance. I dislike looking on at it very much indeed. It's very comfortable, of course, and very gratifying to one's self-esteem, to think one's talents are so extraordinarily important that one simply has to go on using them, but there's something about it that makes one drink a great deal. It's the looking on, you know, and having too much time to think, and not being able to do anything. Because if people avoid issues and haven't the moral stamina to abide by decisions, there's nothing you can do. One's powers of action are at all times intolerably limited."

" I think," said Alice, " you're getting just a little bit mixed up."

" That's true, I am," he said. " That's very true. Thank you for pointing it out, Mrs. Church. Fixedly, all the time he was talking, he was keeping his eyes on the door through which Janet Markland had vanished.

As he went on it occurred to Alice that in Cecily's descriptions of him there had been no mention of the fact that he was in love with Janet Markland. Thinking it over, Alice recognised that in Cecily's eager confidences about the private lives of her friends and in her minute analyses of their

characters, very little was ever said of their relations with one
another. Of Roger Mace she had said that she had known him
for a couple of years, that he was ugly and dynamic, drank
too much, suffered from terrible bouts of morbid depression
but was very gifted, with the rigorous, logical mind of the
scientist. To Alice who had lived most of her adult life with
a scientist and had long ago come to the conclusion that the
minds of scientists are no more logical than anyone else's, are
as subject to emotional interference as those of other people,
function as irrationally, and rely, even to a peculiarly high
degree, on intuition, that had not sounded like very careful
observation. All the same, she could not understand how
Cecily could have managed to spend even a few minutes in the
same room as Roger Mace and Janet Markland without
realising that he was wretchedly, unhappily in love with her,
in a state of bitter conflict with her over some indecision of
hers, and also tense with jealousy over her relations with
Aubrey Ritter. But there again, except that Cecily had
once told Alice how much Ritter owed to Janet's professional
help, Alice would scarcely have guessed that he and Janet
were acquainted. It appeared that it was only what Cecily
felt for her friends and believed that they felt for her that was
interesting enough to her to be mentioned.

It was during a sudden silence that Janet came quickly
back into the room.

At once Roger Mace withdrew his eyes from the door and
turned wholly to Alice, but he immediately lost his way in a
question he started to ask about her husband, fumbled with
the words and said no more.

Janet did not come towards them. She perched on the arm
of Peter Willing's chair and said something in his ear which
made him burst out laughing. But then she looked across at
Roger Mace, held his glance deliberately for a moment and
smiled. There was a strange air of excitement about her and
a glow of red on her cheek-bones; perhaps there was even a
kind of wildness about her. The change that had taken place
in her since she had left the room was astonishing. But when
a moment later she got up and came quickly over to the fire,
holding out her hands to it, they were blue and trembling.

" Ouch," she said, " I'm frozen! "

Just then in the street outside somebody shouted: " Put that light out!"

Janet looked around for the glass she had set down some minutes earlier, filled it and drank it off quickly.

" Well, Mrs. Church," she said, turning her new, excited smile on Alice, " you and I haven't got very far in the business of getting to know one another, have we? I'll tell you what we must do—parties aren't any good—you must come and have lunch with me. It would be a pity to disappoint Cecily, wouldn't it, when she's arranged things so well? One can always trust Cecily, you know, to arrange things. It's part of her genius——"

" What happened to you just now?" Roger Mace interrupted her harshly. " Where did you go?"

" To telephone," she answered. " I suddenly thought of somebody I'd promised to telephone."

" Couldn't you have done it from here? "

" Rather public, isn't it? And I didn't want to disturb everyone with a lot of dull business conversation." She shivered. " It's horribly cold outside. But it's a beautiful night, the rain's quite stopped and the sky's all stars. You know, that's really one good thing that's come out of the black-out—you can see the stars . . ." She pulled herself up with a sudden look of uneasiness as if she had just remembered that Alice had said something of that sort earlier. " Well, Mrs. Church," she went on, " what about my suggestion? Shall we have lunch together? "

" Will you put that light out! "

The cry came from directly outside one of the tall, thickly curtained windows of Cecily's sitting-room.

Cecily looked in from the kitchen.

" Can he mean us? " she said. " You haven't any of you moved any of the curtains, have you? " Then she added in a tone of annoyance: " Hasn't Rit come down yet? I do believe he really doesn't mean to."

Peter Willing replied that nobody had touched the curtains. Shrugging her shoulders and muttering: " Damn fools, they're always plaguing one," Cecily disappeared into the kitchen again.

Kitty Roper remarked: " You've no idea how fussy they are about the black-out round us. One day a poor policeman had to cycle all the way out from Aylesbury to tell us that a light had been reported in one of our windows, and all it actually was was one of the boys hunting around with a torch in the playroom, after he was supposed to be in bed, for a book to read. Neighbours are such ridiculous busybodies. In London, where you haven't got any neighbours—real ones, I mean—you never realise what a mixed blessing——"

Just then several things happened.

Of some of those things, particularly of the sounds that she heard at that moment, Alice afterwards retained the clearest recollection. The bell tinkling sharply and the voice, high up in the house, shouting, left some mark in her mind that never faded. Yet most of what happened then became blank, a blank that had a feeling of the deepest horror attached to it, yet which had in itself no meaning.

It always made her think of an occasion when she had been knocked down by a car. Of that she could remember standing at the edge of the pavement and then finding herself lying in the road, and she had a curious, physical sort of memory of screaming, a memory of her throat opening to force out the sound. But she had no memory whatever, not the most fugitive image, of the approach of the car itself nor of the feeling of the blow as it struck her.

Thus, in Cecily's room, she knew that all of a sudden there was a commotion. She knew that she herself jumped to her feet and then that everyone, crushing together, crowded out into the passage. She knew that the bell started ringing and was reinforced by the impatient clattering of the knocker, and that that voice upstairs, followed by the rush of feet on the staircase, sent a wave of horrifying panic through everyone in the room. But how they all moved, what their faces told, who opened the door, who reached the passage first, who spoke or what they said, all vanished, all were as completely missing from her experience, as the impact with the moving car.

The point at which memory emerged from the blank was when she suddenly realised that Frank Lely was holding a slight, khaki-clad figure in his grip and with his long, pale face thrust close to the stranger's, was bellowing something at him, while the stranger, writhing in his long arms, was shouting back: " It's murder, that's what it is! Can't you get that?— it's murder!"

CHAPTER TWO

NONE of them believed it. None of them doubted that Aubrey
Ritter was dead, but it was suicide that they feared. They had
had that fear in their minds ever since the death of Aubrey
Ritter's wife. From the way that they had reacted to the
shouting of the strange voice upstairs, it looked as if they had
almost consciously been waiting for the tragedy of self-
destruction to repeat itself.

It was a pity that Alice could not remember what her eyes
actually saw at the moment when the shouting started. She
had been looking at Janet Markland's face and it must have
been some change there that she saw before she saw anything
else. If she could have remembered it she might have had
something of interest to tell. But in fact she remembered
nothing of Janet until some minutes later, when she happened
to notice her, looking stunned and uncomprehending, standing
in the middle of the passage, with Cecily, who had just come
out through the door that led directly from the passage into
the kitchen, putting an arm round her shoulders and
exclaiming softly: " Oh God, oh God, Janet. . . !"

The stranger whom Frank Lely was still gripping by the
arms was a young American airman. He was still trying to
make them take in what he was saying: " It's murder! The
guy up there, he's dead, he's been hit with something, it's
murder—can't you get that?—it's murder! "

" Now then, now then, what's all this? " asked a voice
from the doorway.

The front-door had been opened by Peter Willing. On the
doorstep stood a warden and a constable. Under their helmets,
silhouetted against the starry darkness of the sky, their faces
showed the greatest astonishment. The warden still had a
finger on the doorbell.

As the group in the hall fell silent, the policeman stepped
inside. Closing the door firmly, in spite of an exclamation
of annoyance from the warden, he repeated: " Now then,
what's all this? "

" I've been trying to tell them, but they don't seem to take it in! " the American burst out. " There's a guy up there with his skull smashed in."

" *Who's* got his skull smashed in? " asked the constable sternly.

" I dunno—a guy I've never seen in my life," said the American. " I was coming to see some friends of mine— friends of my folks, that is—and what I find is this guy I've never seen in my life, lying up there with his skull smashed in." He looked very young, twenty-one or -two perhaps, and was smallish and slenderly built. His face, which had flamed angrily while he was struggling with Lely, had taken on a look of strained excitement and pallor. " I'm not feeling so good," he added uneasily. " All I was expecting to see was some friends of my folks and what I find is this big guy with his brains all over the carpet."

A snarling exclamation broke from Frank Lely. He plunged at the stairs.

" Stop that! " shouted the constable.

But Lely went leaping up the stairs, turning the bend in them and disappearing. From the hall they could hear the rapid pounding of his feet as he mounted to the top floor.

For a moment the constable hesitated, then he opened the door again and spoke hurriedly to the warden. Turning back to the group at the bottom of the stairs, he went on: " None of you's to leave here; you're all to stay where you are! " Then he strode after Lely and disappeared upstairs.

One of the most horrible silences that Alice had ever experienced settled on the people who stood waiting in the cold, empty passage. It was a gloomy place with old, dreary decorations. Chocolate-brown lincrusta covered the lower half of the walls, while the upper half was papered in faded greys and greens, picked out with what had once been gold but which was now so tarnished that in most places it looked like splashes of dark mud that had clung to the paper in wavering lines and splashes. Red and green linoleum covered the floor and a dull red carpet the staircase. The only light hung just inside the front-door, close to the fanlight which had been permanently blacked-out with brown paper. Since the lamp itself was sheathed in a long cone of paper, the whole place looked so shadowy, so bleak and sad, that to wait there, shivering with the cold and the half-knowledge of what had happened upstairs, was like standing in one of those terrible ante-rooms that occur in nightmares.

The silence was broken by the warden who started rattling the letter-box to attract attention and when the door was opened said: " Hey, you in there—that light's still on! "

Cecily asked angrily: " What light? There isn't any light!"

" It's the light on the stairs, Miss Lightwood," said the warden.

" There isn't any light on the stairs," said Cecily.

" I'm afraid there is," he said. " I've been trying to draw your attention to it for the last ten minutes. It shows distinctly through the curtain. Murder or not, I must ask you to put it out, or else to screen it more efficiently."

" I don't know what you're talking about, there isn't any light, it's just the same as usual," Cecily snapped and shut the door in the man's face. But as she was turning back to the others her glance fell on the young American. " You," she said sharply, " did you do anything to the light or the black-out on the staircase? "

" No, ma'am," he said.

" Are you sure? You didn't twitch the curtain back or anything? "

" Why would I do that? " he asked.

" I don't know why you would do it. Did you? "

" No."

" Then I don't know what that fool of a man's talking about," said Cecily, and shrugging her shoulders, returned to Janet and started whispering to her.

Janet made no response and looked as if she was not taking in anything that Cecily was saying to her. She stood there rigidly with the stunned look on her face, a look which made it appear dull and stupid and tired. The young American whose eyes had been examining one face after another, seemed suddenly to see her. Perhaps he had not noticed her before because of the shadows and her black dress. As soon as he saw her he stirred sharply. His mouth opened as if he were about to exclaim, but then, as if he had suddenly comprehended something horrifying about what he had intended to say, he clamped his lips shut. A wave of red flooded over his neck and face.

Janet saw none of it. Nor did Roger Mace, who was staring vacantly up the stairs after Frank Lely and the constable. Frowning heavily, Roger looked as if he were trying to decide how much of what appeared to be happening could be real and how much was the result of the whisky he had drunk. The only one besides Alice who noticed the American's behaviour was Peter Willing. As he saw it and pondered it a look of bewildered alarm clouded his small, kind blue eyes.

Presently more police arrived.

As they tramped upstairs, Cecily exclaimed: " Well, for the Lord's sake, I don't know why we're all standing here! We could anyway go back to the fire and keep warm."

They trooped back into the sitting-room. As the American lingered behind, Cecily turned to him. " Come along," she said brusquely, " they're going to keep you hanging about heaven knows how long, you'd better come in with us."

" Thank you, ma'am," he replied politely and followed her in.

Peter Willing, who had gone straight to the table where the drinks were, poured out a glass of whisky and brought it across to him.

" Here," he said, " I expect you'd like this. That must have been a very upsetting experience you've just had."

The boy said nothing until he had drunk. Then he observed laconically: " That's pretty good Scotch." He was still very cautious, very wary and suspicious. His pleasant, sensitive face was aloof and pale. Alice looked at his sleeve and saw that he was a sergeant. Also she noticed that instead of the usual array of ribbons on his uniform, he wore only the blue combat-ribbon and she liked him for it.

Roger Mace and Janet Markland had sat down side by side on the couch. Cecily had dropped into a chair and was sitting with her head in her hands. Kitty Roper had disappeared into the kitchen and from the sound of things was making tea.

Peter Willing started walking about, apparently assuming that he must help and sustain people and smoothe out their difficulties for them, but not quite knowing how to set about it.

The truth was that at that moment nobody needed help. They were all in that state of stupor in which, like people who have just received concussion, they were still able to move about and think and speak with deceptive normality. It is usual for the first moments of a calamity to be quite easy to bear. Habit opposes the uprising of too great a distress, the old mode of existence has not yet pased over into the new, and at such times trivial actions, like making a cup of tea or lighting a cigarette, seem sufficient to protect the thin little crust of consciousness to which life, without our fully realising it, has been reduced.

Uneasily Alice recognised that far more of her own feelings than she liked to admit were taken up with reflecting that if only something had happened to prevent her coming to Cecily's party, she need never have become involved in the horror of it. She felt almost glad that the American obviously felt the same. When Peter Willing went on trying to make friendly conversation with him, he gave monosyllabic answers and stared at the floor. Yet now and then, as if he were powerless to help himself, his glance slid back with puzzled concentration to the face of Janet Markland.

When the police and Frank Lely returned from the flat upstairs it was the American whom the Detective Inspector, who had arrived by then, first wanted to question.

The questions and answers, tersely given, ran something like this :

" Your name? "

" Ed Larg—Edward J. Larg."

" Address? "

He gave it.

" It was you who found the body? "

" Yes."

" Did you recognise the dead man? "

" No, I've never seen him in my life."

" Then what were you doing in his flat? "

" I didn't know it was his. I thought it belonged to some
folks called Smith. They're some friends of my folks back
home. It said Smith on the bell."

" You rang the bell, did you? "

" Sure."

" Who answered it? "

" Nobody."

" Then how did you get in? "

" Through the door. It was open."

" What, wide open? "

" No, it just wasn't closed. I rang a few times and then
I saw the door wasn't closed so I thought maybe I was meant
to walk right in, so I did. I knew the Smiths lived right up at
the top, so I went right on up."

" Did you see anybody? "

" Yes."

" You did? " This question came quickly.

" Sure."

" Whom did you see? "

" A woman."

The Inspector stirred, settling his big body more comfortably
in the chair he had taken. In the rest of the room there was
absolute stillness.

" Where was this woman? " was the next question.

" On the stairs."

" Near the foot of the stairs? "

" No, up at the top of them."

" What, you saw this woman near the top-floor flat? "

" Yes, just coming out of it."

" You mean you actually saw this woman come out of the
flat in which you found the dead body? Please be very careful
in your answer. If you find you cannot remember exactly
what you saw, please say so."

" I remember all right. I saw her on the landing. There
isn't any door, so I don't know if you can say she was in the
place or not, but she was right there on the landing. I was
on the half-landing below. She ran down past me and into
one of the rooms of the second-floor apartment."

" The empty one? "

" Oh, it's empty? "

" Yes."

" Well, she ran straight into one of the rooms. I reckoned she lived there."

" Can you describe her? "

Ed Larg hesitated. He stared so hard at the Inspector that it was obvious he was taking pains not to let his glance slip round to anyone else in the room.

" I didn't see her very well," he said eventually. " I didn't look very hard. You know the way it is—I reckoned from the way she acted she didn't want to be seen."

" Oh, did she try to hide her face or something like that? "

" That's right. As soon as she saw me she threw an arm up over her face and ran right down past me."

" But didn't you catch sight of her clearly while she was up there on the landing above you? "

" There wasn't any light up there. I only saw her properly when she was passing under the light on the landing below me, and then she had her back towards me."

" Then perhaps you can describe how she was dressed and the colour of her hair."

" Sure, I can do that."

" Well? "

" She was wearing a black dress and her hair was kinda brown." And as if he could not control himself any longer, Ed Larg flicked a quick glance at Janet Markland.

Though he saw the glance, the Inspector went on impassively: " Could you recognise this woman if you saw her again? "

" I told you," said Ed Larg, " I never saw her face. I only saw her properly when she went under the light below me and then all I saw was that she was wearing a black dress and that her hair was kinda brown. Honest, that's all I can tell you."

The Inspector accepted it. " Well, sergeant," he said, " when you got up to the top flat, what happened then? "

" I found one of the doors was open," said Ed Larg, " and I called out, ' Is anybody home?' but I didn't get any answer, so I went in the room and switched on the light and then I saw this guy on the floor, this big guy with the black hair, and the way he was lying with his head all covered with blood, I thought he was dead, but then I saw his hand was twitching and I heard what sounded like he was saying something, so I bent over him. He went on mumbling but I couldn't make anything of it, and then I heard him say a word . . . And then he gave a jerk and went limp and I reckon that that was really when he died."

" How long had you been in the room before that happened? "

" I don't know. Two or three minutes, maybe. I was thinking maybe I could do something for him."

" And he said a word, did he? "

" Yes."

" You heard it distinctly? "

" Sure."

" What was it? "

" ' Janet.' "

" He said ' Janet '? "

" Yes, that's what he said."

" You're certain of that? Janet? Simply Janet? "

Ed Larg nodded. His face was wooden as if he wished to make it clear that he had no concern with the implications of his evidence.

It was about then that the Inspector began to wear a slightly hurried air as if, since everything was turning out to be much simpler than he had expected, he could afford to feel impatient.

" Just one more question, sergeant," he said. " When you ran downstairs you were shouting ' Murder! ' What made you leap to the conclusion that the man you found had been murdered? Didn't you think of accident or suicide? "

" If a guy wants to kill himself on purpose or by accident," said Ed Larg, " he doesn't usually do it by smashing his head in with a poker, does he? "

Cecily gave a long sigh which had a strangled sound in it as if it might turn into a scream at any moment.

" Thank you, sergeant," said the Inspector, " you've been very helpful."

He had plainly been about to say more, but before he could bring it out an interruption came from the couch where Janet Markland, sitting very upright with her hands locked together in her lap, had been listening to the quick questions and answers with eyes shifting backwards and forwards from one face to the other as if she were watching a tennis-match. There had still been the dull, hurt, stupid expression on her colourless face. When Ed Larg had spoken of the woman in the black dress there had been no change in her rigidity or her vacant attentiveness. In everyone else in the room there had been some change, some movement, but in Janet there had been no sign that she had even understood what had been said. When Ed Larg first said that Aubrey Ritter had died mumbling the word " Janet " there had still been no change. It had not been until a moment later that the quick movement of her eyes had stopped, that they had widened suddenly with a stare of unbearable realisation, and that, starting to rise but collapsing instead in a limp heap on the couch, she shrieked out in a high cracked voice: " Yes, yes, it's true, I did it! "

What followed had a gruesome inevitability.

She was given water to drink, she was soothed, comforted, begged to control herself, asked if she wanted to make a statement and warned that anything she said might be taken down in writing and used as evidence, and then she was questioned.

Afterwards everyone else was questioned in turn, the facts piled up, the unavoidable conclusion was reached.

Perhaps even if Janet Markland had never made her terrible admission, if she had kept her nerve and her wits about her and had insisted on reserving her defence, she would still have found the evidence too strong against her. The evidence of the American by itself would have been almost enough to cause her arrest. But as it turned out, his story was backed up by that of the warden and the constable who had been talking together on the pavement and who stated that they had seen no one but the American enter or leave the house later than the arrival of Mrs. Roper. This was also backed up by all those who had been in Cecily's sitting-room, all of them having to admit that Janet had been gone from the room

at the relevant time. True, Cecily also had been out of the
room then; she had been in the kitchen, and the kitchen,
besides the door that led straight into the sitting-room, had a
door into the passage; she could have slipped out and gone
upstairs without anything being known of it. But Cecily's
bright blue dress, under the landing light, could not possibly
have been taken for black.

To check this last point, the Inspector made Ed Larg go
back to where he had been standing on the stairs when he saw
the woman, and then made Cecily, Janet, Alice and Kitty run
down the stairs in turn and pass under the light. The boy
became reluctant to say anything more, looked troubled and
said that somehow it all seemed quite different now, and that
he didn't want anything he might say to hang anybody. But
finally he had to admit that the only dress that looked black
was Janet's; Kitty's looked red, Cecily's blue and Alice's pale
grey. Further, Kitty's hair was a dazzling blonde, and
Cecily's and Alice's noticeably grey, and Ed was quite certain
that the woman he had seen had had brown hair.

A long careful search followed through the house and all
round it for any black garment that might have been snatched
up by the woman before she went up to Aubrey Ritter's flat
and discarded later. The search was excruciating to the nerves
of all who were waiting and revealed nothing. Cecily had a
black velvet evening dress hanging in her cupboard but it
was covered with small silver stars which gleamed in the light
and which Ed Larg was positive he could not have missed
if he had seen them. She had a black and white check suit,
but at that also he shook his head. Nothing like a black coat
or shawl was found, nor even one of a very dark brown or
blue or green which might have been mistaken for black.
Cecily, as it happened, nearly always wore bright colours.
The coats of her visitors were, one grey lamb, one camelhair,
one red and green tweed, one khaki and two light-coloured
raincoats.

Janet watched, listened and answered with a vague,
bewildered resignation. Sometimes she screwed up her eyes
as if she were making a tense effort to understand and often
she passed the tip of her tongue along her lips, but when

one after the other her friends burst out that it was impossible, that there was some dreadful mistake and that it was certain that someone else must have come in from outside, she looked from one face to the next with almost as much bewilderment at their defence of her as at the police accusations.

Even her own answers did not help her. If she had admitted more or admitted less she would have done herself less harm. But all discretion seemed to have left her. It might actually have helped her, for instance, if she had admitted going up to Aubrey Ritter's flat, but though the Inspector gave her several opportunities to alter what she had told him of her absence from the sitting-room, she stuck stubbornly to her first story.

" I went outside—I went to the corner to the telephone-box," she said, growing more excited each time she repeated it. She was not far from hysteria. " I did go outside—I can only tell you I *did*!"

" But the constable and the warden testify that nobody left the house, Mrs. Markland," the Inspector reminded her patiently.

" But I did go out," she cried with a thin note of agony in her voice.

" But, Mrs. Markland——"

" I did, I did, I went out and telephoned. I didn't want to use the telephone here, I didn't want to disturb anyone, so I slipped out—I just went out and went to the corner and came back again. I dare say they didn't see me. They were talking. They were looking up at the sky and talking about the stars. Probably they just didn't notice me. I didn't think they noticed me at the time. They were engrossed, they were arguing—it's quite likely they shouldn't have noticed me, isn't it? Isn't it, Inspector? You know it's quite easy not to notice a person if you're arguing. That's all that happened— they simply didn't notice me."

The Inspector said: " You can be quite sure all that will be taken into consideration, Mrs. Markland. Now please tell me, to whom did you telephone? "

From the start she gave it might have been thought that she had not expected this question to be put to her. She frowned.

After a moment she started to look more collected. " It was about a private matter," she said coldly.

" But it might provide you with a valuable alibi if you were able to tell me who answered your call," the Inspector explained quite kindly.

" Oh? " she said, surprised. " Oh, yes, I see." Then she shook her head. " No," she said.

" No? Was there no answer? "

" Yes, he answered. He——" A look of pain crossed her face. " No," she said again.

" Please, Mrs. Markland——"

" I don't want to answer any more questions."

" You are not obliged to do so, of course, yet it might be in your interests to tell us more about this."

" It wouldn't help, he couldn't say——" She stopped herself. Her gaze grew fixed once more with a queer, bright blankness, the result of her effort to fight back her tears. " No," she muttered.

" Are you implying that it was Aubrey Ritter to whom you spoke? " asked the Inspector.

" Careful, Janet! " begged Peter Willing, moving forwards. " There's no need for you to say anything. Don't —please don't! You should have a lawyer."

She shook her head. A few tears overflowed, trickled down her face and splashed on to her fidgeting hands. But suddenly she seemed to grow weary of resistance; she sighed and resignedly admitted : " Yes, it was Rit."

" It was Mr. Ritter to whom you spoke on the telephone? "

" Yes, he was supposed to be coming down to the party and I rang him up," she said, " and told him that it would be better if he didn't come."

The sound of a quick little intake of breath came from Cecily. She was sitting hunched up and wretched in one of her deep armchairs.

" Why did you do that, Mrs. Markland? " asked the Inspector.

Janet had started dabbing at her tears. She went on dabbing at them as if she had nothing else to think about at the moment. Yet at length, without prompting, she replied simply: " I didn't want to see him."

" Why didn't you want to see him? "

" That doesn't matter. It was just something . . . It doesn't matter. But I shouldn't have done it. That's so clear now. It seemed a good thing to do, it seemed so inevitable, but it was wrong—oh, God, it was wrong, it was a terrible thing to do! " Her voice rose wildly.

" Janet! " implored Peter Willing.

Roger Mace suddenly got up, sat down again and put his face in his hands, starting to mumble inaudible words into his fingers.

" It was an awful mistake! " Janet cried, her whole body beginning to shake. " I shan't ever be able to forget it or forgive myself. I don't know how I shall be able to live with that in my mind. I can't—I can't think—think—what I— think—I said—I can't, I can't! " It had sunk to an unintelligible mutter, then rose shrilly to a scream. She struck both her fists against her temples.

The Inspector spoke sharply; " Mrs. Markland! "

Several people started speaking all at once, protesting and arguing. He stopped the outburst with a stern gesture.

" Mrs. Markland," he went on, " you began this with a voluntary statement that you had murdered Aubrey Ritter. Do you wish to add to or retract that statement? "

With a jerk Janet Markland stood upright. The wild stare she fixed on him made it easy to wonder how Janet Markland could ever have been taken for a clever woman, a shrewd, controlled woman, a woman of the world. Standing there she simply looked terrified, bewildered and ill. But it is a fact that torment does not conduce to an appearance of dignity; pain always has an element of the humiliating in it.

" But I didn't say that," she said almost childlishly.

" There are many witnesses to the fact that you did say it," said the Inspector.

" No," she cried, " there can't be! "

" There are."

" But I didn't say it, I never said it! "

She stuck to that and nothing could shift her. Shaking her head like a frightened but stubborn child, and reiterating that she had never said it, had never said anything like it, she only grew more excited when the precise words she had been heard to use were repeated to her. She went on denying them. At last she started weeping again, helplessly this time, with great shaking sobs. Mercifully that put an end to the interrogation.

Soon after that her coat was fetched, her bag was thrust into her hand and with her head bowed and no glance for anybody in the room, she was taken away. There was a look of extreme solitariness about her as she went out in the midst of the group of burly men.

Another silence began after the policeman had gone. The room had a feeling of cold and emptiness. The silence was shattered by Roger Mace who suddenly jumped up, hurled his glass straight at a mirror on the wall, added to the clatter of smashing glass a couple of shouted curses and dashed out of the room.

Cecily leapt to her feet.

" My mirror! " she screamed. " Oh, God, my mirror! "

" The man," said Frank Lely with sardonic pity, " shows his feelings."

" My mirror—he shouldn't have done that! Oh, damn him, damn him! " cried Cecily, running across the room and gathering up several shards of glass. She held them out with a tragic gesture. " Oh, I'll never forgive that as long as I live! That mirror was two hundred years old."

" Never mind, love, I'm sure you can have it mended," said Kitty Roper placidly. " I'm going to make some tea. Anybody want some tea? "

" Of course it can't be mended," said Cecily, her face red with anger. " Oh, God, how I hate that man! I've always loathed him, he's a coarse brute. I only had him here to please Janet, and now. . . . One simply can't afford to be decent to people. Something like this always happens."

" Give him a chance," said Frank Lely. " He's been going through it to-night."

" But my mirror——"

" To hell with your mirror."

" Oh, you're a brute too, you're as bad as he is, you're all callous, unbalanced people without a shred of decent self-control. It means nothing to you that something really beautiful's been broken. This mirror——" She let the fragments of glass fall to the ground again, rather as if she were scattering earth on a coffin. " D'you know, it had been in my family for five generations. But that wouldn't mean anything to you."

" Cecily, I'm going to use your telephone," said Peter Willing. Crossing the room, he picked up the directory and started searching through it. " I ought to have done this at once," he said. " I oughtn't to have let her open her mouth, I ought to have taken charge. The way things happened, she couldn't have done herself more harm. I just don't understand any of it, but I ought to have seen what sort of state she was in and insisted that she shouldn't speak. I shall blame myself always . . . Ah, here we are, Blundell and Blundell."

" Who are Blundell and Blundell? " asked Lely.

" Lawyers," said Willing.

While he was speaking into the telephone, Kitty put her head in through the kitchen door and announced again: " I'm making tea." She sounded comfortably certain that tea would make everything look different. Yet she had been having a short cry to herself in the kitchen; her cheeks were moist and her eyes red.

As she disappeared again the American said to Cecily: " Pardon me, ma'am, I don't like to raise the point at a time like this, but could you tell me how I could find out where Mr. and Mrs. Smith have gone? "

Cecily did not reply. Peter Wililng went on talking rapidly into the telephone.

After a moment Frank Lely said: " Cecily! "

" Yes? " she said vaguely.

" The gentleman's talking to you."

" Oh? " She looked dully at the boy.

" I was just wondering if maybe you could tell me the address of Mr. and Mrs. Smith," he said. " I've had an invitation to visit them ever since I've been in England and

this is the first time I've got around to it. And now they're
not there.''

'' They've gone to Sheffield,'' said Cecily. '' Wait a
minute, I've got their address somewhere. I promised I'd
forward letters for them.'' She went to the desk and hunted
about in a drawer. '' Here it is.'' She handed him a card.

'' Thanks,'' he said, '' thanks a lot. Now I guess I'll be
going.'' He looked around, adding gravely: '' I'd like you
to know, I'm sorry about everything.''

Kitty came hurrying in from the kitchen.

'' You aren't going! '' she exclaimed. '' You can't go till
you've had some tea. It'll make you feel better. The kettle's
just boiling.''

His face wrinkling with embarrassment, Ed Larg shook his
head. '' I guess I'd better go,'' he said. '' Thanks a lot all
the same. I'd rather not miss my bus.''

'' Nonsense,'' said Kitty, '' the buses go on for ages. It's
a wretched cold night, so of course you'd like some tea before
you start out in it.''

'' For the Lord's sake,'' said Cecily irritably, '' Americans
don't *like* tea—don't you know that? And he doesn't like us
and being mixed up in a murder.''

'' Nonsense,'' said Kitty again with decision.

Ed Larg reached for the door-handle. '' I guess I'd better
go,'' he said quietly. '' I know the way you're all feeling
and I reckon you don't want strangers around. Good night.''
With a sudden quick smile for Kitty, he let himself out.

'' What a shame,'' said Kitty on her way back to the
kitchen. '' The poor boy, walking into a thing like this in the
middle of his leave—it's horrible, really. I feel awfully sorry
for him. All the time he was giving his evidence and trying
so hard to keep himself, so to speak, apart from it all, I kept
wanting to tell him how sorry I felt about it, sort of as if I
were to blame, if you know what I mean, that he'd got mixed
up in it and had his leave spoiled.''

'' God, what a fool you still are, Kitty,'' said Cecily with a
sigh. '' It was his own darned fault for walking in, poking
his nose in . . . Oh,''—her tone changed—'' I'm sorry, I'm

sorry, of course it was hard luck on him. But all the same, if
only he hadn't . . .''

Peter Willing had finished with the telephone. He put it
down and went over to the fire.

" Frank," he said hesitantly, " you went up there, you
saw Rit. What—what was it like? ''

It was almost the first direct reference that had been made
to the murder since Janet Markland had been taken away.

Lely did not reply at once and Willing, holding out his
hands to the fire, went on: " That boy couldn't have made
some sort of mistake, I suppose? You know, I still can't
believe it. Rit and Janet . . . Janet and Rit . . . What was
her motive? If she did it—if she really did do it—*in God's
name, what was her motive?* ''

Frank Lely said with a lift of one eyebrow: " Don't tell
me you're asking that question in good faith, Peter? ''

" In good faith? '' said Willing angrily. " Of course I am!
D'you think I can understand what's happened? There's
nothing, there's absolutely nothing I can grasp in the whole
business except the evidence. And that's damning—I admit
it, I admit it! But *why* should Janet suddenly murder Rit?
They've been the best of friends for years. I know that, I've
seen them together I don't know how often, I've heard the
way they spoke of one another. I always envied them in a
way, having that sort of relationship. It isn't a common thing
to see. I thought it was a great help to Rit in his difficulties
with poor Rosamund—and, of course, in his work. I'm dead
certain he was sincere when he said he owed almost everything
to Janet. As a matter of fact, I rather admired Janet for the
way she managed it. Rit wasn't an easy person; he wasn't
an easy kind of friend to have. But her patience and understanding were extraordinary, truly extraordinary.''

Frank Lely's lips curled under his little moustache. He
studied the other man's troubled face with far more curiosity
and detachment than sympathy.

" You don't honestly mean to tell me, Peter,'' he said,
" that you didn't know Janet was Rit's mistress? ''

" *Janet?* ''

Utter incredulity showed on the small, pinched face of Peter Willing.

Lely went on watching him.

" Why d'you think Rosamund killed herself? " he asked equably after a moment.

Peter Willing looked as if someone had punched him hard in the middle.

Lely groped for a cigarette in a box on the mantelpiece. His long, white, bony hand with the ring on it gripped a small silver lighter and flicked it into flame. It struck Alice suddenly that he was enjoying the hurt he had just given Peter Willing; more still, that he was interested in it.

As Peter Willing, in stricken silence, turned away and blundered to a chair, Kitty came in, carrying a tray with tea-things.

" I heard what you were saying," she said sombrely. Putting the tray down, she began to pour out the tea. " I can't believe it."

Cecily said nothing. She had her lower lip sucked in under her teeth and was staring pensively at the fire.

Lely looked at her. " Cecily can believe it," he said.

Slowly she shook her head. " No . . . No, there are some things too . . . Besides, you're an awful liar, Frank. You've probably just made it up."

" I have not." His voice grew hotter. " I knew Rit well for a good many years, you know. I should think, though I know it's a claim that lays one open to being laughed at for an impertinent fool, that I knew him rather better than anybody else did. Janet never really knew him at all. She ran him, she controlled him, sucked the juice out of him and took a commission on the transaction—she'd a good practical sense, oh, a grand one—but if she'd really known anything about him she wouldn't have handled his life as she did and mishandled his talent. When he started out he had potentialities, real ones, he had something to say, he had convictions and courage, but once he'd got into the hands of that woman——"

" You're getting excited, Frank," said Peter Willing quietly. " Don't—I can't stand it at the moment."

"All right," said Lely. He puffed out a mouthful of smoke, rounding his lips to a small, red circle to do it. "All I intended to say is that I did know Rit pretty intimately and . . . oh, it doesn't matter."

"I can't believe it," said Kitty again as she handed round the cups of tea. "I don't know about Rit—I'm inclined to think that he was ready to take anything he could from any woman and not quite understand that sometimes you can't have everything all at the same time. But I can't believe it of Janet. She was always rather puritanical really. She wasn't exactly prudish but she was awfully serious about sex, even after she got married. We used to argue about it, at least I used to argue because I knew she disapproved of me, and she used to say she just didn't know, and she'd look sort of cold and unhappy and change the subject."

"And how long ago was all that?" asked Frank Lely with his sardonic smile.

"Oh, ages ago—ten years or so," she answered.

"Ten years do change a person," he said.

"Yes—but," said Kitty, "the moment I saw Janet I thought to myself, she hasn't changed at all, really not at all. And Cecily hasn't either. I think I've changed the most of us three; I've grown old and staid with my husband and my three children and my cups of tea and my mind on the last bus and all. Incidentally, when does the last bus go, Cecily? I mustn't miss it."

"Don't worry about that," said Lely, "I've got a car here."

"Have you? Oh, how lovely," cried Kitty, "a car! But how d'you manage that? Are you allowed it for something special?"

"Oh, I do manage it," he answered, shrugging.

"And you can take me to Baker Street?"

"With pleasure."

"That'll be lovely," she said, with a warm smile at him. "I'm in luck this evening."

"Oh, you—you two!" cried Cecily fiercely. Her chin jutted forward and her mouth was tight and bitter. "Can't you wait to make your assignations at least until you've got away from here? I think it's disgusting, I think it's utterly horrible. Rit's dead and Janet's—Janet's as good as dead, I suppose, and all you two can do is start plotting how to get away together. Well, go now—why don't you? I don't want you here if that's the way you're going to behave. Go, go, for the Lord's sake, go!"

Lely and Kitty looked at her in astonishment.

" Why, Cecily! " said Kitty.

" Good heavens, I only offered Mrs. Roper a lift to the station," said Lely. " Whatever's the matter with that? "

" Ugh," said Cecily, " I know both of you! You make me sick. But don't stand about, you're wasting your opportunities —besides, I can't stand the sight of you. Go! "

" But you must be quite crazy, love," said Kitty, looking round to see if anyone wanted more tea. " You're making me feel very embarrassed. Major Lely just offered me a lift to Baker Street in his car."

" Yes," said Lely, " that's all. Of course if you think she should walk it instead——"

" Oh, all right, all right, I'm sorry, I apologise. I'm always wrong," said Cecily sulkily. " But let me tell you all the same, there are some things I just can't bear."

Kitty laid a hand on her hair. " You're such a dear," she said. " You haven't changed a bit. Poor Cecily, you can't believe it about Janet any more than I can, can you? And Rit . . . I was going to see Rit to-night, wasn't I? It's about five years since I saw him. I met him and Rosamund one summer in Paris, you know. It was the only time I ever met Rosamund. They were driving each other nearly mad even then, and they were both so desperate and concerned about it, each planning miracles of self-control for the sake of the other that never worked. Rit had changed a great deal already. He was haggard and nervy and always talking about war. You'd have thought he never thought of anything but war. He said if it started he'd clear out immediately to South America or Malay or somewhere. Malay! . . . Oh, why am I talking like this? I used to love Rit so much when he was quite young; he was so beautiful and brilliant——"

" Be quiet, can't you? " gasped Cecily.

" Yes, yes, I'm sorry, I'm an awful fool," said Kitty with a sigh. She turned to Frank Lely again. " You never told us, what was it like up there? What—had actually happened? "

" Oh, it was just as that fellow Larg said," he answered. " Perhaps the professional eye picked up some interesting details, but mine didn't. There was a poker on the floor. The police took a lot of photographs and fingerprints and so on."

" A poker," said Kitty thoughtfully. " A poker and Janet . . ."

" I can't believe it! " said Peter Willing wildly. " It's all incredible—I can't believe it! "

It was then that it occurred to Alice that although, one after the other, Janet's friends had been saying: " I can't believe it!" not one of them had said: " I *don't* believe it."

She herself was feeling a deep incredulity, but it was mostly at the thought that she, Alice Church, had spent the evening in the same room with, had shaken hands and talked with a murderess. She had often found it hard enough to realise that soldiers she knew had actually killed people, that some young man in uniform with a sensitive and kindly face might in fact have the blood of hundreds of human beings on his hands. The young man in uniform, however, would have acted not only on his own impulse but as the result of a complicated tradition of moral action, and so could not really be compared with a pale, slender woman in a black dress who at one moment had been sitting there, asking one how many children one had, and at the next moment murdering her lover with a poker. In everyday life the springs of violence are hidden in even grosser darkness than those of sex. Alice could make nothing of her strange experience; she could not bring the two aspects of Janet Markland together; she could no longer make herself realise that Janet Markland was one consistent personality. But then, she suddenly thought, for Janet's friends, how much harder it must be, how much more incredible.

That evening little more was said.

A move to leave was started by Peter Willing. Cecily's guests got into their coats, said good night to her and filed down the steps to the gate. The night was still bright with stars and the street empty and silent.

Alice was halfway down the steps when Cecily came hurrying out after her. The others were ahead already; Frank Lely was unlocking his car, while Kitty Roper, clutching her grey lamb coat around her, was shaking hands with Peter Willing, who had just been refusing a lift.

" Alice, don't go," whispered Cecily, catching Alice by the arm. " Stay here—do please stay here with me! "

" Well, I don't know, Cecily," said Alice reluctantly. " It's a bit difficult. I'm expected at home."

" For God's sake, Alice! " Cecily begged. " You can telephone—your husband won't worry. It's not as if we're having raids at the moment. And just think what it's going to be like in this house alone."

" Yes," said Alice, " I know, I shouldn't care about that myself."

" Then stay. Be an angel, Alice." Cecily's face was strained and grey-white in the. darkness. " I just can't bear the thought of it alone. I feel frightened. I want to run away."

" Then why not come home with me? " Alice suggested. " There's plenty of room with the children away."

Cecily began: " Well, that's awfully kind of you, Alice; I think I will if I may." But then the two little hard lines appeared between her eyes and she shook her head. " No—no, I won't, if you don't mind. I'd better not. Your husband'll be there, won't he? I feel just now as if I couldn't bear meeting anybody—anybody new. In a way I'd really like to be quite alone, even without you, only I can't face it. And I don't feel very well, I feel as if I might be sick or something. So I'd better not go out. But I wish you'd stay with me, Alice. I'll be everlastingly grateful. Think of the darkness in the house and the silence and being alone. . . . I've always been a bit silly about being alone in places, I've never liked it. *Please,* Alice——" There was the desperation of a child, frightened of the dark, in the words. " Didn't you hear the tramping of the men on the stairs when they carried the—the body out? I'm going to sit listening to that, and listening and listening——"

So Alice stayed the night with Cecily Lightwood. Peter Willing walked away into the night, Kitty Roper and Frank Lely drove off together, Cecily and Alice went back into the sitting-room, stoked up the fire and sat down at either side of it.

Alice was very tired and wondered if Cecily would insist on sitting up all night or if she would be able to think of sleeping. But though Cecily looked dreadfully exhausted, she was tense and restless. They had a small, quiet supper together, Cecily fetching in from the kitchen some of the food she had prepared for her guests. There were sandwiches and some pretty little home-made biscuits set out on some old Worcester dishes. Arranging the plates on the floor between herself and Alice, Cecily poured out some whisky and said: " This'll do us more good than Kitty's tea." Sighing, she went on: " How extraordinary it is to think that Kitty should have turned into the sort of woman who instantly makes tea in a crisis. You should have known her when she was young, Alice—the most beautiful, immoral bitch you ever saw. Always a bit on the coarse side, of course, and definitely vulgar, but that can be quite refreshing when it comes from real vitality. Anyway, I was always very fond of Kitty. She's always been good for me, I think; she sort of counteracts my damned bad temper and nerves. I ought to have seen more of her all this time. One can always be as foul to her as one likes and it never matters. Of course, that's partly because really she's as hard as nails; she doesn't give a curse for anyone—she never did. She never cared much about things either, or ideas. I don't think you could even say if she cared much whether she enjoyed herself or not, because she just always did enjoy herself somehow, in any circumstances. Look at to-night ——" She checked herself, then after a moment added speculatively: " I wonder if she did go home with Frank. What d'you think?"

" Well, I shouldn't dream of leaping to that conclusion myself," said Alice.

" Ah, but then you don't know them both as I do," said Cecily quickly. " Mind you, I don't care what they do, it's not my business and I'm not curious or censorious, and I know I oughtn't to have burst out at them as I did. I know I ought to be able to stop myself being so outspoken. But I was disgusted, I really was. There are decencies in these things. They might at least have waited till they got away from here before they started making their arrangements."

" But all they did——"

" Yes, yes, I know—all they did was arrange for Frank to take Kitty to Baker Street! What an innocent you are, Alice! That's something I rather like about you really—you're an intelligent woman and yet you don't see into the meaning of things. Somehow it makes you very soothing to be with. You're good for me too, I think. You're one of the people I never want to quarrel with, almost like Janet——" She stopped. A look of horror spread over her face.

Alice pretended not to notice and said: " Well, I've never mixed much in circles like yours, so perhaps the meanings of things in them do rather escape me. To me a lift in a car is just a lift in a car."

Cecily smiled rather scornfully and lapsed into silence.

Presently she asked: " Aren't you tired? I am, I've that hurting sort of tiredness that keeps you wide awake. I think this has been the most horrible night of my life."

" I hope it has been," said Alice. " I shouldn't like to think you'd had many like it."

" Oh, my life hasn't been much good, I've made too many mistakes," said Cecily.

" Who hasn't? " said Alice.

But Cecily shook her head; the mistakes of others were not to be compared in magnitude with hers.

The fire was burning warmly. Long flames were curling against the back of the chimney and soft, busy cracklings were issuing out of the banked up, black and copper coals. Those soft sounds made the room seem very quiet, with a deceptive, weary peacefulness.

" No," said Cecily dully, " that's it—I've made too many mistakes in my life."

" I suppose you're thinking of Mrs. Markland," said Alice.

" It doesn't matter what I'm thinking of! " It was exclaimed with one of the sudden bursts of fierceness that

could always come from Cecily without any warning. " All
my life . . . I've known Janet all my life. *All my life,*
Alice! "

" Don't talk about it," said Alice.

" No," said Cecily, " I won't—but for Christ's sake, let's
talk about something else then! "

So they talked about the war; one can always talk about
the war. After a while they shifted on to food, which is easier
still and more companionable; there is no limit to the amount
that two women in wartime can say about food. But Alice
did most of the talking. Cecily spoke occasionally, bringing
her words out in quick little rushes, but sometimes in the
middle of a sentence she forgot what she had been about to
say, and looked away with a troubled, half-scared frown on
her forehead. Sometimes she interrupted Alice with something
quite irrelevant, so that Alice knew she was scarcely listening.

One of these interruptions came in the midst of some
nostalgic memories of Alice's about eggs and oranges.

" My stupidity! " Cecily suddenly exclaimed, hissing the
words bitterly at the fire. " My stupidity and blindness! The
way I've been taken in! And there I was, talking about your
not seeing into the meanings of things . . . That's different,
of course, but how you must have wanted to laugh at me
when I said it. Why didn't you, Alice? Why didn't you
throw it back at me? That's what you ought to have done.
Why aren't people ever honest with one? Why do they always
try to keep one all comfortable in one's own stupidity? So
that they can laugh at one when one isn't there, I suppose. I
never do that with people, I'm straight with them, I say what
comes into my head—and so I'm told I hurt people's feelings,
and I'm tactless, and God knows what other rubbish. But I
don't lie and cover things up and deceive my best friends so
that I can laugh at them afterwards—that isn't my idea of
friendship. Look at that beast, Frank Lely. God, how I
loathe that man! You know, I only put up with him because
of Rit. But look at the way he seems to have known—well,
known the whole thing, and never said—damn him, never
said a word . . . Yes, yes, I know, I know, don't say it,
Alice—I can see what you're going to say. He hadn't any

right to say anything, it was a confidence, wasn't it? Of course, it was very fine and honourable of him to keep such very, very interesting gossip to himself. Oh, hell, what nonsense, what bloody nonsense! But it's no use crying over —over spilt blood, is it, Alice? After all, it's much commoner than spilt milk. Nobody spills milk, it's far too precious. Only two and a half pints a week—think of that! Only two and a half pints of milk a week . . . There you are, Alice, I've got back to food. Isn't that clever of me? We can go on talking about food now as long as you like. D'you know that food's a wonderful safeguard against emotion? If people are hungry enough they can't be unhappy about much else. And even if they aren't hungry, they can always bury themselves in the buying of food and the preparing of food and washing it up and thinking of the next meal. I envy domestic women, you know. They're wonderfully protected——"

She had not meant to stop there but that was where the tears burst through. As noisy sobs choked her, her whole body started shaking. She went on muttering short phrases, gutterally indistinct. Alice caught one of them more than once repeated: " All my life . . . I've known her all my life . . ."

Later that night as Alice lay awake in Cecily's bedroom, which Cecily had insisted that Alice should take while she herself made up a bed on the couch in the sitting-room, this phrase kept coming back to Alice.

" All my life . . ."

What, Alice wondered, had a woman who had been friends with a murderess all her life honestly thought of her all those years? What had the other friends of the murderess thought of her? Although they all seemed so stunned and bewildered now, would they all soon be saying, as they had said of the suicide of Rosamund Ritter, that they had expected something of the sort all along?

It would be interesting, thought Alice, lying there sleepless, to know what Dr. Crippen's intimate friends had thought of him before he murdered Mrs. Crippen. And what had those who had known Madeleine Smith believed about that attractive young woman? Had Constance Kent been considered a normal girl? Once or twice during the night Alice thought she heard Cecily moving about, and once she even thought she heard her on the stairs and considered getting up to go to her, but decided against it.

Alice herself did not sleep at all. Some time before it was light she grew tired of lying in bed and got up and went to the bathroom. Fumbling around in the dark, for there seemed to be no bulb in the lamp-socket, she managed to light the geyser and had a bath by the light of a small electric torch which she had in her bag. After she had dressed she crept softly into the sitting-room. Cecily was alseep then, lying almost face downwards on the couch, her head turned slightly to one side with her arms flung up loosely across the pillows. The position looked strained and uncomfortable and yet had the abandonment of complete exhaustion.

Alice did not like to disturb her, but she did not like to leave either until Cecily had awakened, so she went back to the bedroom and sat there reading for an hour or so. It was very cold, for though there was a point for a portable gas-fire beside the old grate, there was no gas-fire there. It was about ten o'clock before Cecily, looking sullen and unkempt in a beautiful green velvet dressing-gown, trimmed with panels of her own lovely embroidery, came looking for her.

Cecily was in an abominable temper. She appeared to wonder what on earth Alice was doing there and asked her if she hadn't had enough *News of the World* sensationalism to last her for a bit. She said she wished to God Alice would go. They almost parted like that, but at the last moment, when Alice was at the door, Cecily slipped a hand through her arm.

" Oh, I'm sorry, I'm sorry," she said wearily. " There I go again. I didn't mean any of it, Alice—you know that, don't you? You were an angel to stay here. I don't know what I'd have done if you hadn't. But listen—don't ever talk about any of it to me again. I've got to cut it right out somehow. I've got to find out somehow how not even to think about it, and I'm beginning by cutting out the talk. I thought it all out last night after you'd gone to bed. I never slept a wink all night and I did a lot of thinking. I'm not going to have a word to say about it all to anybody. If they've the impertinence to try and make me talk about it, I simply shan't answer. So remember that, will you? Because I think you're really the best friend I've got now, Alice, and I want to keep that. You understand, don't you? '' She leant nearer suddenly and kissed Alice on the cheek.

Alice felt a stir of pity and embarrassment. She escaped as quickly as she could. Since her first meeting with Cecily she had always felt more pity than friendship for her; she seemed to be a person whose exaggerations, anxieties and perpetual tension had a numbing effect on the emotions of all who came in close contact with her.

When Alice looked back from the gate Cecily was still standing on the doorstep The sight of her with her uncombed grey hair, her ravaged, handsome, immature face and the beautifully embroidered dressing-gown held close to her slender, almost girlish body, gave Alice a sudden pang of fear for her. She wondered if she ought to turn back. But with a smile and a wave of her hand Cecily stepped back and closed the door. Alice went on down the street and caught the trolley-bus at the end of it.

CHAPTER THREE

ALICE saw Cecily and her friends at the inquest. After that she saw none of them again for some time. Cecily stopped going to the Citizens' Advice Bureau. Alice rang her up once or twice, but first Cecily said she had 'flu, and when Alice asked her if she had anyone to look after her, assured her over-hastily that she was being splendidly taken care of by a charwoman; later she said simply that she would be frantically busy for at least the next fortnight but would ring Alice up as soon as she had a moment to spare. Since she never did ring up, Alice concluded that in spite of her declaration of friendship she was determined to be left to herself.

At the inquest a verdict of wilful murder had been brought in against Janet Markland. Sergeant Larg had been there and had had to give his evidence over again, and so had the warden and the constable. Peter Willing and Frank Lely had been selected to give evidence on the length of time that Janet had been out of Cecily's sitting-room, and some servants and neighbours had been found who between them built up a picture of Janet's relationship with Aubrey Ritter, which confirmed what Frank Lely had said of it. That she had been Ritter's mistress was beyond any doubt. In 1936 the two of them had spent a fortnight together at an hotel in North Wales under the names of Mr. and Mrs. Ritter, and since that time had seen one another constantly; Ritter, a very rich man since the productions of *Coal Dust, The Angry Heart*, and *Black Harvest*—a point which the police had not failed to emphasise—had frequently given Janet extravagant presents, and had sometimes spent days and nights at a time at her flat.

The police claim was that following the suicide of Rosamund Ritter, a change had come over the relationship. Suffering from remorse at his wife's death, Ritter had attempted to break off his connection with Janet. A letter had been found, written on the day of the discovery of his wife's body, in which he had told Janet that he felt they would both find it intolerable to go on seeing one another after what had happened. But Janet, it had appeared, had put up a good deal of resistance. The police had produced a charwoman of hers who had overheard part of a telephone conversation between her and Ritter on the morning when the letter had arrived. Janet had been weeping, so the woman had said, and had accused Ritter of weakness and called him a fool. The same woman had said that Ritter had come to Janet's flat in the afternoon and that there had been a quarrel; she had heard raised voices, though not, she had admitted, what had been said. But as Ritter had left she had heard him say: " We ought to have got married years ago, you know, Janet." Mrs. Markland had replied: " Was that my fault? " Ritter had said: " It's really no use now." Janet had said no more and Ritter had gone. Apparently they had not met again after that until the night of the murder, when, it had been claimed, Janet Markland, hearing that Aubrey Ritter was in the top-floor flat of the house in which Cecily Lightwood was living, had gone upstairs to persuade him to resume his relations with her, that Ritter, as before, had refused to see any more of her, and that Janet, in a fit of rage, had snatched up the poker and killed him. There had been no suggestion that the murder had been premeditated, but the police had been able to show that Janet's fingerprints were on the poker. In spite of the fact that on closer questioning both the warden and the constable had admitted that just possibly Mrs. Markland might have slipped out of the house and back again without their noticing her, since they had not, in fact, actually stood still at the gate the whole time, but had walked up and down a certain amount and had frequently gazed up at the sky, the jury found the story of adultery and violence convincing and brought in the verdict of wilful murder.

The day after the inquest had been a Saturday. Alice had had a great many things to do. There had been the shopping for the week-end, some ironing and mending, her usual afternoon at the Citizens' Advice Bureau, and dinner to cook for some friends who had been expected in the evening. She had slept badly the night before and had gone through the day in a tired torpor.

She had kept thinking of the problem of the character of Janet Markland. But it had been stupid, repetitive thinking and had always come round to the same point. She had got sick of it. She wanted to think of other things, some of her C.A.B. problems, for instance. There was one, the problem of a deserter's wife who had kept her husband hidden in the house for eight months, feeding him on her own rations and never letting him out of doors except in the black-out, until suddenly the man, unable to bear the existence any longer, had given himself up, only to make the bitter discovery that he had received his discharge from the army on the grounds of health only three weeks after his desertion. His sentence for desertion had not been heavy, but his wife had been drawing his pay all the time he had been in hiding and now, with her husband ill and two young children on her hands so that she could not go out to work, had to refund all the money she had drawn. What, she had asked Alice in terror, was she to do about it? She hadn't meant to be dishonest, and didn't the army owe her husband something for ruining his health? She had tried sending the children to a day-nursery, but they had both immediately developed chickenpox.

This story of foolish, anguished people had wrung Alice's heart and she knew she ought to have been thinking about it, trying to find ways of helping the devoted, distracted woman in her ignorance and fear, but instead her mind kept clouding with misty images of Janet Markland. Could that quiet, tired woman whom Alice had met at Cecily's party really be the grasping, hysterical creature revealed by the police. It felt important to Alice that she should clear this matter up for herself. It nagged at her all day with an exhausting drain on her energy. Nothing sucks the imagination so dry and leaves behind such a sense of frustration as a problem of human character which cannot be solved simply by emotion and faith.

Once she tried talking it over with her husband. But Oliver Church never cared much for discussing people except as their idiosyncrasies might happen to affect the intrigues of the scientific world. Alice returned to her own thoughts. She found herself remembering much more of Janet Markland than she realised she had noticed; she began to find the pale,

weary face with the look of melancholy remoteness about it
a constant intruder into her mind. She began to feel a curious
disquiet. When she looked at the faces she saw around her,
familiar faces or strange faces in the street, she had moments
of fantastic suspicion, sometimes almost of panic, because of
all the dreadful potentialities that might be hidden by them.
Sometimes she found herself shot through with an agonising
distrust of her own perceptions.

One day, on an impulse, she rang up Peter Willing.

She made no attempt to be honest with him. It seemed to
her that he was most likely to agree to tell her what he knew
of Janet Markland if she went to him with doubts of Janet's
guilt. Of all Janet's friends, he had seemed the most incredu-
lous of it. That she might be doing something very cruel did
occur to Alice, but she stifled her conscience, telling him on the
telephone that there were several points in the evidence which
she could not understand. He sounded eager to see her. They
made an appointment for lunch the next day and at twelve-
thirty Alice went to pick him up at his office.

It was on the second floor of a building in Essex Street.
After climbing a great many steep stairs, Alice found a room
labelled " Willing and Markland, Inquiries." In the room
a young woman with fluffed-out red hair and a very short skirt
who was seated at a switchboard, rang through to Peter
Willing that Mrs. Church had arrived, and he came running
in at once with his hand outstretched.

" How *very* nice of you to come, how *very* nice to see
you! " he sang out warmly, as if Alice were a favourite author
up from the country for a day. But his eyes were tired and
expressionless and his hand was limp. He seemed to be trying
to put over a little act of urbane normality. Perhaps it was as
much for his own sake as for that of the girl at the switchboard
or for Alice, but it was as mechanical as the actions of a
sick man forcing himself through a ceremony.

In his own office he kept it up for a minute or two. Flinging
himself into the chair behind the big desk, he thrust a box of
cigarettes towards Alice, leant back, jerked one short leg over
the other, beamed at her as if nothing in the world mattered
to him now that she was there, and said: " Well now, Mrs.

Church, what's troubling you? Tell me all about it, and then we'll put our two heads together and see what we can do. Two heads are always better than one, eh? Anyway, there's no problem that isn't lessened by a good discussion. I never believe in bottling things up and keeping them to oneself. Half the difficulties in the world come from that. I believe in getting as many people as possible to share my troubles and asking for all the advice I can get—even if I never take it, ha, ha! Now what's it all about, Mrs. Church?"

Alice had no acquaintance amongst writers but concluded that Peter Willing had found that they respond to a good bedside manner as well as anybody else. Yet his manner that day, though he plainly intended it should seem reassuring and kindly, only seemed strained and excitable and a little absurd. His small figure behind the big desk was tense; he could not stay still for a moment.

Alice accepted a cigarette and waited while Peter Willing lit it for her, then she sat back and took a quick look round before she spoke.

The room was full of books, ranged along painted shelves. The books gave the room an oddly raffish appearance, for they were all in their shiny paper jackets, as colourful as the heaped counter in a sale in a silk department. The desk was very orderly. Above the bookshelves hung a row of photographs; several of them were of famous faces and all were inscribed with messages of friendship to Peter Willing.

It was because of one of the photographs that Alice forgot how she had intended to open the conversation. Getting up, she crossed over to the bookshelves and reached for the photograph.

" This is Aubrey Ritter, isn't it? " she said.

" Yes, yes, poor old Rit," said Willing. " Of course you never met him, did you? "

" No," she said, " and this is the first good photograph of him I've seen."

" Ah, yes, those smudges in the papers are pretty appalling, aren't they? They never tell one anything unless one already knows the face."

" He was very good-looking," said Alice.

" Yes indeed!" said Willing. " Of course, that photograph was taken three or four years ago and he'd rather altered lately. He'd grown a good deal older-looking—more drawn, you know, and nervy—though which of us hasn't, if it comes to that, during this horrible war? Poor old Rit, he felt the war terribly, he took it very hard. He wasn't the kind of person who can live on a daily ration of horror and not show it. If he had been he couldn't have written as he did. It was because he felt so intensely what other people suffered that he produced such wonderful work. A grand person, Mrs. Church." Willing's voice shook slightly. " He was really. I wish you'd known him."

Alice went on looking at the photograph. It had obviously been a snapshot, enlarged, showing Ritter standing in a low cottage doorway. There was a look of hot sunshine in the picture; the walls of the cottage looked dazzlingly bright, the shadows were deep and rich. The way the man stood there, a pipe in his mouth, a book under his arm, looking out smilingly from the cool, dark doorway, brought thoughts of peace and leisure very vividly to mind He had on a loose shirt of some dark colour and corduroy trousers. A silk handkerchief was knotted round his neck; the handkerchief had a gay pattern of overlapping circles which showed as distinctly in that sharp light as the fine muscles of his forearms. His hair, in an attractive disorder of loose, dark curls, fell forward across his forehead. He had a long, narrow face with thin, delicately moulded features and in spite of his smile, it had a look of aloofness and gravity. From the way that he was stooping in the doorway he seemed to be a big man; his shoulders were broad and he had a graceful, easy way of standing. The odd thing about the picture though, thought Alice, as she propped it up against the wall, was that in spite of the corduroys and the gaudy scarf and the beautifully tumbled curls, it made her think of a schoolmaster rather than of a successful dramatist. Perhaps it was a lack of vitality about the figure and some suggestion of somewhat strained and conscious good nature. Suddenly she thought of a remark of her husband's: Oliver had said that he would never trust a man who had himself photographed with a pipe in his mouth.

As she went back to her chair she realised that she was feeling very nervous She still did not know how to explain her presence.

" You're sure you don't mind if—if I start talking about all this? " she said.

" I'll be glad! " said Willing forcefully. He jerked back in his chair, folding his hands. " I'll be glad to hear what an intelligent person who isn't personally involved with any of the people in this whole ghastly business has to say about it. I'm still utterly bewildered myself—though that's a ludicrously inadequate word for it. I say to myself twenty times a day that I still can't believe in it. Janet and Rit! . . . We always called him Rit, you know—I suppose because we couldn't take the Aubrey. Poor old Rit, he had such a terrible lot of things to contend with all his life, even that impossible name. And then his wife . . . Poor Rosamund, she was a grand person too in her way. I wish you'd known her. She and Rit were really so devoted to each other—and Janet was so attached to them both. And so . . . But there's the evidence—there's the evidence, God damn it! "

Raking his fingers through his rough, fair hair, he scowled across the desk at Alice.

" If only Janet hadn't insisted that she never went up to his room! " he exclaimed. " I'm not sure what difference it would have made, but I'm sure it would have made some difference; I'm sure it would have helped.. That's the part of her story that so obviously can't be true, because after all, the American boy saw her—he *saw* her. And there isn't any reason why he should lie. It isn't as if he could conceivably be mixed up in the thing himself or have any malice against her. Actually I think he hated having to say what he did. Yet Janet goes on saying he never saw her and that she never went upstairs! Of course, I can understand her saying it at first—she was terrified, poor girl, and said the first thing that came into her head to defend herself. But why does she have to stick to it? Why doesn't she simply admit she went upstairs? Dangerous as that might be, I'm sure it'd be less damaging than such an obvious lie——" He broke off as the telephone at his elbow rang. " Sorry," he said, " forgive me a moment."

His manner changed completely as he spoke into the telephone. The nervous torrent of words stopped; his voice grew smooth and firm. The conversation concerned some writer whose name was Pat; the speaker at the other end of the line seemed to be accusing Pat of having over-written himself; Peter Willing defended him with a bland sort of sternness. How could a writer who produced only one book a year possibly overwrite himself, he demanded? As he put down the telephone again he said: " You've read Pat's *Green Geese*, of course, Mrs. Church? A lovely book, isn't it? Beautifully written, so subtle, so discerning—sold twelve thousand copies—oh, a *lovely* book in every way. Now what about going out? If we don't we'll be interrupted every few minutes. It's impossible to talk here."

" I suppose you're pretty rushed with work," said Alice, standing up, " now that you haven't got——" She stopped, feeling she was saying something rather foolish.

But Willing picked her words up: " Haven't got Janet?— Oh, I'm overwhelmed, utterly overwhelmed! But it isn't simply the quantity of work, it's all the decisions that have to be taken. You'd never guess how I used to rely on her judgment. Of course, we divided the work up and each had our special branches—Janet handled the film and dramatic stuff—but still we used to discuss everything. I relied on her completely. And apart from that, of course, I've got worries. I haven't any idea yet how this thing will affect us —financially, you know. And how long I shall have the heart to carry on if . . ." He made an uncertain gesture. " Well, where would you like to have lunch, Mrs. Church? "

She left that to him and he took her to the coffee-room of a small hotel, tucked away down an obscure passageway above the Embankment. It was the sort of place where the food is excellent and incredibly expensive and Anglo-Indians approve of the curry. The room was dim and quiet, with the white tablecloths gleaming like lilies on the surface of a black pool of shadows, and all voices and all footfalls sounding deadened.

" We can talk comfortably here," said Peter Willing.

If the hushed whispers in which everyone there seemed to feel impelled to talk could be described as talking comfortably, there was certainly nothing to prevent it.

" I always come here when I want to talk over something important," he went on. " Now to go back to what we were saying . . ."

But before they could do that there was lunch to be ordered. With the coming and going of the waiter it was some minutes before Peter Willing, with a momentary return of the bedside manner, murmured just audibly in Alice's ear: " And now, Mrs. Church, what is it? Do tell me just what's worrying you."

" As a matter of fact," Alice whispered back, " that point you were speaking of yourself, I mean Mrs. Markland's queer insistence that she never went upstairs—that's one of the things that's been puzzling me."

Willing nodded.

She went on more boldly: " It's such an obvious suicidal line to take. It's made me wonder if. . . . Well, not exactly if there'd been a mistake in the evidence, but if there mightn't be something behind her insistence, some reason for it— something which might just possibly help her if it could be dragged out into the light. And I thought that you, knowing her probably better than anyone else, might be able to explain. . . ." She paused suggestively.

But Willing only nodded again and said: " Ah."

" I'm afraid I'm putting this very badly," Alice said, beginning to grow nervous again. " You see, I find the whole thing so incomprehensible. But I thought that you might know enough about Mrs. Markland to be able to guess why she took the line she did, and—and why she——"

" Wait a minute," said Willing. " Let's deal with that point fully before you go on. I'll tell you everything I've thought about it, and—well, done about it, because, you see, there was just one thing that struck me right away. That was that everything hung on the American's evidence and that possibly—not probably, but still it seemed to me the sort of thing that simply had to be cleared up—just possibly that evidence might not be true. You'll probably think it fantastic of me to have bothered about it, because that boy was quite unconnected with any of us, and so very honest. But I—I was looking for every conceivable way out. Besides that, I'm methodical, I like to tidy up and put loose ends away. And now I'll tell you something just in case you're wasting time racking your brains over the same point. That very same evening, after I'd left Cecily's place, I went and knocked up a good firm of detectives and I had them hunt up everything about that boy. It didn't take them long. He comes from St. Louis. He's of French descent, his father's a miner—incidentally, none of the family has even been in New York—and Larg had never been in this country before he came here about three months ago. Smith, the friend of his father's whom he was trying to find, was some sort of skilled mechanic who'd spent about twenty years in America. The enquiry didn't lead anywhere. I'm afraid there's nothing wrong with Larg. There isn't even a chance that he's a crazed and disappointed dramatist whose work Janet had politely declined to handle and who'd planned a clever double murder—of Ritter first, the motive jealousy, and then of Janet, the motive revenge. I've seen a letter of Larg's, concerned with what he calls ' more than sampling ' our beer, and excellent though his style is in its own way, it doesn't belong to a person with literary ambitions. No—don't laugh at me, Mrs. Church. I had lots of other ideas quite as fantastic as that. I've thought of everything, absolutely everything. I tell you, I'd have jumped at anything that would have brought a little order and sanity back into my own world. I've been lost, I've been drowning in horror and blackness all these days. I'm never going to have any faith in anything again."

Suddenly Alice found herself wondering how much faith he had ever had anyway except on the surface. Watching him curiously, she said: " And now that you've proved that there's nothing wrong with Ed Larg's story, do you still want to help Mrs. Markland? "

" But of course! "

" Even though, apparently, she must have killed Aubrey Ritter? "

His worried forehead contracted still more.

" Yes," he said after a moment, " even so."

" Ritter was a friend of yours? "

" Yes, yes—but you know, I believe Rit himself would have wanted it, in fact, I'm sure of it. He had an extraordinary understanding of other people and a sort of—of *mercy* towards the weak and the evil in them, the sort of quality that you associate more with women than with men usually, though he wasn't at all effeminate. He'd a really amazing, unobtrusive charity. I suppose it arose out of all the troubles he'd had himself. Anyway, I'm sure, I'm absolutely certain that he'd have wanted us all to give Janet all the help we could."

" I wish you'd tell me more about him," said Alice, " I mean about the sort of person he really was."

Willing gave a quick smile. " A grand person, Mrs. Church, a really grand person. With all his brilliance he was so simple and warm and spontaneus—he always admired other people so sincerely and humbly—that was wonderfully attractive. Take his attitude to poor Mace. Roger was bitterly jealous of him on Janet's account—Roger's the type that always is jealous, don't you think? He's got so much self-distrust. Rit spoke to me about it once or twice and told me it worried him. You see, apart from its being quite unfounded, he'd an immense admiration for Roger. He was always saying how brilliant he was and how he'd give anything in the world to have a really penetrating mind like his. There wasn't a trace of envy or jealousy in Rit's own character. Oh, God, when I think what's happened——"

Alice broke in quickly: " Unfounded? Did you say Dr. Mace's jealousy was quite unfounded? "

" Indeed, yes! "

" You mean you don't believe what the police have stated about the relationship between Mrs. Markland and Aubrey Ritter? "

" I certainly do not! " said Willing in a violent whisper.

" But in that case—— "

" I know, I know, why did she kill him? Why, why? I tell you it was the finest, easiest relationship, the most perfectly mutual, balanced . . . Oh, I can't put it into words! "

" Yes, but why *did* she kill him, Mr. Willing—why, if it wasn't to revenge herself for his having abandoned her? "

For an instant Alice had an odd feeling that she had frightened the little man. He looked round vaguely, found the waiter's eye on him, beckoned and asked for more bread. The hush in the shadowy room seemed to grow heavier. Alice suddenly found herself wishing that they had gone somewhere noisier and brighter. Too much, in that muted atmosphere, seemed to hang on their words. The room seemed to listen and wait for what they said.

Peter Willing started crumbling the bread with shaking fingers.

" There's only one explanation," he muttered, avoiding Alice's eyes. " You won't believe me, you'll say it's not possible, but knowing Janet and Rit as I did, I stick to it that there's only one explanation."

" And that is? "

" Accident."

He raised his head; his light blue eyes stared at Alice defiantly.

" Accident? " she said thoughtfully. " Well? "

" Oh, I know, I know—I know everything you're going to say! " he exclaimed excitedly. " How does one kill a person accidentally with a poker? Why didn't she say it was accident and explain how it happened? That might get her a verdict of manslaughter at least. And why, why does she go on insisting that she never went up to the flat? I know all about those questions and I can't answer one of them. But all the same, accident's the only possible explanation."

Alice said nothing. Willing looked at her anxiously and waited for her to speak, but her mind had gone blank. The idea of accident simply did not make sense.

At length she said: " That's it—why *does* she insist that she never went upstairs? That's what one always comes back to. You know, there must be a reason."

He nodded eagerly. " Of course. And as a matter of fact, I've been wondering if—well, if, Janet being the sort of person she is, might not be in some way protecting somebody by saying that. I haven't the faintest idea how saying it could in fact protect anybody, but still, you see, there's Janet's character, isn't there? For me that's the fundamental thing. I've known her for years, I've worked with her, I've trusted her judgment, I've relied utterly on her integrity. All that's so important to me that the logical side of things hardly seems to me to matter very much. You, I'm sure, have a very clear, incisive mind and you'll feel sorry for me for being driven to talk such nonsense—yet I know, I simply *know*, Mrs. Church, that the only way Janet could kill a person is by accident.''

Alice did feel sorry for him; she felt very sorry indeed, and it struck her that in a world inhabited, as his seemed to be, by '' grand people,'' there was little room for an explanation of a good many human actions except on a basis of accident.

While she was thinking about it he leant towards her. There was a slightly feverish look in his eyes. '' I think I'm going to try and tell you all about Janet,'' he said. '' Then perhaps you'll understand what I mean. I'll tell you about how I got to know her and how we started working together and about Rit and poor Rosamund and all that. I'd like to be able to make you see. . . . Because, after all, if only I could make you understand . . . As I was saying, two heads are better than one, and if only I could get you to see what's so clear to me, you with your clear brain and dispassionate view might be able to point out something I've missed, something in the evidence that's got just a tiny hole in it, and then between us, perhaps, we could actually do something to help Janet. What d'you say?''

Alice was so surprised and so impressed by the thought of her incisiveness and dispassionateness that she nodded readily, giving him at the same time what she hoped was a comforting smile. He responded with a sudden, quite sunny beam and went on talking rapidly.

'' As a matter of fact, it was my wife who first got to know Janet. She met her at the house of some friends and liked her. I can still remember what Evelyn said about her when she got home. She said: ' I met an awfully charming woman to-day

—one of the calmest people I've ever met.' I made some remark about never believing in the calmness of calm people and Evelyn said: ' You'd believe in Mrs. Markland's.' It's funny I've never forgotten that—I suppose it's because, when I did meet Janet, her calm struck me as something absolutely real and balanced. It seemed to come out of an extraordinary understanding of herself. And she was very young, you know, only twenty-four or five. It was quite soon after she'd separated from Ian Markland—you never met him, I suppose? ''

Alice shook her head, wondering why she had never heard till this moment that Peter Willing had a wife.

'' Neither did I,'' he said. '' He was killed in nineteen-forty, you know, at Calais. I don't think Janet had seen him for years. She never spoke much about him and I never heard her blame him for the way things had turned out. My belief is that he was probably quite a grand person—I'm sure Janet would never have thought of marrying him if he hadn't been—but that they just weren't suited to each other. The most I ever heard Janet say was that she didn't believe in early marriages. I know Markland was in advertising when they married, and doing very well. But he gave it up fairly soon and went to live in the country to write. It was soon after that that Janet left him. She was writing too, scraping along on magazine stories, when Evelyn and I first got to know her. I was trying to write a bit myself in those days, as I suppose all of us have done some time or other, but I'd a wife and two children and had to take life seriously. I don't know how long Markland stuck to it—I know I never heard anything of him.''

So Peter Willing had not only a wife but two children down in Surrey. For some reason this gave Alice a feeling of reassurance. She had thought, that evening at Cecily's party, that she was amongst a group of utterly rootless people, living on their nerves, their gifts and their overstrung emotions in two-room flats. She was glad that Peter Willing at least had taken time to supply himself with some of the normal interests and responsibilities of mankind. However, she was not at all sure that it made him any more likely to be reliable in his interpretation of Janet Markland's character.

" But don't you know at all the reason why they separated? " she asked.

He shrugged. " Janet always said it was her fault for marrying him. Cecily Lightwood once told me a lot about it, but, you know, I never know how much one can believe of what Cecily tells one. She's a dear, good soul with a heart of gold—absolutely of gold—but her interest in other people is always so melodramatic. She told me a dreadful story of women and drink and extravagance and cruelty. She said Markland was a sort of spoiled, vicious child with a colossal opinion of his own abilities that took Janet in at first, but that once she was married to him she began to see through him, and once she realised his excesses weren't the offshoots of genius she couldn't bear them any more. But to me that story's never quite made sense. I simply can't see Janet being attracted by that type of person. She hated unkindness and selfishness. One of the things, she's told me, which she's always liked so about poor Cecily is her immense generosity. Cecily's the kind of person, you know, who gets really offended if you don't let her help you. And poor Roger too—he's the kindest soul alive; he keeps inadvertently giving his last shilling away, hardly knowing that he's doing it. And Rit, of course . . . And Janet herself has always been a wonderfully considerate person. I'm not at all easy to get on with, you know—I'm very nervous and irritable and sometimes I have a foul temper. It's all my digestion, of course; it's been rotten ever since the war, the last war. There are days at a time when I feel as if I were carrying a ton weight inside me and I go right down into a black pit of depression. I don't think much about other people then, I just think of myself and become one revolting lump of self-pity, and I don't get my work done—and Janet's always wonderful about it. D'you know, I've never in my life seen her lose her temper? A murderess? Good God Almighty——" He seized one of Alice's hands and thumped it on the table, " I tell you, it can't be, it simply can't be, it just *has* to be accident! "

Alice did not take up that point again. She inquired: " When did Ritter appear on the scene? "

" About a year or two after Janet and I got started here,"

Willing replied. " As a matter of fact, he was our first real success. He was just what we were both waiting for. We hadn't even kept our heads above water before that. If Rit hadn't turned up we'd have had to throw our hands in. All my wife's capital—she'd had a legacy from a grand-aunt which was what we'd relied on when we started up—it had all gone. Times were pretty bleak, and I remember I'd been having a particularly bad time with my rotten old inside— d'you know, without exaggeration, I did think of the gas-oven once or twice. Then Rit turned up one day. He turned up without any appointment. I found him hanging about on the stairs with a roll of paper under his arm which was obviously a manuscript, and looking as if he couldn't pluck up courage to go on. He didn't make me feel in the least hopeful when I saw him. He looked like an undergraduate-poet. He always kept rather that look except that he didn't go in for being dirty or dishevelled. It was simply that he had a passion for colour. Perhaps that's why he was so unhappy in the north. Think of it—the drabness and grimness and squalor of those ghastly black slums and the almost equally soot-grimed provincial suburbia! And then the harsh, dour temperament of the people! He always said he could never really feel it was England at all and that he felt far more foreign there than he ever had in France or Italy. I imagine he must have looked pretty conspicuous going about in his coloured shirts and scarves and corduroys. He was really like a child about his clothes. It was a sort of exhibitionism, of course, but so simple and naive and spontaneous—I don't think I've ever known anyone so open and spontaneous as Rit—that it attracted you, it charmed you. Anyway, there he was on the stairs, asking me very nervously if there was any chance that he could see Janet, who might just possibly remember him, he thought, as they'd been at college together, and all the time he talked he twisted the manuscript round and round under his arm. I looked at it and saw that it was typed in red on thick grey paper and tied up with emerald green ribbon, and I thought, oh Lord, why does it always have to be this sort of thing? And I gave one of my passing thoughts to the gas-oven. Well,"—he leant back with a faint smile—" that was the manuscript of *Coal Dust*."

The waiter had cleared the table and put coffee in front of them. Peter Willing brought out a cigarette-case. It was of gold. As he slid it back into his pocket he went on: " Not that the play was much use in the form it was in then. He did a lot more work on it before we got it accepted by Jan Sterne. It was Janet who made him do the revision—only it was more than revision, really, it was almost a complete re-writing. I took him in to see her—after putting on the air of a busy executive and keeping him waiting for a quite unnecessary ten minutes. That's funny to look back on, you know!—and Janet took the manuscript home with her and read it that night. Next day she told me that she thought there was something in it though it would never do as it stood; it was much too precious and full of quite undramatic reflections on the horrors of industrialism. Rit had gone back to Manchester already. She wrote to him and told him what she thought and he began by taking offence and blowing up. Then he came up to London again and the two of them came down to us in Surrey for a week-end and argued and worked, and gradually the thing took shape. I think I began to feel even then that something exciting was happening. Rit was very modest really and eager for criticism and very easy to influence—too easy perhaps, considering his gifts—and he'd an amazing capacity for work and concentration. Of course he was terribly impeded at that time by his job. I've always thought schoolmastering must be one of the ghastliest lives on earth and for a person like Rit it was positive torture. He was simply squandering himself on it, working himself dog-tired and then trying to write—just to save his soul, you know; he hadn't the faintest idea that he'd ever make money out of his writing. Yet the queer thing is, considering the conditions he was working under, that I've always felt *Coal Dust* was the best thing he ever did. I wonder if you agree with me. I know it's immature and emotionally perhaps rather trite at times, but it has a freshness and power and sincerity . . . Well, that's how it's always struck me, at any rate."

As he paused, Alice asked: " Was he married already at that time? "

" Oh, indeed, yes," said Willing. " He'd married Rosamund during his first year in Manchester. He'd met her in Vienna in the summer holidays; she'd been studying music there. At first he never spoke of her and then one day Janet told me they'd sat up half the night together, talking of his marriage. Once he let himself go, apparently it all just poured out—and, of course, Janet, was a marvellous listener. She didn't tell me much of what he'd said, though I gathered his marriage was a mess and I thought of all the usual reasons for that, of a wife who didn't sympathise with his writing and wanted him to stick to the safety of schoolmastering and so on . . . I was absolutely wrong. I realised that the moment I saw Rosamund. She came to London to his first night . . ."

His voice trailed off oddly as he said that. Fingering his empty coffee-cup, he gazed down into it with narrowed eyes, visualising something long ago, something that still seemed to stir him deeply.

" What was she like? " Alice asked.

" Beautiful! " he answered softly. The hush in his voice seemed suddenly to be less because of the silent, cavernous room than because of something he felt which still shook and dismayed him. But immediately he forced an unconvincing flippancy into his tone. " If I hadn't been in love with my wife, I really believe I'd have fallen in love with Rosamund at first sight. Perhaps I did in a way anyhow. Yes, I'd better confess it, I dreamt of her for three nights running! She was very slender and graceful with chestnut hair and very pale colouring. I'm no hand at describing people and if I say things like ' she was like a flame,' and so on, you'll think me ridiculous—yet sometimes I say just that phrase to myself and feel quite pleased with it. I know I can't possibly give you any idea of what she was like, but she really was lovely. Rit was enormously proud of her—you could see that—and she of him. She was very excited that night; she was wild with pleasure at his success and gave the impression of being the gayest, simplest creature in the world. Unfortunately, that was only one side of her. She'd a hysterical temper and she went in for attacks of depression which made one almost think . . . Well, perhaps in view of what happened, one would have been right in thinking that she wasn't really quite normal. She seemed to take a delight in making scenes, she'd storm and weep in public so that it could be pretty terrifying to go about with her, and afterwards she'd have terrible fits of remorse and hate herself for the way she'd behaved; she'd be like a child then, trying to propitiate you for what she'd done to you. Poor Rit simply lived in a state of terror. But he knew she was devoted to him and absolutely dependent on him, and for anyone as soft-hearted as he was that was a tie from which there wasn't any escape. I dare say it would have been better for him, in a way, better for his writing anyhow, if he'd had the ruthlessness to leave her. I've always thought it was the strain under which he lived and the fact that he had to hold himself in all the time that brought the touch of artificiality, you might almost call it superficiality, into his later work—because I'm afraid there *was* a certain superficiality about it—much as I admired it, I thought there was something about it that didn't ring quite true. Of course, it may just have been that he'd left the scene he was writing about . . . Perhaps he'd lost his human feeling about it and let it turn into a theory. But I still believe that the strain of trying to make a good job of his marriage to Rosamund was the real trouble. I do believe there's a lot to be said for the idea that artists shouldn't let themselves be too concerned, too *morally* concerned, as it were, with their human relationships. If he'd left Rosamund perhaps he wouldn't have been quite such a lovable human being, but posterity might have been grateful for it."

This last speech of Willing's puzzled Alice considerably. She sat thinking about it for some time, then at length said hesitantly: " But there was Janet, wasn't there? "

She thought his body tensed slightly. Lowering his eyelids, he started tapping his cigarette mechanically on the edge of the ashtray.

She went on: " For instance, the fortnight in Wales . . . Did you know about that at the time? "

" No," he answered.

" But—it did happen, didn't it? "

He snatched a quick glance at her face, looking momentarily as if he hated her.

" It hurt," he muttered, " I'll confess to you, it hurt, finding out about it like that. I couldn't understand why she'd never told me about it. I shouldn't have been censorious—she knew that—she could have trusted me. After all, it might have affected her future, our future, quite considerably. But it's not just that . . ." Little wrinkles of distress fanned out round his eyes. " It's that I can't *understand* why she didn't tell me. There wasn't any *reason* why she shouldn't."

Alice thought there was no need just then to remind him that if most of us had any inkling of all the things that our best friends never dream of telling us there would be very little friendship and perhaps very little love.

She said: " D'you think Rosamund ever suspected it? "

He frowned, raking about the ash in the ashtray with the stub of his cigarette.

" No," he said, " no, I'm sure she didn't. I'm sure Frank was wrong there. She could never have kept it to herself if she'd had any real suspicions. She was jealous of Janet, of course, as she was of almost anyone who had any part in Rit's life—even of dear, loyal Cecily sometimes, and me. Once she even had a storm with my wife because Evelyn had taken it into her head to knit Rit a pullover. He'd been extravagantly admiring of some she'd knitted for the boys, so she'd made him one just like them. Rit was delighted with it, and Rosamund was utterly furious—ending, of course, in tears and pleadings for forgiveness. But the point is, it wasn't a sex-jealousy. It was all because her own life had absolutely nothing in it but Rit. As I told you, she was studying music when they first met. She played the violin, and I've often thought that if only she'd gone on with that everything might have turned out differently. But unfortnuately she hadn't the necessary pertinacity and self-discipline. Every now and then she'd get out her violin again and arrange to take lessons and make all sorts of resolutions, and then she wouldn't go to the lessons and she'd leave her music lying about all over everything and never touch it, and Rit would get mad at the mess

—he was an awfully tidy soul—and perhaps they'd have one
of their rows, and it would end with Rit in sheer desperation
going to hide for two or three days in Janet's flat . . . Of
course, I knew about how he used to do that, but for some
reason I never thought . . ." He swallowed, then shrugged
that thought aside again. " But isn't it a terrible thing, Mrs.
Church," he added, " what two people, whose one desire
in life is to help one another, can actually do to each
other? Poor, lovely Rosamund. Such a grand person really,
so kind and generous in her intentions, and always so utterly
helpless."

" Was there any particular cause for her suicide? " asked
Alice. " I mean, was there any particular event that drove her
to it?"

" I don't think so," he answered. " I think it was just
there waiting all the time. I think it was the only possible
outcome. But I don't know—perhaps there was something.
Cecily could tell you more about it than anyone. She was
closer to Rosamund than any of the rest of us, unless perhaps
Frank Lely. He was devoted to her and wonderfully kind to
her in his queer way. It was he who found her, you know.
Sometimes I've wondered if there was a note or anything, but
if so, he destroyed it and never said anything about it. He'd
be capable of that. He's a strange character; he's got the
ruthlessness Rit lacked, and perhaps in the end he's the more
gifted of the two—Janet always said he was, though she's
never liked him. She always said he'd do big things some day
and that he was wise enough not to be in a hurry, but she said
you couldn't trust him as a human being. I don't know about
that; I've always found him easy enough to get along with,
and he always did have a curiously steadying effect on
Rosamund. Anyway, I should think he probably knows more
than anyone else of what was going on in the mind of that
poor, tortured soul before she died."

" And was it the gas-oven that was her way out?"

" No, she took an overdose of some sleeping-tablets. She
was hours dying. As a matter of fact. . . ." His voice shook
slightly in a sound which might have been sob or laugh.
" As a matter of fact, there wasn't a gas-oven. It was

electric. They'd an awfully expensive flat in a new block
where every conceivable gadget was electric. She and Rit
took such a charming, childish pride in it when they first
moved in. They were like that, both of them. Money meant
nothing to them in the ordinary way, it was just a delightful
toy to play with. It never made them the least bit pretentious,
and they gave it away with both hands to everybody. When
Rit first gave up his teaching and they moved to London
they were both very cautious still; they took a little flat on the
top-floor in Fitzroy Square—I remember there wasn't even a
sink in the kitchen—and they decorated it themselves and
furnished it beautifully out of junkshops, and lived there as
if their income was about three pounds a week. And then
suddenly it seemed to strike them that they were rich and all
in one day they rented a new flat and bought a car and a fur
coat for Rosamund and Lord knows what else. Janet and
I had to go over the flat with them and turn all the switches
on and off and admire all the exciting things that happened.
It seems terribly pathetic, somehow, thinking back to it. For
about a month they seemed to be happy, but it didn't last.
Rosamund had to live all the time on a peak of emotional
excitement, and that's something which just isn't feasible.
Soon all the old scenes were happening again. I believe it
must have been just about then that Rit spent that fortnight
in Wales with Janet . . ." He stopped suddenly. Leaning
back, he stared straight ahead of him, and for the first time
Alice realised that his mild, pleasant face could look hard,
almost stonily hard.

Yet when he looked at her again he had a deprecating
little smile on his lips.

" You mustn't think that I resent the fact that Janet never
told me about that, Mrs. Church," he said. " It hurt, I
confess it, but I do understand really that she might have had
all sorts of reasons for saying nothing about it. We live in an
outspoken age, and I'm used, I suppose, to a particularly outspoken circle of people, but actually Janet always said very
little about herself. One could have taken her for rather a
puritan—perhaps subconsciously that's what I always thought
she was—except that she was always so ready to take other

people as they were and to sympathise with their efforts to make hashes of their lives. She's shrewd, mind you, and wonderfully good at assessing their possibilities—that's why I'm missing her so terribly in the office—but she's too inately kind to be a puritan. Take her affection for poor Roger, for instance, or even poor, dear Cecily."

" And all in all," said Alice, feeling it was time to do some summing up of all that she had gathered from him, " you're perfectly certain that there was nothing in her nature to explain the murder? "

He exclaimed excitedly: " I've told you, it can't have been murder, it simply can't have been! It was an accident— that's the only possible explanation."

" An accident with a poker? "

" Yes, yes, I've told you, I don't pretend to have the slightest idea of how it could have happened, but accident's what it simply has to be! But as a matter of fact, I *have* had an idea . . ." Flinging himself back in his chair again, he cast his eyes up to the ceiling. " I *have* had an idea how a person might be killed by accident with a poker, *provided that person was a dramatist!* "

Alice waited.

After a pause, he went on rapidly: " Suppose the real reason why Rit didn't want to come down to Cecily's party that evening was that he was working. Suppose he'd started working on a new play. Suppose there was a murder in it . . . D'you see what I'm getting at? When Rit was working everything else went out of his head. He lived his scenes and his characters. If you interrupted him he simply swept you into it too. You'd find yourself acting little impromptu passages with him. And so, you see, I'm wondering if it isn't just possible that that evening when Janet arrived he—I know it sounds fantastic, but I do believe there's something in it——"

" He put a poker into her hand and said, ' Now hit me over the head with it, please, and let's see what happens '? "

" Yes," he said eagerly, " yes, that's it, that's just it! "

But the next moment his excitement had collapsed and he was eyeing Alice with a weary, embarrassed air.

" It *is* possible," he said defensively. " Of course he must have slipped, or perhaps Janet did—something went wrong, anyway. But I do think it's a far more plausible explanation than that Janet deliberately murdered him."

" But if anything of that sort did happen," said Alice, " there'd have been a manuscript somewhere, wouldn't there, or at least notes of some sort? "

" Yes, by jove," he said, " of course there would! "

" And was there? "

He gave a sigh. " Not that I know of."

" What happened to Ritter's papers? "

" I went through them with the police, then they were sent off to his mother in Gloucester. He left everything to her. There were a few short stories and the beginnings of several novels—he was always meaning to write a novel—but there wasn't anything about a murder. Of course, it might have got lost, or been removed, or . . . Mrs. Church! " He jerked in his chair and one of his hands shot out and gripped Alice's wrist again. " Mrs. Church, Frank Lely was the first on the scene of that death also! "

Perhaps, if Alice had been more impressed than she was by the theory of an accidental killing, she would have responded more than she did to this suggestion.

" But then there would still be the question, wouldn't there," she said, " of why Janet denies having gone up to Ritter's flat? "

" Yes," said Willing, " yes, there would still be that."

And that, though they still went on talking for some time, was what they always came back to. Janet Markland had condemned herself by her own stupid, stubborn lying. For her fingerprints were on the poker and Ed Larg had seen her on the staircase. Alice did not feel that her lunch with Peter Willing had clarified anything for her.

CHAPTER FOUR

ALICE pondered a good deal during the next few weeks on what Peter Willing had told her of Janet Markland and the Ritters, but she found in the end that she only felt more confused than ever. Certainly she felt no nearer to any understanding of the murderess. How could a woman such as the little literary agent had described ever have snatched up a poker and killed anybody with it? Not that the woman whom he had described struck Alice as particularly likely ever to have existed. Janet Markland, according to her partner, was a reserved but entirely balanced individual who could be gently considerate to the weaknesses of others because she was so secure in her own strength. But few really reserved people, Alice thought, are as balanced as they appear; at the back of the reserve there is nearly always something they are afraid to give away, and where there is fear there is tension and instability. Peter Willing had either failed completely to penetrate the character of his friend, or else out of loyalty had concealed half of what he knew. On the whole, Alice thought, it was the more likely that he had been deceived himself, although at least partly with his own co-operation; he liked to think everyone he knew charming, sensitive and benevolent. Eventually Alice decided that it would be best for her to think as little as possible about the problem and to sever her connection with the group of people amongst whom she had been brought in contact with passions that could lead to murder. She tried to give her mind entirely to the problem of running a home in wartime and to the problems of the people who came asking for her help at the Citizens' Advice Bureau. Solving these problems would at least make some difference in the lives of a number of people.

But one day Cecily Lightwood rang up and asked Alice in a strained, offended tone when she was next coming to see her.

Cecily made it sound as if she felt that Alice had been avoiding her. The truth probably was that Cecily had found herself suddenly wanting to see Alice, but feeling uncertain of how Alice had taken her own earlier avoidance of her, had convinced herself that the blame was all Alice's. She kept Alice talking so long on the telephone that Alice guessed she was feeling lonely, and arranged to have tea with her the following Sunday.

But she did not look forward to it. Cecily was not likely to be cheerful, and Cecily depressed had the art of clawing all the emotional stuffing out of people. Alice had recognised earlier that the only feeling Cecily roused in her, apart from admiration for her work and a slight warmth at the charm she could occasionally show, was pity, and pity is an enervating element in any relationship.

So preparing to be clawed at and reduced to the depths of depression herself, Alice set out on the Sunday afternoon for the house near Parliament Hill Fields.

She arrived at four o'clock. Nothing about the house seemed altered except that both the upper flats were occupied. The housing-shortage in London was already growing acute and the fact that a murder had been committed in a flat seemed to count as less of a disadvantage than broken windows or a gaping roof.

Alice rang and had to wait a long time before the door was opened. When at length Cecily appeared she looked as if she had forgotten that she had invited anyone. She was in one of her slovenly phases; her grey hair was limply out of curl and straggling loose round her shoulders, she had no make-up on and was wearing a soiled scarlet blouse, blue slacks and bed-room slippers.

She stared at Alice expressionlessly then slouched ahead of her into the sitting-room without saying a word.

As soon as Alice had closed the sitting-room door, Cecily turned on her.

" Why did you come? " she asked sharply. " You didn't want to! I could tell that by your voice on the telephone. I suppose you prefer not to have anything to do with the dis-reputable sort of people whose friends get murdered! "

" Don't be ridiculous," said Alice uncomfortably. She felt that in spite of the fact that this time Cecily was surprisingly near the truth, her attacks of distrust were always absurd and pitiable. " You've been avoiding me."

" Only because you showed pretty plainly you didn't want to have anything to do with me. Oh, I don't blame you." Cecily flung herself into a chair by the fire. " I suppose you're fed up with me too for dropping the C.A.B., but—oh God, I just couldn't face it! Other people's troubles started looking a bit too silly to me compared with some of my own. Those damn fools, the stupid sort of things they make a fuss about! I got fed up with trying to sympathise with them. People who can't handle their own troubles without dashing off to some miserable bureau to get themselves spoon-fed with good advice ought to be—well, I'll tell you what ought to be done with them! I've got a window-cleaner who turns up about once in six months. He's got his own ideas about what ought to be done with all the people he doesn't like—particularly politicians in his case. He always says, ' Tike 'em up on top of Parliament 'ill Fields and blow 'em sky 'igh! ' Well, that's what ought to be done with a lot of people. That's what ought to be done with all the soft, stupid fools who want everything done for them. ' Tike 'em up on top of Parliament 'ill Fields and blow 'em sky 'igh! ' '' Throwing back her head she went off into guffaws of harsh laughter.

Alice knew this mood in Cecily. She also knew, in spite of what Cecily had just said, that the intensity of sympathy which Cecily had felt for everyone who had come to her at the C.A.B. with problems concerning rationing, clothing, ruined homes, war-injuries and all those more personal problems such as the infidelity of husbands or the awkwardness of difficult children which sometimes lay behind some apparently simple query, had made her work almost valueless. All her enormous capacity for indignation had always been ready to burst out on behalf of anyone who had happened to come to her; then everyone else in the office had had to listen and help and agree that this particular case was far more urgent and difficult and infamous than any other, and Cecily had spent herself in promising assistance which she had no power to give.

As she sat down, noticing that the big, pleasant room, like

Cecily herself, looked neglected, with cigarette-ash spilling about out of over-filled ash-trays, crumbs on the carpet and faded flowers in a bowl, Alice remarked: " I wondered if you'd move away from here. I thought probably you would."

" Why should I? " asked Cecily. " I hate moving. Besides it's hell trying to find a new place nowadays. And none of your things fit and you get things broken. I did wonder just at first if I wouldn't move, but what difference would it have made? One can't leave one's thoughts behind, can one? Aren't we told hell's inside us, or something of that sort? No, I don't believe in running away from things."

" I see the upper flats are taken," said Alice.

" Yes, damned sensation-seekers! Aren't people foul? My God," snarled Cecily bitterly, " I hate the human race! I loathe everything about it, its looks and lies and bestialities and treacheries! There's no one you can trust. You keep kidding yourself you've found someone who's straight and decent and then you find that it's just that very person who's . . ." She pulled herself up. Lurching on to her feet, she grabbed at a packet of cigarettes on the mantelpiece. " Kitty's coming," she said abruptly.

The words brought back to Alice that other evening with rather a shock.

" D'you see her often? " she asked.

" Heavens, no, why should I? " said Cecily, sprawling back in the chair again, drawing fiercely at her cigarette. " The woman's a complete fool, she always was. I've no patience with her at all. She used to have a good deal of charm when she was young and hadn't got so blousy and fat, but she was always sex-mad and she hasn't grown out of it. She rang me up this morning and said she was in town having lunch with somebody and could she come on here afterwards. I had to say all right, though I didn't want to see her in the least. I know whom she's been having lunch with, it's that beast Frank Lely. Did you see the two of them go off together after the inquest? Even after the inquest! Good God, aren't people unspeakable? "

" But why should that disturb you so? " said Alice. " It's

quite natural to want to talk to somebody after a horrible thing like that.''

'' Talk! '' said Cecily and laughed.

'' But——''

'' My dear Alice, Kitty can't look at a man without thinking of getting into bed with him. Someone like you, who's probably got a normal amount of self-control, although—well, I swore I'd never trust my own judgment about that again. I thought Janet had self-control and . . .'' Her voice grated and she drew a sharp breath. '' The point is, someone like you just can't understand a dirty little bitch like Kitty. But you know . . . about Janet . . . I thought she had all sorts of things. You remember all the things I used to tell you about her? I thought she had all the qualities I hadn't, self-control and a calm, reasoned way of thinking things out and an ability to have friendships without getting them all mixed up with sex. But that's done with—I'm never going to let myself get taken in like that again. I'm not going to give anyone the chance to do it. If Janet, if Janet of *all* people, was just a treacherous fake . . .'' She stopped again and sat glowering at the fire.

'' But I never realised you were so proper about sex,'' said Alice. '' You used always to—to display the attractions of freedom, so to speak.''

'' I'm not in the least proper! '' said Cecily indignantly. '' If only Janet had been honest about things, I'd never have criticised her at all. Good Lord, there aren't many women who'd have resisted Rit if he'd wanted them. He'd more charm than any man I've ever met, and besides that he always needed help so much. That's a fatal combination, you know,''—she laughed sardonically—'' it's a simple knock-out! Oh, if Janet hadn't been so secretive about it, if she'd had the courage of her convictions, if she'd only told me . . .'' She sucked in a swift mouthful of smoke. '' I wonder if you know what it's like, Alice, to think you're somebody's best friend and then discover you don't know the first thing about them. You tell them everything about yourself, *everything*— and you think they're doing the same with you, and then you find they've left out every single important thing. They've

treated you like a. child, they've taken you in absolutely,
they've made the most utter fool of you! ''

With her brows drawn together in a puzzled frown, Alice
reflected that perhaps it was not really as surprising as it felt
at first that Cecily should obviously care more about the fact
that Janet had deceived her than about the murder of Aubrey
Ritter.

After a moment Cecily went on reflectively: '' You know,
there's only one person who saw through Janet, and that's
Frank Lely. It's queer, I've always loathed him, I've always
thought him an evil-minded brute, yet I did realise he wasn't
a fool. I always used to wonder why he didn't like Janet—
he never did, you know, he never trusted her. He told me
once he never trusted repressed people; he said they were
always controlled by some internal compulsions of which an
ordinary person couldn't know anything at all. Janet was
awfully repressed, of course, I see that now; I used to think
it was reason and self-control, but it wasn't, it was simply
repression. I've been thinking that her sexual relationship
with Rit can't really have been a bit satisfactory. I'm rather
inclined to think she must have been quite frigid. I never
used to think about it at the time, I never thought of her at
all in connection with men, but looking back now I'm sure
that must have been the trouble always. One can *feel* it, you
know . . . I shouldn't be surprised, anyway, if that was why
things went wrong straight away with Ian Markland.''

This was the kind of discussion that always made Alice feel
uncomfortable, and she was glad that the bell rang just then.

Kitty Roper came in looking as bouyant, as beautiful and as
flashy as ever. She had on an emerald green suit, trimmed
with black fur, a red and green checked blouse, and a silk
handkerchief, patterned with overlapping circles in all the
colours of the rainbow, tied under her plump chin.

She greeted Alice as if she were delighted to see her again,
then she exclaimed: '' What a horrible mess, love! Poor old
Cecily, I know just how it is—you're simply knocked to pieces,
aren't you? When I'm knocked over by something I always
let the place get in a mess too—and then of course I curse
myself, because it's much worse straightening up than it would

have been keeping on top of things all the time, especially with a husband and children, not to mention Americans, though mine are lambs and very helpful, but I simply hate domestic work, you see, and only get through it by the exercise of an iron will. You'd never think to look at me that I'd got an iron will, would you, Mrs. Church? "

She laughed. Throwing down her bag and gloves, she started unbuttoning her green jacket.

" Let's tidy up a bit for Cecily, shall we? " she went on, looking round thoughtfully. " Then the poor old thing can put her feet up on the couch and have a nice rest. Come along, love——" She fastened a plump hand round one of Cecily's arms and pushed her down on to the couch. " You're looking like the wreck of the *Hesperus*. You put your feet up and look on while Mrs. Church and I tidy up. There's nothing so beautifully restful as looking on while other people tidy up."

Cecily gazed at her for a moment, too astonished to say anything. She watched Kitty pick up an overflowing ash-tray and empty it into the fireplace. Then she screamed at her: " Stop it, you fool! Leave my things alone! What the hell d'you think you're doing? You're a fool, Kitty, a complete fool! Leave my things alone, damn you! "

Kitty calmly picked up the bowl of faded flowers and carried it away into the kitchen. In her checked blouse and gaudy green skirt, broad hipped, full-breasted, and with the vivid silk handkerchief tied under her chin, she looked like a Ruritanian peasant-girl out of a musical comedy.

Tense and pale, Cecily started whipping herself up into a rage. But she did not get up from the sofa, and by degrees, as Kitty returned with a dustpan and brush and started sweeping up the crumbs from the carpet, Cecily's repeated assertions that Kitty was a fool, an utter, complete, unspeakable, unmentionable fool became quite good-humoured. At last she actually smiled. Alice reflected that certainly there was something of iron in Kitty.

Presently Kitty said: " There, love, things look much nicer now, don't they? You'll find it'll do you good. And d'you know what, first thing to-morrow you must go to the hairdresser and make yourself look decent. You're looking like the wreck of the *Hesperus*."

Cecily gave a cackle of laughter.

" ' The wreck of the *Hesperus*,'—you always used that ridiculous phrase when you were at school. Aren't you ever going to grow up? "

Kitty grinned. " I'm ever so grown up really," she said. " You ought to see me at home, managing my huge family. You'd just never believe it."

" Alice," said Cecily sharply, " why d'you keep staring at Kitty? "

Alice gave a start. " Do I? " she asked.

" You do. She's a sight, of course; she gets herself up outrageously. But why d'you go on staring at her? "

" It's my beauty," said Kitty, " or else my fat. I'll get some tea now. No, no, love—you stay still." She vanished again into the kitchen.

Alice tried to avoid Cecily's eye. She was feeling flustered and disturbed. But Cecily leant towards her and whispered: " You *were* looking at her awfully queerly."

Alice shook her head. " I'm sorry, I didn't realise . . ."

" You know, I like Kitty," said Cecily. " She's so open and direct. She always does me good."

Alice nodded vaguely. She knew quite well that she had been staring at Kitty, though for the life of her she could not tell what it was that had held her gaze so helplessly. There was something about Kitty that worried her like a scrap of tune that she could not identify. She felt that she had to go on looking, puzzling, trying to name what it was that reminded her of—what?

Kitty came back into the sitting-room with the tea-tray. She put it down on the little table at Cecily's elbow. Straightening up, she untied the handkerchief over her hair, tossed it aside and pushed her fingers up into her coarse blonde curls to loosen them. She had enormous earrings clamped on to her ears shaped like water-lilies and painted white and gold. The handkerchief missed the table at which she had aimed it and fell at Alice's feet. Alice picked it up. She started to say: " What a gorgeous——"

But as she held the square of silk in her hands, something about the pattern, a pattern of overlapping circles, plucked at her memory. Something started vibrating. A scarf—a scarf, she remembered, with a pattern just like this one—she was ready to swear it was exactly the same as this one—that had been tied round the neck of a man in a photograph . . .

Kitty, as she took the scarf from her, seemed a little puzzled at the look on Alice's face. Alice wondered if she was looking as excited as she felt. Kitty had said that she had not seen Aubrey Ritter since an occasion in Paris about five years before, but Peter Willing had said that the photograph in his office had been taken three or four years ago. Then how had Kitty got hold of the scarf?

But plenty of answers to that question immediately flocked into Alice's mind. There might easily be two scarves. Both might have been bought in Paris one day when Ritter, Rosamund and Kitty were out shopping together. Again, either Kitty or Willing or both, might have been careless about dates; the meeting in Paris might have taken place less than five years ago, or the photograph be older than Willing had said. Again, perhaps the scarves were not really the same; that, after all, was only too probable. Finally, even if Alice had made no mistake about that, it was possible that the whole thing was coincidence. There could be two identical scarves bought separately at different shops at different times by two different people. . . .

But this was a case of murder.

In a case of murder a good working assumption to make is that there are no such things as coincidences.

Kitty and Cecily had gone on talking, that is to say, Kitty was talking. She was the only person Alice knew of who reduced Cecily to a listener. She was talking about her children, her home, her house-keeping.

Alice suddenly made up her mind. "Mrs. Roper," she said, "just how long ago was it that you met the Ritters in Paris?"

She knew that it sounded queer. She intended that it should.

Kitty checked what she had been about to say and with her eyebrows raised and her blue eyes wide and blank, gave

Alice a stare of bewilderment. But it seemed to Alice that it had taken her just a moment to adjust that look to complete naturalness. Alice herself simply stared at the scarf.

Cecily burst out: " Damn, now that's come up again! I believe we'd managed not to mention the bloody business for almost ten minutes." Jumping to her feet, she strode about the room. " In God's name, how long will it be before we're free of it again? "

" Never, love," said Kitty softly, still looking at Alice. She was smiling a vague, sweet smile. " Let me see now, when *did* I meet them? It was in the summer of thirty-seven, I think. Yes, that was it, it was thirty-seven. My mother-in-law was looking after the family and I was having a fortnight on my own. I've always insisted on getting rid of family cares for at least two weeks in the year. But that was the last time I went abroad. Next year John was so certain there was going to be a war that he went up in smoke when I said I was thinking of going to Italy, so I agreed to make it Torquay—and then, of course, there wasn't a war that year." She paused. She had been twisting the scarf round and round one hand while she was speaking; now she made a fist of the hand and struck a blow with it at the air before her. Then she began mechanically unwinding the scarf. " And Torquay was the last flicker of freedom. The year after there really was a war and I lost my mother-in-law's services because she became something awfully indispensable in a hospital, and I lost my maid, of course, and so I'm stuck at Long Clinton all the year round. D'you know Long Clinton, Mrs. Church? It's near Aylesbury. It's very pretty really; I love it. You should come out and visit us there. Come for a week-end. I wish you would." She looked at Alice questioningly and steadily. Her lips still smiled rather vacuously.

Alice murmured politely: " I should love to."

" Really? You will? " There was curious eagerness in Kitty's tone. " Then let's fix it up straight away, shall we? We mustn't let it slide. When can you come? Can you come next week-end? "

Alice said she thought she could manage the next week-end. Kitty said she would ring up during the week to arrange details. She talked a great deal after that, with exaggerated inconsequence, and then quite soon found a reason for leaving. She did not tie the scarf over her hair but bundled it into a pocket and went out bare-headed.

As soon as she had gone Cecily burst out in amazement: " Good heavens, what on earth came over the two of you all of a sudden? You aren't really going to Long Clinton, are you? "

" Why not? " asked Alice.

" Her husband's the most sickening bore," said Cecily, " and the house'll be full of squawling kids and drunk Yanks."

" Kids don't always squawl," said Alice.

" But——"

" And Yanks aren't always drunk."

" But still——"

" And even husbands," said Alice, " don't always bore."

Cecily shook her head. " But I'd never have expected you to be attracted by Kitty."

" Why not? " asked Alice again.

" She's such a fool."

" She's got a very quick mind," said Alice.

" I don't understand it," said Cecily. " There's something funny about it."

There certainly was, and like Cecily, Alice did not understand it either. She wondered if Kitty really would ring up during the week. She had been frightened, that had been obvious, and the way she had acted had removed any doubt that Alice might have continued to feel that the scarf Kitty had worn that afternoon and the scarf Ritter had worn in the photograph were the same one. But what if they were? Kitty, on second thoughts, might realise that it would be difficult to make anything much of the discovery.

However, she did ring up, letting less than twenty-four hours pass before she did so. Reminding Alice breezily of her promise to spend the next week-end at Long Clinton, she asked if her husband would like to come as well. But when Alice handed the invitation on to Oliver he made a face which suggested that he entertained more or less the same ideas about

Kitty's household as Cecily. Alice, replying with the glibness of practice that her husband had to go on working right over the week-end, arranged that she should go alone to Long Clinton.

She went on the Saturday evening, after an afternoon at the C.A.B. She arrived at Aylesbury at about six o'clock. It was dusk already. Long Clinton was another twenty minutes' journey by bus and it was dark when she reached it, so it was not until the next morning that she saw that the house where Kitty Roper lived was a small, neat, modern affair set about halfway up a rather bare hillside, with only three or four other houses, more or less of the same type, dotted over the slopes nearby At that time of the year it was all bleak and cruelly swept by the wind. It seemed much colder than London.

Kitty's family consisted of three blonde, noisy, handsome children, aged from four to eight, and a very quiet husband. The children seemed to be good tempered, friendly and surprisingly helpful about the house; the husband seemed to be irritable, obstinate and determined to be waited upon. The house was very well run; when Kitty had said that she loathed domestic work she had certainly been talking nonsense, for it was easy to see that she enjoyed it, as she would have enjoyed anything that gave her an outlet for her energies. Her children adored her and trusted her; her husband, Alice thought, did not trust her in the least; he watched her with a curious, jealous steadiness nearly all the time she was in the room with him. He seemed to depend on her entirely but always spoke to her condescendingly, as if they both took it for granted that he should think her stupid. Kitty, obviously untroubled by this, used her bouyant good humour to protect her husband and children from having a too wearing contact with one another.

Dr. Roper was a thin, hollow-chested individual with a cold, precise manner. Perhaps his aloofness was only the result of shyness, but it had the appearance of conceit. He never looked at Alice when he spoke to her; he either went on looking at his wife or up at a corner of the ceiling. He gave Alice the impression of someone who was holding himself in all the time, waiting, listening, watching. He dressed very neatly in well-cut, dark clothes and wore rimless pince-nez behind which his brown eyes looked large and liquid and blank. He was not a bore; he spoke too little to be a bore, but he had all the arrogance of the medical man without the redeeming humanity.

The household was completed by two American soldiers. One was a solemn young man who, whenever Alice saw him, was reading the *Quarterly Review of Biology*. The other was a blythe youngster who crooned a good deal and had serious views about Dorothy Lamour. Both were on excellent terms with the children, and like everyone else in the house, even in the end Dr. Roper, did everything that Kitty told them.

During the first evening Kitty acted as if she had had no reason for asking Alice to Long Clinton except that she had taken a sudden, exceptional liking to her. Alice was led up almost immediately to see the children in bed, then she was swept into the kitchen, " to talk to me while I cook," as Kitty put it. As usual, however, it was Kitty who did all the talking. She talked about the children; she talked of them with joy and pride. " Aren't they lambs, aren't they wonderful? Oh, Lord, I do think they're wonderful! " she said without any self-consciousness. She asked Alice's advice as to whether she should have another child, or whether she should at least wait until the war was over. " John says wait," she said, " though what he really means is, we've got enough already, but of course I can manage that." All the time her hands were busy; she was an excellent cook and the dinner that evening was delicious. Kitty at Long Clinton dressed very differently from Kitty in London: she wore a brown knitted jumper and tweed skirt. But she had the scarf with the overlapping circles knotted round her throat and fastened with an old-fashioned garnet brooch. Alice felt sure the gesture was deliberate, and its bravado intrigued her.

After dinner they did the washing-up, then sat round a pleasant fire of logs in the sitting-room. Kitty knitted while her husband kept his eyes on her and asked Alice questions about her husband's work. With a little cutting edge on his voice, he spoke of the sheltered life of the laboratory; Alice did not miss the envy in his tone. They went to bed early.

It was only when Alice was in bed, feeling uncomfortably wakeful in the strange room and wondering why, after all, she had accepted Kitty's invitation so eagerly, that it occurred to her as strange that Dr. Roper had not made a single reference to the murder. Altogether a rather strange man, Dr. Roper. Or was he by any chance quite a commonplace one who had landed himself with a very strange wife? But the thought of all the children in the house made Alice desperately homesick for her own who were in Canada, and half of whose childhood she was losing. She thought how fortunate Kitty was to live in Long Clinton instead of in London and to have been able to keep her children safely about her. By the time that Alice fell asleep her mind was filled with thoughts as unconnected with the murder of Aubrey Ritter as the conversation of Dr. Roper.

The next day Kitty was not wearing the scarf though she wore the same brown jumper and skirt and a flowered apron. There were tomatoes and bacon for breakfast. After breakfast Dr. Roper went off in his car to visit some patients, the daily maid arrived from the village and took over the care of the children, and Kitty suggested to Alice that they should go for a walk.

" Gladys doesn't usually come on Sundays," Kitty explained as she put on her coat, " but I managed to persuade her to come to-day as we had a visitor. I wanted you and me to have some time alone together." Her voice altered slightly on that sentence. Buttoning up her old tweed coat and drawing on some sheepskin gauntlets, she pulled the door open and they set off walking briskly into the crisp, bright morning.

For some minutes they walked in silence. There was hoar-frost on the hedges and the ground was frozen hard. The sky was a faint, chill blue and there was the hard sparkle of wintry sunshine in the air; the grass crackled underfoot as if it were made of paper.

Presently Kitty began to hum a tune under her breath and Alice knew that something was coming.

" Well," Kitty burst out at length, " it *was* Rit's scarf, and he gave it to me, and of course I did see him after that meeting in Paris—I saw him often! I don't know how you knew about it—and I don't see what difference it would have made to anyone if I'd told them about it. It would have made an awful lot of difference to me, I can tell you that—it would probably have smashed my life up—but it wouldn't have made any difference to Janet. Her relations with Rit were her own affair and mine don't come into it."

She spoke with passion. Her eyes sought Alice's fiercely.

Alice explained: " I saw the scarf in a photograph in Peter Willing's office."

Kitty stared at her disbelievingly. " Is that true? Is that really true? "

Alice nodded.

" I know the photograph, of course," said Kitty. Then she laughed and the laugh sounded angry. " So it was just in that photograph! And I thought . . ."

" What?" asked Alice.

" Why, that you'd known him yourself rather better than you were letting on. If I'd realised . . ."

" You wouldn't have asked me down here? "

" No," said Kitty frankly, " I shouldn't. I should simply have taken care that you didn't see the scarf again. I might even have destroyed it, though I should have been sorry to do that; it's such a beauty, and I don't suppose one'll be able to get anything of the sort again for years and years. Besides, it's the only memento I have of . . ." She paused, reaching out to snap off a dry twig in the hedge with a wrench of her strong fingers. ". . . of some pleasant times," she ended.

Alice did not say anything. She had all the guilty feeings of a sensitive person who knows that she is interfering in someone else's business, and she was not all clear with herself what justification she had for doing so.

After a moment Kitty went on thoughtfully: " Now I suppose I'll have to tell you about everything or you'll make trouble for me. You could easily uncover it all if you wanted to. But if I'd realised it was only a photograph . . . But then," she exclaimed in a new tone, " what on earth are you worried about? I thought you were jealous, probably. I

thought perhaps you were another of——'' She broke the
sentence off to stare at Alice curiously.

" Another of Ritter's mistresses? " said Alice at a venture,
though she could hardly believe her ears as she brought out the
staggering suggestion.

Kitty gave a matter-of-fact nod.

" Then," said Alice, " were there really so many of
them? "

" Oh, I don't know," said Kitty, " but I did always
rather take that for granted. Rit was always awful about
women, even at college, and then getting tied up to someone
like Rosamund, which gave him the idea he was a martyred
saint, made him ever so much worse. Actually I got fed up
with him pretty quickly; he expected too damn much. He
tried to wring such a frantic amount of emotion out of one.
I'd made it quite clear I wasn't in love with him this time,
and I thought we were just going to enjoy ourselves for a
week-end or two and no fuss, but he wanted me to be
agonisingly sorry for him all the time, and sympathise with
him and mother him. Well, I happen to have a normal outlet
for my maternal instincts and I found it all horribly morbid,
so though I went on seeing him now and then it wasn't very
often. I don't regret it. I did have quite a good time with
him really. He was very attractive and when he got too
morbid I just didn't take any notice of him. But, you know,
I never had the faintest idea he was playing the same game
with Janet! When Frank came out with it that night at
Cecily's, you could have knocked me down with a feather.
Janet! I just couldn't believe it at first. She was always
such a stiff, aloof, little thing—though I suppose people do
alter, and I suppose the sympathy line went over big with her.
Of course I knew he saw an awful lot of her but I always
thought it was just a smoke-screen. What a cunning old devil
he was, wasn't he? You know, I'm sure he never realised how
many lies he told us all, he did it so naturally.''

Alice listened in astonishment. She wondered what would
happen if Kitty Roper and Peter Willing started comparing
their impressions of the dead dramatist. Floundering around
among the implications of all that Kitty had tossed off so

casually, Alice picked on one point haphazard. " Then you were in love with him once? " she said.

" Oh, I don't think so—not really," Kitty answered. " I kidded myself I was, naturally. One does at that age."

" What age? " asked Alice.

" Nineteen, twenty, thereabouts—when we were at college. That's when I first met him. I was at school with Janet and Cecily and then went on to college with them, that is, I went a year later. The three of them were always around together already, with several others. I got admitted to the gang and . . ." She made another of her sudden pauses.

Their pace had been slowing down while they talked. Kitty's blue eyes, wide and thoughtful, had a hard gleam in them; her cheeks had been whipped into vivid colour by the cold. She looked very beautiful in her rough, simple clothes, but at the same time tough and rather dangerous.

" It's not much good regretting things, and I don't, so I'm not going to start pretending I do," she said. " But if I hadn't turned up, Rit would probably have married one of those two, I'm not sure which, but I should think probably Janet. Cecily was much the better looking, in fact, she was rather magnificent, and she was athletic and a marvellous dancer and she dressed awfully well, but she was all nerves and explosions even then and fearfully dependent on Janet. Janet was a calm, quiet, determined little thing, sort of shy on top but awfully sure of herself underneath, at least that's what I used to think. I thought the two of them marvellous and tacked myself on to them like a hero-worshipping child. They were both much cleverer than me, and seemed much older and more sophisticated—and I suppose that's why it seemed so exciting when I got Rit away from them, though it was too easy actually. But I've often thought that if I'd steered clear of him he'd have gone ahead and married Janet —he was very much the marrying sort—and then she'd never have married Ian Markland, and Rit would never have married Rosamund, and . . ." She seemed to be a person of very incomplete thoughts; sooner or later she always came to a sentence which she seemed unable to finish.

Curiously Alice said: " Then I suppose you knew Ian Markland? "

" Ian? Oh, yes," Kitty answered carelessly. " I liked him rather, but he was the last person Janet ought to have married. I could have told her so."

From her tone, Alice leapt to the conclusion that this left a great deal unsaid. " And didn't you? " she asked.

" Heavens, no! " said Kitty. " I don't believe in interfering in other people's lives. Live and let live is my idea of getting along. Don't you agree? "

" Not altogether," said Alice.

Kitty gave her a surprised look as if it had never occurred to her that anyone could disagree on this point.

" Well, I don't want other people interfering with me," she said, " and I take damn good care that they don't. So I don't see why I should interfere with them. Or do you mean——? " Her voice sharpened suddenly. " Do you mean that you think I did interfere with Rit and Janet? Is that what you mean? Because if it is I think you're talking through your hat. You can't think for other people in these things, they have to look out for themselves. If she wanted Rit she should have put up a fight for him." Her tone was angry but there was a sound of fear in it, fear that if she did not harden herself she might not find regret as absent from her mind as she preferred to believe.

" No, that isn't at all what I meant," said Alice, thinking, however, that in such discussions as these one always comes sooner or later to that bitter, resentful and unanswerable question, am I my sister's keeper? " I meant that—that sometimes one has the feeling that one has to interfere, that——"

" And that's what you're doing now, isn't it? " Kitty broke in harshly. One of her hands shot out and grabbed Alice's wrist. It hurt, she gripped so fiercely. " Well, let me tell you something straight away, you aren't going to interfere with me, d'you understand? That's why I asked you down here. I asked you down here to show you that there are a lot of things in my life that I'm ready to fight for to the last—my children and my home and my security. You've got children yourself, you ought to understand me. I hope you aren't going to make me fight, but if I have to I will. When I was young I was a fool, I didn't know what I really wanted. I played around a lot and made a fool of myself with every other man I met and thought that that was what I was after. And then one day I got myself in a mess—I found I was having a baby. Of course I did the obvious thing; I scrounged all the money I could off my friends, dug up a shady doctor and got rid of it. And as soon as I lost it . . . Well, it was the most ghastly thing I've ever been through! I don't mean the operation itself, that went off all right, but it was what I felt when I realised I'd lost my baby . . . As soon as I'd lost it, anyway, I came to my senses and knew what I wanted. And I went ahead and got it. And I'm going to keep it. And if I'm a fool without any self-control and do damn silly things sometimes that put it all in danger—well, I'm still going to fight for it, d'you understand? I'm not going to let it get taken away from me. I'll fight any way I can. I don't care what I do, but I'm not going to let you walk in here, smashing my life up for me! "

Disengaging her wrist, Alice said: " I'd better try to explain, if you'll listen to me. But first, I've no wish to smash up anything for anybody."

" Then what *do* you want? "

" Perhaps your help—I'm not sure."

Her face suspicious, Kitty put a hand in a pocket, brought out a packet of cigarettes and held it out.

" Well," she said, " go on, what's troubling you? "

Alice found it very difficult to put into words. " It's something like this," she said. " I can't pretend there's much reason about it, it's mostly just a queer feeling that won't let me alone. I met Janet Markland only once. I was asked to that party of Cecily's on purpose to meet her. Cecily'd told me an awful lot about her. But Janet didn't in fact make much impression on me—there wasn't time. Then I saw her again at the inquest and she puzzled me. Her story puzzled me. I couldn't understand why she went on saying that she'd gone out to telephone and never gone upstairs instead of admitting that she'd been up to Ritter's flat. If she'd admitted that, she might have claimed that Ritter was already dying when she got there; it would have looked bad, but not as bad as telling a lie which it's so very easy to disprove. And I—I couldn't get used to the idea that that quiet, quite pleasant woman had actually murdered somebody . . ."

" Ah, yes," said Kitty, " I know! "

" And then," Alice went on, " I had a talk with Peter Willing. He told me a lot about her. He refuses to believe that she murdered Ritter, he thinks she killed him by accident. Certainly the person he described to me couldn't have been a murderess. But she couldn't quite have existed either. She couldn't have been anybody's mistress. So I only felt more puzzled than before, trying to imagine what Janet Markland was really like, and how it was that she'd managed to deceive so many people about so many things for so long. And then I recognised that scarf of yours . . ."

Kitty laughed. " And you thought, here's the solution to the mystery, Janet Markland is not a murderess at all—the real murderess is that bold, brazen, immoral woman whom it's quite easy to imagine lashing out with a poker! But may I remind you, it wasn't me the American boy saw on the stairs, and it wasn't my fingerprints that got on the poker! "

" All right, I did think that just at first," Alice admitted quietly. " I did think . . . Well, it doesn't matter, because of course one can't get round the evidence."

" But you do want to know what I know? "

" Yes."

" And you're in a position to force me to tell you."

" No, I don't want to force you. But I'd be very grateful if you'd help me to understand what sort of a person Janet Markland is. I might try talking to Cecily, only she seems so bitter at the discovery that Janet didn't tell her everything about herself that she can't think beyond that at present. Somehow it seems to matter much more to her than the death of Ritter."

Kitty nodded. " Yes, it would be like that . . . Here, let's walk a bit faster, shall we? It's so damn cold. All right,

I'll tell you what I think about Janet, if that's what you want, but you've got to remember, I've hardly seen her for years and though we were pretty good friends once, I don't suppose we'd find we've got much in common now. Still, I'll tell you what I can." She trod her cigarette-stub into the ground.

They had started down a rutted lane, shut in by high brown hedges. Shabby remnants of last year's traveller's joy, looking like the tufts of wool that sheep leave on barbed wire, hung in clumps high up on the bare twigs. The dull green of brambles was woven through the branches. Here and there some shrivelled beech-leaves made rusty smudges on the brown. It was melancholy and very quiet except for the drone of aircraft overhead which soon became easy to forget, it went on so constantly.

" It's difficult to know where to begin," said Kitty. " I got to know Janet when I was about twelve years old. We were in the same dormitory my first term at school. I had a funny sort of hero-worship of her at first; I'd never been away from home before and she was awfully nice to me. Besides, her mother had just died, which made her seem sort of pathetic and romantic; I couldn't think of anything as terrible as losing one's mother. Then I found out that her father was dead too—he'd died when she was five or six— and she was living with two old aunts, sisters of her father's. And apparently she was half-French; her father had run some sort of hotel for English people in Paris and had married a Frenchwoman. When he died the mother had a breakdown and so had to sell up instead of keeping the place going, and afterwards there was hardly any money, so then the two aunts had turned up from England and taken Janet and her mother home with them and been awfully good to them. But the mother'd always loathed living in England —the French are so unadaptable, aren't they?—and she'd always been awfully delicate, and then when Janet was fourteen she died. I know Janet was very fond of her aunts and awfully grateful to them, and when they lost their money —they lost it all somehow when Janet was at college so she couldn't finish there and had to look for a job straight away, only instead she got married to Ian Markland—well, she always sent them as much as she could afford. They were very austere and vegetarian, and talked a lot about Beauty and Love, and wore hand-woven smocks and sandals and carved beads, and they dressed Janet awfully queerly in shapeless sort of sacks covered with embroidery, which they kept going into ecstasies of admiration over, so that I know she simply hated it, and was awfully glad that she had to wear uniform at school. I'd have gone absolutely crazy myself if I'd had to stay with them more than a fortnight—I did stay with them once in the holidays. They were ever so sweet and kind all the time and never said we mustn't do things, and at first, after my own home which was pretty stern yet somehow comfortably rowdy, it seemed wonderful and strange and perfect. But then I began to get the feeling that one couldn't be natural for a moment—one couldn't raise one's voice or curse or smash anything or even really laugh, because Beauty and Love were always getting in the way. Yet the two funny old things always talked an awful lot about things being ' natural.' They'd a special way of saying the word, sort of in hushed italics. I remember my hair'd been shingled—the fashion had just come in—and so's not to hurt my feelings they said it was very pretty but that bobbed hair like Janet's looked more ' natural.' And there sat Janet, looking aloof and unconcerned as if hair didn't interest her anyhow, and really envying me my shingle like hell—she told me so years afterwards. She told me it was an appalling struggle for her later on to start dressing as she wanted to and using make-up and wearing high-heeled shoes instead of sandals. It wasn't exactly a struggle with the aunts because they never said no to anything, it was a struggle with what they'd made her into. Poor Janet, she was always very shy and subdued, she never ragged or made a row. I'm sure that an awful lot of that quiet dignity that used to impress me so was simply that she was terrified of giving herself away. Even when she was grown up she never worked up the courage to be really smart. She always stuck to dark colours, navy and brown and black. Black . . . well, you remember how she was dressed that evening at Cecily's? "

" I'm not likely to forget it," said Alice.

" Well, that was just typical of her," said Kitty. " And her underclothes too—they were always awfully *good*. You know what I mean, good heavy silk, well cut but no frivolity. She'd simply never had dared to wear a pair of pink satin cami-knickers or a chiffon nightdress. She'd have said in a slightly embarrassed way that she couldn't see what use they were." Kitty laughed. " I tried to tell her once what use they were and she just looked cool and interested in my psychological peculiarities and rather amused—by then, I suppose, she must have been able not to give away even her embarrassment. I thought marriage to Ian would cure her, but she seemed to go on being just as aloof and serious about everything. . . . I say, I'm sure I'm not telling you the sort of things you want to know. I'm sure Janet's underclothes can't have anything to do with the murder."

" I'm not so sure," said Alice. " The way a woman dresses and what she thinks about it always tell one a good deal about her."

" Yes, that's true," said Kitty. " Take Cecily, for instance. As far back as I can remember her she always dressed marvellously except for sudden attacks of going about with holes in her stockings and her clothes crumpled and spotty and her hair all in knots. And she was always particularly peevish and depressed when she was like that. And then take me. At home I dress all quiet and sensible in jumpers and tweeds and things, and then suddenly I get the feeling I've simply got to get into something loud and flashy, just as—just as I get the feeling I have to break loose and do silly things. Something works up inside me. . . . Frank says—Frank Lely, you know—that I'm just as much of a psychological case as the other two." She stopped. Her lips with their haphazard splashes of scarlet lipstick suddenly closed firmly on one another. Then she went on : " I'm being absolutely frank with you, Alice. But if you ever let John know any of the things I'm telling you—because he trusts me, you see, he trusts me absolutely, and in everything that counts I *am* faithful to him, but he might not understand that—so if ever

you breathe a word about anything I'm saying, I'll—I'll kill
you, I will really! "

Alice thought of several things to say. Among them was
the suggestion that to threaten murder at the moment was
singularly inept. But was it really possible, she wondered,
and this thought got in the way of all the others that presented
themselves, that Kitty believed that her husband did not know
of or at least suspect her infidelities? Trusted her, did he,
that man? Was she a complete fool?

After a moment Kitty continued: " What was I talking
about? Clothes . . . Cecily . . . me. Isn't it funny the way
Janet was always attracted to people who were so completely
different from her? Take just Cecily and me. I was everything that Janet disapproved of and when she was quite young
and still rather inhuman she was always telling me so. I was
lazy and frightfully stupid and always stuffing sweets and
smoking on the quiet and telling any lie that'd make life more
comfortable for me. Cecily told lies too but hers were to
impress people or make them sympathise with her. She was
very bossy and fearfully good at games and always having
crushes on mistresses. She was rich and spoiled with a mother
who was a tremendous beauty, who used to come and visit
Cecily wrapped to the eyes in mink, with diamond clips
glittering all over the place. She married again when Cecily
was about fifteen and Cecily dramatised it terrifically, I
remember. She told us all how her stepfather hated her and
how cruel he was to her. I'm sure it wasn't true. Poor old
Cecily, I've always been sorry for her somehow. This affair
of Janet, it must have been a ghastly blow for her. Worse,
I should think, than for anyone else."

" Worse than for Roger Mace? "

Kitty raised her eyebrows. " Oh, him. . . . Well, I don't
know—d'you think he was really much in love with Janet?
Horrible for him, of course, poor thing, but I expect he'll get
over it."

Alice did not think she meant it to sound callous. Rather
it was that Kitty was unable to imagine that Janet Markland
might be capable of rousing any strength of passion in a man,

perhaps also that she was utterly unconvinced that sexual passion itself could have any intensity.

" You said you knew her husband," Alice said after a pause. " What sort of man was he? "

" A slick little devil, quite bright and clever in his way," said Kitty, " not at all the sort of person you'd think would appeal to Janet. I've a sort of idea, though—well, I told you her aunts lost their money, and—I don't mean she married him for his money, I don't mean that at all—but he was doing pretty well for himself in advertising, making six or seven hundred a year already at the age of twenty-four, and Janet had awfully little faith in herself, so. . . . But it wasn't his *money*—you do see what I mean, don't you? And of course he was awfully attractive. But about that time he was getting an enormous opinion of himself. Everyone flattered him for having got so far so young, and he began to think he was a genius and much too good for advertising and insisted on throwing it up and settling down in the country to be a poet. But that didn't suit Janet too well, I imagine. For one thing, she's very intelligent, and she'd have known he was a rotten poet. And then there were other things. He'd a wicked temper and he was horribly vain; though I must say I always liked him rather, he was such good company, and he took it for granted that he should be unfaithful to her—I mean, absolutely took it for *granted*. I don't really know what it was he liked about Janet—her serenity, I suppose, and believing he'd got her away from Rit. But anyway, Janet didn't want to have to depend for life on a bad poet, did she? I think it was very sensible of her to clear out; I'd have done the same. After all, one does want to be able to count on one's husband and know one can have children and everything."

It was, thought Alice, extremely difficult to decide how naïve Kitty was. They had crossed a stile and started down a path across a meadow. Had she deliberately tried to give the impression that Janet had married Ian Markland for his six or seven hundred a year and then left him as soon as that income ceased to exist? Aubrey Ritter had been very rich.

Was there then in Janet's character a streak of the purely mercenary? Had the rage which had made her kill Ritter been roused by frustrated avarice rather than by frustrated passion? Was that the explanation? In a way, thought Alice, that made the more reasonable story. She began to think that Kitty might have given her the clue to the truth. But had she done so on purpose? Alice looked at her curiously.

She was, thought Alice, that most difficult of types to understand, a complicated but stupid woman. She was naturally dishonest, yet she was frank about her dishonesty, and to one person, whom she might easily be deceiving at the moment, she told the truth about the lies she had told someone else. She assumed that her lies would always be accepted. She assumed that she was trusted. She was good-natured, ready to devote her immense vitality to the physical well-being of others, but except concerning her children she seemed to have few strong feelings. She seemed to care very little for her husband, and obviously the death of her lover did not mean much to her. Had she ever cared about Ritter, Alice wondered, even when, long ago, she had snatched him away from Janet and Cecily? How many other lovers had there been, and who were they and what had happened to them? And what *had* she intended that Alice should think about Janet?

Perhaps nothing in particular.

Probably the fact was that so long as she felt secure that Alice would not tell her husband how she had acquired her pretty silk scarf, Kitty did not care one way or the other.

John Roper had just got back to the house when Kitty and Alice turned in at the gate. He had driven the car into the garage and came out of it to meet them. He was carrying the traditional black bag and wore a neat, double-breasted black overcoat and a grey homburg with curled up edges. He looked prim, elderly and harassed. He made a remark, full of a sarcasm which Alice failed to understand, about their having been of course for a ten mile walk; she concluded, in spite of the unpleasant tone in which he had spoken, that he meant it to be a friendly joke. With sudden whoops and cries the children tore out of the house and surrounded them.

Alice stayed until the next morning. All the time she was at Long Clinton she heard Dr. Roper make only one reference to the murder. It was at dinner in the evening. Suddenly he asked Alice what she thought the sentence on Mrs Markland would be if she were found guilty when she came up for trial. Alice replied that she had not the faintest idea.

With his eyes as usual on his wife, Dr. Roper said: " I don't think anyone should hang for killing a man like that." It was said simply, without heat, and then he went on eating. Kitty acted as if she had not heard him.

That evening Cecily was vindicated, for one of the American soldiers did come in slightly drunk. It was the solemn young man, and the only effect his drunkenness had on him was that he wanted to tell everybody all the things that he had been reading in the *Quarterly Review of Biology*. His friend saw him off to bed. The next morning Kitty and two of the children accompanied Alice to the station in Aylesbury. The children were very charming, and Alice, thinking she had got all she could out of Kitty, enjoyed that part of her visit far more than all the rest. The children, at any rate, were a credit to Kitty.

But after all, Kitty had one thing more to say on the subject of Janet Markland. She saved it up for the very last moment when Alice was leaning out of the train-window to say good-bye.

" You know, Alice,"—Kitty seemed to hesitate a moment —" you know, you ought to see Frank—Frank Lely. He's got a theory."

" A theory?" said Alice.

" Yes, about Janet."

" What sort of theory? "

" A psychological theory."

" Oh, you mean something about her being so repressed that she had to murder somebody sooner or later? Don't you think there are rather too many of those theories around already? "

" N-no," said Kitty, " it's not like that. It's. . . . He always loathed her, you know, or anyway disliked her. And so . . ."

Doors were being slammed. A whistle was blown.

" And so? " said Alice impatiently.

" So it's queer that he thinks she didn't do it," said Kitty. " It doesn't make sense, of course, because there's the evidence, but still he says,"—the train began to move—" he says he's sure, now he's thought it over, that she couldn't kill anybody—and I do believe that's actually why he dislikes her! Good-bye, Alice—good-bye! Come again sometime— the children loved having you! "

CHAPTER FIVE

THE SENTENCE which Janet Markland received at her trial was hanging by the neck until she was dead.

Of the points that her counsel attempted to make in her defence, only one had any noticeable effect on the jury; it was the fact that Ed Larg, on arriving at the house, had found the front-door open. This, counsel suggested, coupled with the admission of the warden and the constable that it was just conceivably possible that a very light-stepping person, dressed in black, might have left the house and returned to it without their noticing her, supported Mrs. Markland's story that she had gone out to telephone, leaving the door unlatched so that she could get into the house again. Cecily, however, on being questioned, had to admit that the latch, particularly since the air-raids, did occasionally stick, so that the door, after being closed, presently came open again on its own. The faint doubt which had been roused in the minds of the jury was settled again.

Janet tried to explain away the story of her relations with Ritter by admitting that she had spent the fortnight in Wales with him, but claiming that she had gone away with him in the belief that he was leaving his wife and that a divorce was to follow; when, she said, she discovered that in fact he had not had the courage to say a word of the matter to his wife, and that he felt an utter inability to break the tie with her, she herself had returned to London. Since that time, whatever appearances might suggest, there had been no more than friendliness between them. Continuing to the charwoman's story of the letter and the telephone conversation, Janet's explanation was that Ritter had written the letter in a fit of remorse immediately after his wife's death, apparently believing that an unfounded jealousy of his friendship with Janet had contributed to Rosamund's unbalanced state; that as soon as he had sent it he had become horrified at what he had done, and had telephoned to tell Janet to take no notice

of what he had written; she, however, having believed for
some time past that it would be best for them both to end a
relationship which had really put a great strain on them,
had told him that he was a fool and weak to change his mind
so quickly. It was a reply, she said, which had cost her an
effort and some tears; it was not surprising that the charwoman had interpreted what she had heard as a quarrel.
Ritter had straight away rushed round to see Janet and it was
true that then they had quarrelled, but the cause of the quarrel
had been Janet's continued insistence that she wanted to see
no more of him; their words, as they separated, had been
correctly reported by the charwoman, but she had misunderstood them; Ritter's last remark had been a question: " It's
really no use now? "—in fact, it had been a proposal of
marriage. Janet had never seen him again after that. Twice
she had spoken to him on the telephone, once when he had
rung her up at her home and asked her if she would not recon-
sider her decision, and once on the night of the murder when
she had slipped out of the house, rung him up from the box
at the corner and told him that if he came down to the party
she would immediately leave it. He had assured her that he
would not come. As for those desperate words that had been
torn out of her when she heard of his death: " Yes, yes, it's
true, I did it! "—she could not, she said, remember having
said them; she could not remember anything of that moment;
but if it was true that that was what she had said, then what
she must have meant was that she believed her refusal to see
him had been the cause of his death. She had, she told the
jury, still been suffering from the shock of believing that he
had killed himself. She added that she had never been up to
his new flat, had never seen Sergeant Larg on the staircase,
had never been on the staircase, and could not imagine how
her fingerprints had come to be on the poker. The whole story
was received by the jury with almost uninterested incredulity.

When it was all over Alice managed to lose the others in the
crowd and slip away by herself. She turned into a teashop,
sat down in a corner and ordered a pot of tea. She felt sick
and very tired. For a murder trial, she supposed, it had
been unusually simple and short, but she felt deeply shaken.

Janet had looked nervous, wretched and ill—the newspapers later described it as quietly composed—and it had been horrible watching her dread and her misery. Catching sight of her own face in a mirror, Alice was startled to see how haggard and exhausted she looked herself.

She was ravenous for a cigarette, her head was aching and she felt a strung-up, nervous excitement. The teashop was fairly full. It had been the first she had happened to find as she hurried away from the crowd, and it had turned out to be a dingy little place with greasy, green walls, a smell of fish and chips and sauce and cabbage, and dusty paper chrysanthemums on each table.

At the next table an old man was reading an evening paper. Alice saw the headlines; they were about the fighting in Tunisia. That was one thing about wartime, she thought; even in later editions Janet Markland was unlikely to compete for space with the Eighth Army.

A shadow fell across her table. She looked up and saw Roger Mace standing there. He had been at the trial, though he had not had to give evidence. He had on an old raincoat over his usual tweed coat and flannels, and a shirt that was none too clean. His face was grey and dull and tired. He looked as if he had forgotten what sleep was.

Hesitantly he asked: " Mind if I sit down, Mrs. Church? "

" Please do," said Alice quickly, filled with pity. As he pulled out a chair and slumped into it, she added stupidly: " How are you feeling? "

" I—oh, all right. . . . It's another twenty minutes before the pubs open." It sounded like an explanation of what he was doing there. He sat sideways at the table, leaning against the wall, and as he glanced listlessly about the room, he took hold of the chair next to him and began to tilt it backwards and forwards. " Well," he said, " that's over. Thank God it's over."

" Was it—as you expected? " asked Alice.

" Oh, yes," he said, " yes, yes."

" The appeal——"

" Not a chance, you know. It just delays things. I suppose she wants that."

Alice pushed her cigarette towards him. " She'll be reprieved, of course. They'll never hang her—not when there was so little calculation behind it."

" Thanks," he said, taking a cigarette. He seemed to take no notice of her words. He repeated : " Well, it's over."

Her pity for him made Alice's tongue feel as heavy as lead.

" Isn't there a chance—just a chance," she said, " that the verdict's the wrong one? " She had an idea it was what he wanted her to say.

" Oh, yes, there's a chance, isn't there? " he said. " There's always a chance. Nothing's complete. There's nothing that can't be assailed by new knowledge. . . . *What?* " He looked up startled, his features twitching convulsively as the waitress stopped before him, asking him for his order. " Oh, yes, of course, yes—well, tea, please."

" A pot of tea? ' '

" Yes, a pot—a cup—anything. . . . D'you know, Mrs. Church, I've been doing a lot of thinking lately. It seems to me. . . . By the way, d'you mind my talking? "

" Of course not," she replied.

He looked at her with the steady, probing stare that she remembered. " Quite sure?"

" Quite sure," said Alice.

" I thought I shouldn't want to talk to a soul for months," he said, " but in fact I can't stand the thought of not talkng. I saw you come in here and I followed you. You're someone it feels all right to talk to. But if you mind——"

" Of course I don't mind," said Alice. " I wish I could help. I know what it's all meant to you."

" Do you? " he said. " Do you really? " It seemed to strike him as a surprising thought. " Yes, and so do most people, don't they? That's the queer thing, we all have our labels in this trial and the whole world knows about us. It's a horrible experience. It gives one a sort of unreality in one's own eyes. I'm used to the idea that what I feel and what I go through is a pretty complicated business that I myself couldn't find words for even if I tried, but now everyone seems to know everything, and there's this label. . . . I'm the man who was in love with the murderess, aren't I? "

"*Was?*" said Alice. She said it quickly, before she thought what she was saying.

He looked confused and stopped tilting the chair backwards and forwards. "Look," he said, "she's dead—that's the way I've been looking at it. I've got accustomed to the idea now; she's dead."

"But——"

"Don't you see, thinking of her shut up there, torturing herself and waiting, that wouldn't be bearable?"

"Then at least you're certain she's guilty?"

"Oh, no, I'm not actually certain of anything. Usually I say I'm certain she's not guilty, but . . . I don't know, somehow just now I can't be bothered to say it. What does it matter what I say? If she's got to be hanged or imprisoned for years and years, I'd sooner she was guilty, because otherwise—Look, that'd be another of those unbearable things, wouldn't it? A hundred years hence, if you read the story of it, it'd still be unbearable. So it's best on the whole she should be guilty, and I can forgive her guilt—God, what does it matter to me? I don't mind how guilty she is, it's her suffering I mind, and what she's gone through all these years, and what it's done to her. They got it all wrong at the trial, you know, but it wouldn't have done any good, explaining. They always get that sort of thing wrong. There's a way of discussing things in law-courts, they've a special language almost, that can't be adapted to deal with the things that people actually experience at one another's hands. The law has a special standard of psychological probability that has an incredible melodramatic simplicity. I'm not criticising it; the law's a wonderful business really, but it has to be based on generalities and fairly crude simplifications, and so it inevitably takes an unreal and entirely melodramatic view of human behaviour. If you tried to explain in a law-court what that man Ritter really did to Janet and why she cracked up when she did, they wouldn't listen to you. They couldn't function if they listened to you—and it's very important in the lives of all of us that they should function."

His tea had arrived but he was taking no notice of it. Alice reached over and poured it out for him.

" Look, Mrs. Church," he went on, " I could have explained a lot, but it wouldn't have made any difference, would it? "

" Not if it hasn't affected your own feeling that she probably did kill him," said Alice.

" But that isn't my feeling," he said in surprise. " I didn't say that, I only said I didn't mind if she's guilty. I'm too close to her to mind—and this is a queer thing, I'm too close to her, I've discovered, to be able to feel I know how she may have acted. I'm sorry if that doesn't make sense to you, but if you know a person really well, the truth is you can't guess how they'll act in an altogether new sort of crisis."

Alice understood more or less what he meant. She knew that intimacy creates a special environment for two people, and the deeper the intimacy, the more they both live within it, the closer its boundaries usually are, so that all that lies beyond them becomes with time not less but more and more of a mystery.

She watched Roger Mace driving his spoon round and round in his tea. She felt so sorry for him that she could easily have started crying, tears being one of the easiest, if also one of the most useless ways of showing sympathy. After a moment she said cautiously: " That explaining—I mean about Janet and Ritter—would you like an audience? It's a story I'd be glad to hear."

" I don't know—perhaps—perhaps later." He said it so abruptly that Alice thought she had made a mistake. But he went on: " Perhaps later, when I've had a few drinks. In a way, I know, I'd like to tell you about it, but I'd have to be a bit drunk to do it. One can't talk about oneself stark sober."

" Can't one? " said Alice.

" Well, can you? "

" Sometimes."

" I can't. Perhaps that's what's the matter with me. Anyway, I can't. So wait till we've had a few drinks and then I'll tell you."

" But I ought to be going home pretty soon, I'm afraid," said Alice.

His features twitched again. " Oh," he said, " I'm sorry,
I wasn't thinking. But it's a pity. I. . . . It's to the husband
and family, I suppose?"

" Yes," said Alice.

He looked as if he found this wholly unexpected and
unfamiliar.

" Couldn't they manage just one evening without you?"
he suggested tentatively and held Alice's eyes for a moment
with an odd half-smile.

" Well," said Alice, " as a matter of fact, the children are
in Canada, and perhaps there are times when a grown husband
ought to be able to get his own dinner. But I'll have to
telephone."

" Then go along and do it now," said Roger. " The pubs
should be open by the time you've finished."

When they went out into the street it was half-dusk. It was
moist and cold, with the shadowy forms of low-hanging clouds
changing their shapes with a menacing look of shouldering one
another out of the way in the darkening sky. The pavements
were blocked with the jostling crowds of the rush-hour; over-
loaded buses followed one another closely, their wheels hissing
on the damp surface of the road. A few lights still showed
from doorways and shop windows, but one by one, as unseen
hands tugged at black-out curtains, the lights disappeared.

Alice telephoned to Oliver and then walked along the Strand
with Roger, presently turning up towards Covent Garden.
The side-streets were almost as empty as the Strand had been
crowded, except where queues, already being admitted for
the six o'clock performance, were shuffling in at the side-
entrances of theatres.

Alice and Roger walked quickly as if they were going
somewhere in particular.

Suddenly Roger stopped and said in a hurried, anxious
tone : " Damn, I'm not thinking—we probably ought to go
and eat somewhere. You're hungry, aren't you? I should
think you are."

" I'm not in the least hungry," said Alice.

" But you must be—I just wasn't thinking—I'm awfully
sorry." He looked about with an uneasy frown as if he could

not quite think what he was looking for. " We ought to go and find somewhere to eat," he muttered.

" But I'm not in the least hungry," Alice repeated.

" You must be," he said stubbornly. " After all those hours in there——"

" I know, but I couldn't eat now if I tried."

" You see, I simply forgot about it, I didn't think, I'm awfully sorry, but we'll go and find somewhere now——"

Alice saw that it was because he wanted a drink so badly that he was forcing himself into what was almost a frenzy of consideration for her wishes.

" But I don't *want* to eat now," she said, taking his arm. " Let's go and have this drink."

He asked uncertainly: " Is that really what you want to do?"

" Yes."

He looked as if he deeply doubted her honesty. " No, you'd really sooner go and eat now, wouldn't you?"

" No," said Alice.

" Because if you'd prefer it——"

" We'll eat later," she said. " Come along."

With an air of relief he gave in and they started hurrying on along the twilit pavement.

Presently Roger Mace said: " In here," and stopped and pushed at a door.

They went in, walking into darkness and swaying shrouds of black-out curtain that smelt of dust and old clothes and alcohol. Managing to find the opening, they walked through it into warmth and light. The small saloon bar was almost empty, with shining taps and glasses and panelled walls and a few chairs and tables.

" It's usually quiet in here," said Roger. " It's all right, isn't it? "

" Of course," said Alice.

" If you don't like it we can go on somewhere else," he suggested.

" But it's very pleasant."

" You're sure? "

" Quite sure."

"You'd tell me if you preferred to go on somewhere else, wouldn't you?"

"Yes, yes, yes—don't worry so," she told him.

She sat down at one of the tables. Roger bought their drinks and brought them across to the table, sitting down opposite to Alice, sideways at the table, as before, leaning back against the wall and reaching out at once for a spare chair to tilt backwards and forwards.

"Look," he said earnestly, giving Alice one of his steady, serious stares, "you must tell me what you want to do, you mustn't simply say you want to do what I want to do. I've a way of forgetting about things, I don't think. But that doesn't mean you shouldn't say what you want to do."

"All right," said Alice, "I will, I promise."

"But really," he said, "I don't want you to be sorry for me and think you just have to go around with me. In fact, if you only came along because you were sorry for me— well, we could just have this drink and say good-night, if you like. You'd sooner do that, I believe. You didn't really want to come, did you? You only came along because you were feeling sorry for me."

"Look," said Alice emphatically and then realised she had caught that trick of speech from him and felt embarrassed, "will you please stop worrying. If I weren't sorry for you there'd be something rather queer about me, but I'm interested too, and for my own sake I want to learn all I can about Janet Markland, and I like this pub and I like this drink, and I like a night out too sometimes."

He smiled a little at that and said: "All right, all right, that's nice." Leaning his head back against the panelling, he let his glance wander vaguely round the little room. After a moment his eyes closed.

A small, wizened waiter in a grey cotton jacket came by, polishing the tables. He said something about its turning into a dirty night. When he had passed on Roger gave his eyes a rub as if they were hurting him, then groped for his glass and emptied it.

"What's the biggest mistake you ever made in your life?" he asked abruptly.

After a moment Alice replied: " I'm afraid that isn't quite a question one can answer off-hand."

" I can tell you which my biggest mistake was," said Roger. " It happened when I first met Janet. Shall I tell you about how I met her? It's quite a funny story really; it might have been the opening scene in a comedy. It was just before the outbreak of war—ten days before, as a matter of fact. D'you remember what one felt like then? D'you remember the feeling of certainty that war was coming, mixed up with the feeling that actually it couldn't come—just plain and simply couldn't. I had a sort of feeling that of course it was inevitable, but that to act as if it were, even to cut one's holiday short or anything like that, would be supremely ridiculous and would only make one look a fool. Perhaps other people don't go in for that kind of confusion. My trouble is, I've never found any difficulty in thinking one thing and feeling something quite different; the only difficulty, and that doesn't always appear just at first, is to continue to exist in those conditions. Either the conviction or the rationality always seems to drop out of things——" He stopped. The tired, puzzled look deepened on his face. " I was saying something else," he said. " I didn't start about that. What was I saying? "

" You were talking about the first time you met Janet," said Alice.

" Oh, yes—yes, of course—the funny story."

As he stayed silent Alice prompted him: " Were you abroad at the time? "

" Yes, I was in the south of France," he said. " It was in a little pension right off the fashionable beat that I'd found the year before when I was cycling about there. I'd found the place quite by chance, but they told me, the people who kept it, that there was an English lady who came there every year, and as apparently no other English people had ever come near them, they were certain that this woman must have sent me. When I said I didn't know her they just didn't seem to take it in. Well, when I turned up again the next year— I'd booked in advance this time—they told me at once: ' She is here already, she is here! ' Then before I could stop them they rushed me straight out into the garden—it wasn't really a garden, it was just a bare patch of ground with a few pines, ending in rocks and the sea—and there was Janet, in not very much of a bathing-suit, sitting on the rocks, dabbling her feet in the water. Madame Joubert seemed absolutely delighted about everything and clapped her hands and shouted down at Janet: ' Voila, madame, le moyen de vous amuser est arrivée!' and left us together. It was damnably embarrassing —but it really was quite funny.''

That evening Alice was incapable of laughter. She asked seriously: '' What did you do about it? ''

'' Oh, we just went on feeling embarrassed for a bit and looking foolish. I said something about the Jouberts believing that we were friends, and she said: ' Oh, it's worse than that, you know,' and I said: ' Yes, of course it is,' and then we both laughed and Janet took off her sun-glasses and I saw that she was older than I'd thought, and for some reason that made things seem not quite so difficult. And then she asked me if I liked looking at things in rock-pools, so I went down on to the rocks beside her and looked into the pool there. . . . D'you know, for a long time one of the only things I really knew about Janet was that she liked looking in rock-pools? She'd never say simply what she liked and what she didn't; she'd never let on about herself. She was always trying to find out what I liked and what I wanted to do, and then saying that she really didn't mind herself, and that that was quite all right for her too. She was always saying that she didn't mind. I tried to make her see she'd got to tell me what she wanted, but she wouldn't; she went on saying that she didn't mind, and that it was nice sometimes not having to decide things. But the truth was, she was scared of telling one what she thought. She'd been frightened somehow, and always tried to hide up what she was like. The queer thing was, it got me frightened too. I got awfully scared of what was going on in her mind, rather as if I felt she coudn't want to hide it up all that much if it weren't pretty terrible. I suppose, in a way, I was awfully distrustful of her—only not at first, of course. I didn't notice it for some time. At first. . . . Well, at first I just thought I'd never met anyone it was so easy to talk to on so little alcohol." That seemed to remind him that his glass was empty. Standing up abruptly, he picked up both glasses from the table and bore them away to the bar.

When he came back he went on: " Those were a pretty queer ten days, you know. The Jouberts wouldn't believe there was going to be a war. Madame Joubert jeered at everyone who thought there was and said she would only believe it when the bombs began to fall. The other people there, the French people, one after the other cut short their holidays and went home. Badly printed and somehow awfully unimpressive mobilisation posters kept appearing on walls. There was wonderful sunshine and the sea was as clear as glass and at night there was the sort of moon you used to see in illustrations of fairy-stories. There was one man there, an artist, who talked of committing suicide. I wonder if he did—I don't suppose so, but perhaps he's dead all the same. He had a shrill-voiced, silly little bitch of a wife who felt ashamed of him and used to reproach him in public. Janet was rather nice to him, at least she tried to be, but she spoke French very badly. That's queer, you know, considering she was half-French. She got on all right with French people, though; she was much less reserved with them than she was with the English, and I've an idea that not speaking the language very well had something to do with it. That's always a help to simplicity; you have to go straight to the point because it's too difficult to dither around it. D'you know,"—he stirred suddenly—" I think I'm getting tired of this pub. What about moving on somewhere a bit livelier? "

Alice rose and they fumbled their way out through the black-out curtains into the damp, heavy darkness, filled with thin rain.

The pavements were slimy. Neither of them had a torch, and to Alice the space before her was a wall of blackness, but Roger slipped a hand under her arm and led her along confidently. She did not know where they went but after a little while Roger told her: " Two steps up! " and they pushed their way through swing-doors into more black-out curtains and through them again into light.

After that Alice noticed that at every pub they went to

during the evening's wanderings, Roger was always able, in spite of the darkness, to tell her how many steps up there were at each door. She wondered if he had realised that he possessed this highly specialised, all too revealing knowledge.

The second pub was very much fuller and slightly more colourful than the first. Besides the usual mixture of non-descript civilians and soldiers of a dozen nations with their pick-ups, there was a group of gentle-faced young men in very pretty clothes who were earnestly interested in one another, and some girls in slacks and bright blouses with rather unkempt hair. A stout man with a beard, wearing a camel-hair jacket, was lecturing in a braying, high-pitched voice to two bored-faced women on the subject of his own writings and those of Stendhal.

Roger and Alice managed to find a corner of a table to sit at, though they had to share their bench with one of those queer, toothless old women, bundled up in black clothes, who sit alone in pubs, staring into space. Alice was afraid that the nearness of the old woman might put a stop to Roger's narrative, but except that he nodded at her as they sat down, he took no notice of her.

" Well," he said when they were settled with their drinks, " d'you want me to go on about Janet or shall we talk about something else? You, for instance. Suppose you talk about yourself—you mustn't let me do all the talking." But before Alice could answer he went on hurriedly, as if he were beginning to find it difficult to put a check on his tongue : " D'you know, I grew up with the idea that nobody ever talked about themselves. I didn't really know there was any sort of talk but arguing and making plans. My father never spoke about himself except when he was worried about his relationship to God, and I found that ridiculous and rather indecent. I used to think that to speak about oneself must always be ridiculous and indecent. That one could do it, that in fact it was quite a normal thing to do, and that one could actually like doing it— d'you know, that was a much more startling discovery to me than sex. Can you imagine that? But it took drink to do it— it still does. Drink's wonderful stuff if you've got the right company. It's no good otherwise—I don't drink at all when

I'm with people I don't like. Janet couldn't understand that; she thought I was just sodden. But I couldn't work if I were. But you were going to tell me about yourself, weren't you? Go on—please. You know, you're an awfully silent person Are you always? " He turned sideways, looking thoughtfully into Alice's face. " Tell me a bit about yourself and what you're like," he said.

" Let's go on about Janet," Alice replied.

" But aren't you bored? "

" If you'd really like to know something about me," said Alice, " I'll tell you. The truth about me is, I've got an enormous curiosity about Janet Markland. Call it a morbid sensational curiosity or anything you like, it's become really important to me. I want to find out all I can about her."

" Yes," he said, " yes, I see. . . . I understand, I suppose. Well, all right, I was telling you about those ten days in France, wasn't I? You know, we never managed to clear up the Jouberts' misconception about us. We tried to at first, and they tactfully agreed, with a sort of wink in the eye, that of course we'd never seen each other before, but they used to make lewd jokes that were supposed to have no particular application and everyone laughed and knew just what they meant. So we found we really got most peace if we gave in and pretended that things were as they thought they were. I suggested to Janet that I should move on somewhere else but she didn't seem to want it. That was marvellous, you know, realising that she didn't want it. I was crazily in love with her already, of course. I daresay you could say that was inevitable, given the atmosphere and the odd circumstances, and I didn't notice just at first that there was a—a sort of integrity about it that I'd never known much of before. I kidded myself I was just taking what seemed to be coming my way. At first I worried a bit about her wedding-ring and her being Mrs. Markland, and then one day she told me that she'd been separated from her husband for eight years. She told it to me quite abruptly in the middle of talking about something else, and it sounded as if it were an awful effort to her to say it. Then she frowned and turned away as if she were awfully annoyed about something. . . . You know, in some ways she was really very naïve; she was always giving herself away when she didn't mean to. But she never told me a word about Ritter. Here, for God's sake let's have something more to drink—I can't think why we aren't drinking! ''

Alice, who was beginning to feel worried about the amount she had already drunk, tried to stop him, but he had snatched up both glasses and was elbowing his way through the crowd round the bar before she had had time to do so.

When he returned she asked him: '' When did you hear about Ritter? ''

'' After we got back to England,'' Roger replied. '' We—we practically got engaged one evening, at least it seemed like it at the time. Janet agreed she'd see to getting a divorce from Markland as soon as we got home. Then all of a sudden she turned—I don't know how to describe it—she turned sort of sad. I couldn't make out what had happened. I thought it was something I'd done—I knew I was pretty crude pretty often. But later on, when I knew more, I thought that it was then that she'd started thinking about Ritter again; I believe he'd been right off her mind for some time. Anyway, next day we suddenly came to our senses and packed up quick and came home. The evening papers we got at Dover had the news of the invasion of Poland. Everything was in a muddle after that; my department was being shifted out of London straight away and I had to help with packing and all that, and I didn't see Janet for three days. Then I went to see her at her flat and Ritter was there——''

The way he stopped made it sound as if he had stopped in the middle of a sentence. He started rubbing his eyes again with the fidgety gesture Alice had noticed before. It was only now that she realised, however, that he rubbed them because they had filled with tears.

The old bundle in black suddenly looked round at him.

'' You talking about the Markland trial, Roger? '' she said. Her voice, to Alice's surprise, was sweet and faded and cultured, like something put away in lavender in a country vicarage. Her red-rimmed eyes moved blearily from Roger's face to Alice's.

Roger nodded irritably without replying.

"Bad business that," said the old woman. "Gal couldn't have done it."

"What d'you mean?" Roger snapped at her. "What d'you know about it?"

"Feel it in my bones," said the old woman.

Roger leant back and drew in and let out a long breath. Alice saw that his hands had started shaking.

"What was I talking about?" he asked her hoarsely.

"Ritter," said Alice.

He said one word, a very vicious one.

"Ah, yes," said Alice, "but what was he really like?"

Roger gave a short, angry laugh. "I'm not the person to ask that, am I? I hated him. And hate does prejudice one, you know!"

"I've seen some photographs of him," said Alice, "and of course I know his plays."

"Of course, of course, his plays!" said Roger. "Well, what more d'you want to know then? Don't his plays reveal him as a man of deep understanding and broad sympathies and a realistic comprehension of the tragedies and heroisms and beauties of black, industrial England? . . . He came from somewhere in Gloucestershire, you know. He never went north until he got a job, teaching in some school in Manchester. He was a teacher there for about four years, then he produced *Coal Dust* and handed it over to Janet and Willing, and they got it taken for him. After that he moved pretty quickly to London and used to swear that nothing on God's earth would ever make him go back north again. He hated the place and he hated the people still more, but he made a damned good thing out of pitying them. He used to pity them so hard and so beautifully it was obscene. I don't believe Janet was really taken in, but she was so pleased he was successful because— anyhow, that's how it looked to me—she'd never really expected anything of him. But perhaps I'm wrong there, perhaps that's just my prejudice and she did really think a hell of a lot of him. He was very handsome and perhaps he was quite likeable if you didn't happen to hate him. He really did care about that wife of his in a way, and try to stop her going off her rocker. But he hadn't the nervous stamina himself to take the strain of it, and they used to have horrible scenes with each other. And that's why he had to have Janet, of course, and the others.''

'' Were there many others? '' asked Alice.

'' Look,'' said Roger, as if he were explaining something that ought to have been very obvious to her, '' Ritter was the sort of man who always has to have a mass of women round him. There were always dozens of them around, though I've an idea he wasn't actually unfaithful to Rosamund more than a few times. What he wanted was someone to straighten him out when Rosamund got him all tied up in knots——''

'' Wait a minute, wait! '' said Alice excitedly. '' You've just said that he wasn't unfaithful to his wife more than a few times. Then—then you believe the police had got the story all wrong, do you? ''

'' Isn't that what I've been explaining from the beginning?''

She looked at him in confusion, wishing that she had not started on that last glass of beer. A mere pint and a half was always enough to make her thoughts move so fast that she could not keep up with them. '' Oh,'' she said carefully, '' is it? ''

'' Janet did go away with him once,'' Roger went on, '' but as she said at the trial, she thought he'd broken off with Rosamund. When he insisted on going back to her, Janet wanted to break right off with him straight away. She wanted him to get his affairs handled by a different agent. She was in love with him then all right and she wanted all or nothing. That's a feeling I know something about. . . . However, it was then that Ritter began to show his talent for hanging on. He seems to have made her believe that he'd go right under if he hadn't got her to hold on to. And perhaps he would have, though I think myself he'd simply have found someone else to do the job instead of Janet. But you couldn't expect her to see that; she had her vanity. I used to try telling her that it was mostly vanity on her part and that she needn't be afraid of what would happen if she cut loose from him, but it was

a long time before she'd listen—and when she did, of course
she chose just the wrong time for it. It really was pretty
brutal, walking out on him just when she did. But he'd given
her the opportunity by writing that letter after Rosamund
died, and I suppose Janet had realised by then that if she
missed the chance she'd never manage to make another for
herself. She hasn't a very strong character, you see. That's
one of her troubles, that people always think she has—I did
myself at first—when she hasn't really."

The old woman spoke up again. " That gal never did it,
Roger," she said. " People are fools."

He struck the table with the flat of his hand. " Will you
keep out of it! You don't know anything about it."

" She isn't the murdering sort," said the old woman, " I
remember seeing you and her together. Anyone could see
she's a nice gal, a nice, refined gal, not riff-raff at all."

Just then another voice interrupted them. It was a soft,
fluting voice like that of an agitated dove cooing in a
Bloomsbury gutter.

" Oh dear, oh dear, *have* you seen my Mr. Doyle? " it
asked.

For a moment Alice saw an astonishing vision hovering
before her. It was of a slender young man wearing a bottle-
green suit, a white silk embroidered blouse and an amber
necklace. He had curly chestnut hair to his shoulders, rouge
on his cheeks, mascara on his lashes and polish on his pointed
fingernails. His expression was mild, anxious and benevolent.

" I've been looking everywhere for my Mr. Doyle," he
said plaintively, " *haven't* you seen him? "

The old woman shook her head.

While Alice, feeling a bewildered hope that if only she
looked hard enough he would turn into a woman before her
eyes, gazed up at him, he floated on, his soft voice carrying
through the crowd as he found other acquaintances: " Please,
oh, please, haven't you seen my Mr. Doyle? " A little eddy
of uneasy smiles followed him.

He had made a tour of the place and was almost at the door
again when the stout, bearded man in the camelhair coat
remarked in his braying voice: " I've no moral scruples

against it, mind, naturally not—but when they come in here and drink up our beer, that's what I can't stand."

Roger stood up abruptly.

" Let's go," he muttered in Alice's ear, and with a hand on her arm was hustling her out almost before she had had time to struggle into her coat.

Outside in the rain and the darkness he stood still and cursed. Alice could feel that he was trembling.

" Damn that old woman! " he said. " Damn her, damn her! "

" But why? "

" What does she know about it? Why couldn't she keep her mouth shut? "

" But doesn't it please you at all that——"

"—That that damned ignorant, drink-sodden old woman takes it into her head to say Janet couldn't have committed murder? " He wrenched at Alice's arm and started hurrying her along the pavement. " Janet innocent—innocent and condemned—innocent and going to be hanged or shut away for life! I pray to God she did murder him, that's all! Why can't fools keep their bloody mouths shut?"

" I'm afraid I don't understand you at all," said Alice.

" Don't you? You think it'd be nicer for her to go to Heaven with her conscience lilywhite? "

" Oh, don't be such a fool," said Alice.

He hurried on for a few more yards then suddenly stood still. " I'm sorry," he said softly, " I'm sorry, I'm awfully sorry. You're being awfully good to me." He pressed her arm.

After that they walked on more slowly.

Presently, in a quite different tone—it was level and had some sardonic amusement in it—Roger remarked: " That extraordinary object in there with the necklace and nail-polish—he was simply monstrous and ridiculous until that fat brute made that crack about the beer, and that turned him into a tragedy. I dare say that was really why I felt I'd got to get out then, it wasn't altogether the old woman. If one looks on at a bit of cruelty and doesn't do anything about it, one always feels sick inside and wants to run away. I remember something of that sort that Janet once told me about herself and Ritter. I'll tell you. Perhaps it explains quite a lot about her. . . ." But there he paused once more. " In here," he said, pushing at a door, " Mind—three steps."

" Well," said Alice when they had settled themselves once more, " tell me this story."

" It was something that happened to Janet when she was about twenty," said Roger. " When she told me about it she must have been thirty-three, yet it still seemed to churn something up in her as if she couldn't bear to think of it. I suppose she'd always kept it to herself. I know, when she told me about it, it struck me as completely fantastic that she could still be worrying over it. The thing happened quite soon after she'd got to know Ritter. They were both at London University. It seems that in those days Ritter was rather given to long hair and corduroys—he always was rather—but in those days he had a beard as well, and he was more or less the leader of some aesthetic group in the place, and ran a magazine, and always talked at great length in debates, and generally drew attention to himself. As usual there was some group of hearties, engineers or medicals or something, whose sensibilities were offended, and one day in the middle of some dance about a dozen of them turned up and collared Ritter. He was dancing with Janet at the time. They pushed her out of the way and dragged Ritter out while everyone else looked on and did nothing or grinned in a sheepish sort of way, and they ducked him in some tank there was, and cut his hair for him and shaved off his beard and then brought him back into the hall and dumped him in a chair and danced round him. Nearly everyone laughed and joined in in the usual apish fashion. And Janet didn't do anything. That woman, Cecily Lightwood, went round after it was all over, making a lot of noise protesting and wanting steps of some sort taken against the toughs—and Janet didn't even join in that. She told me she simply went mum and couldn't bear to say a single word about it. And she told me that since then she'd always had a sort of feeling of obligation towards Ritter. She said she knew there wasn't any real sense in it nowadays but that she just couldn't get out of the habit of feeling it."

" Then d'you mean," said Alice, very interested, " that that incident explains the sort of hold you believe Ritter had over her? "

" It wouldn't be as simple as that, would it? " said Roger. " There'd be other things too. There's always more than one thing."

" But all the same, what you believe is that Ritter simply had a hold on her sympathies," said Alice, " and that there wasn't anything else between them? You do believe the story she gave at the trial? "

He looked at her curiously.

" You don't," he said after a moment.

" If it was as you think," she said, " why was there so much secrecy about the relationship? "

" Secrecy? " He wrinkled his forehead. " There wasn't any secrecy. I knew all about it."

" None of Janet's other friends did. Cecily, for instance."

" Oh," he said, " Cecily. Well, you know what that woman's like. She's got a mania for gossip, and she sees sex in everything, and she was a pretty close friend of Rosamund's, and Rosamund could make scenes about anything."

" I see."

One of his eyebrows lifted quizzically. " No—you don't, I'm afraid."

" I simply don't know," said Alice. Watching the signs of strain and torment on his face, she found she was utterly unable to decide whether it was a true understanding of Janet that had given him his faith in her, or whether, because of his love, he had been more deceived than anyone else. " Why didn't you and Janet get married? " she asked.

He gave a sigh, pushing his fingers through his hair. " Well, all sorts of things happened—all sorts of things. First there was Ritter. I told you, Janet had never said a word about him while we were in France—she didn't know how to, I suppose, because if she'd said he was simply a friend that wouldn't really have explained much. Then when I went to see her after we'd got back to England, he was there—he was working at a typewriter while Janet was doing something in the kitchen. He was in his shirt-sleeves—a beautiful shirt,

mind you, a wonderful shirt, and I should think that if I were
a woman I'd be able to describe that shirt in detail, wouldn't
you?—I hated it so hard, you see, because it and the
typewriter and everything all looked so settled in and
domestic. And it was Ritter who welcomed me and fussed
around like hell making me feel absolutely at home. Janet
just sat in the background and said very little. I couldn't
make things out at all. Ritter was immensely friendly. Janet
seemed to have told him a certain amount about me, because
he knew I was a physicist, and as he'd done a bit of physics at
school and had just been reading *Einstein and Infeld* he
seemed to think it'd go down all right if he talked about it.
It was pretty difficult. I made up my mind to stay till he
left, but he just didn't leave, he went on and on with his
bloody conversational charm. As a matter of fact, he was
always like that when I met him; I could always see him
switching on his bloody conscious generosity towards me. I
should think really he hated me as much as I did him. . . ."
He paused. Drinking quickly, he set his glass down again
and looked at Alice with an anxious frown. " Look," he said,
" I told you I was prejudiced. Ritter may have been all
right really. I dare say he had his own way of trying to be
a human being and just found it as hard as most people
do. . . . Well, it was Janet who broke the party up by saying
she knew that Ritter wanted to get on with some work and so
she and I had better go out somewhere. So we went—we went
and had dinner. And I sat there saying nothing, absolutely
nothing. I didn't mean to do it but I didn't manage to say
a word. Then Janet suddenly started telling me the whole
story. She started off quite abruptly, as she had when she
told me about Markland, and she sounded sort of annoyed
with me and hostile, just as she had then, as if she were certain
I'd never believe what she told me. And the queer thing was,
I believed every word she said. I believed it all straight away,
I didn't like it and I couldn't quite make it out and yet
I believed it. I asked her what she wanted to do about things
and she said she wanted me to give her a little time so that
she could break off entirely with Ritter. So then I thought

I'd produce a bit of generosity on my own and asked her if breaking off was necessary; I talked some gup about not wanting to get between her and her friends and so on. Well, she just looked as if she were going to burst into tears, and she actually wrung her hands and said yes, yes, yes, it was absolutely necessary and that if she didn't break off with him completely he'd ruin everything for us. I was worried about it because she couldn't have got so excited if she hadn't been badly scared of something. Anyhow, I asked her how much time she wanted and she said a week or two. . . . That's about three years ago, you know.''

At the pain in his voice Alice felt her throat tighten.

'' What went wrong? '' she asked.

He shrugged his shoulders. '' Ritter didn't want to let go— that was all at first. He urged her to marry me—I believe he really thought it would be a good idea—but he wanted to be in on it, as it were. He started acting as if he were responsible for the whole thing; he was always about the place, and I believe a good many people must have thought that I was some special discovery of his and that it was a beautiful new friendship. He read more and more popular science and his conversation became more and more scientific. He told me his next play was going to be about a scientist—in industry, of course, in the Black North. And I hardly ever saw Janet alone, and it wasn't one week or two, it was about six, and still nothing had happened. I began to see that she was terrified of actually making the break. Ritter'd got a hold on her, a wonderful hold. . . . D'you know, Alice, there are actually people who think they can keep the love of another person by threatening to kill themselves if they're pushed off? D'you know that? God, the number of times *I* wanted to murder that man! ''

'' But—but, Roger,'' Alice broke in quickly, a number of disturbing thoughts hurrying through her mind. '' d'you mean Ritter used actually to threaten to commit suicide? ''

'' I don't know if he did it in so many words,'' said Roger, '' but it was what he'd made Janet afraid of. And then his wife went and played the trick on him. Rather a joke that,''

—he chuckled harshly—" wasn't it? " His tone had become very savage and there was an ugly twist to his mouth.

" What happened then? " Alice urged him.

" Nothing," he answered. " Not a single damned thing."

" But——"

" You see, while Janet was trying to make herself do something about Ritter, she was finding out more things about me. She was finding out that I'm not very good company when I haven't had a drink, I'm morose and suspicious and I don't listen to what's said to me, and I forget to do things I've promised, and I put off all sorts of things, and I tell a good many lies too when I'm in the mood—I lead a mess of an existence. It made her quite unhappy, the business of finding it out bit by bit. She kept telling me she was sure I didn't have to be like that if I didn't want to be—and that's true, I suppose, and so I got angry and said all right, perhaps it was how I wanted to be. And so things changed by degrees. It was mostly my fault. I wasn't what she needed and it was just another of her bloody misfortunes that she really did care for me. After a bit I began to realise that I—well, in a way I was another Ritter to her. I was someone she felt responsible for and had to do something about. . . . No, perhaps it wasn't as bad as that. I don't know. I don't know anything much about this sort of thing. But something went wrong." He shuddered suddenly, emptied his glass then leant forward and put his head between his hands.

He had got himself fairly drunk by that time, though the only way he showed it was in the way his words ran on, sounding as if he could not have put a check on them even if he had tried. His eyes were red-veined, but that might have been from sleeplessness and from the tears that had kept starting in them.

Alice had thought of a question she wanted to ask him. Though he started talking again almost immediately, she went on thinking about her question, wondering if it might not be very important, very important indeed. Along with wondering about that she began to ask herself how drunk she might be herself. She had not attempted to keep pace with

Roger, but still she had drunk a great deal more than she was used to. This question then, she thought, and the way it had suddenly gripped her imagination, might that not be due to beer and tiredness and the emotional atmosphere? She held it back, waiting for Roger to finish.

" I always kept on urging Janet to make the break with Ritter because I was jealous, and besides, I could see the way it was draining the vitality out of her. And she kept promising and almost doing it, and then Ritter would produce another crisis, and she'd put things off till it was over. For instance, there was a time that began with Cecily bursting into Janet's flat one day and telling us all that Rosamund was going to have a baby. Rosamund had just been telling her about it. You'd have thought, from the way Cecily carried on, that having a baby was one of the world's major calamities. She seemed to be furious about it. She said that a woman with Rosamund's rotten health and nerves hadn't any right to have a baby, and that anyway it was a crime to have children in the middle of a war, when they'd probably be bombed and half-starved and grow up dangerous neurotics who'd certainly want to destroy civilisation the moment they got the chance, and she said that Rosamund was behaving as if she were crazy, wandering around singing and smiling at nothing and wanting to leave their lovely electrified flat and dash straight off to some loathsome house in the suburbs, and that having a family and a house in the suburbs and all would absolutely ruin Ritter—it was an extraordinary rigmarole. Janet put a stop to it fairly firmly. She really seemed annoyed. Cecily took offence, telling Janet that she'd obviously never understood how disastrous domestic responsibilities were for an artist, and Janet snapped back that she understood that all right but that just this once she was going to think of Rosamund. So then Cecily left and later Ritter arrived and brought out all the same stuff that Cecily had been saying. He'd got it into his head that Rosamund's health really wouldn't stand it, and he said he was going to persuade her to have an abortion. Janet asked him if he wanted Rosamund to go right off her head and managed to calm him down a bit, but he did seem absolutely desperate at the idea of having to have a child and I don't know what he really said about it to his wife. Anyway, there wasn't any child, and Rosamund had one of her nerve-storms, and Ritter had one of the attacks of remorse that always went with them, and came and sat in Janet's flat for days, saying it was all his fault, which was bloody nonsense because actually the whole thing had been a mistake, as Janet managed to find out. But Ritter didn't want to listen to that, he just wanted to go on lacerating his feelings and have Janet comfort him—which she did, the damned fool! I couldn't stand those scenes, you know. There was a sort of obscenity about them, they made me feel ill. It was that sort of thing I couldn't have stood if we'd got married. Janet was right; she'd have had to break off with Ritter first. . . . But now, here's something that I keep on asking myself. Why, that's what I want to know, why did she have to go and break off with him just when she did? It *was* brutal to do it to the poor devil just then—though I suppose, with the two of us pulling at her all the time, her nerves had got to a state where she hadn't really any choice of action or much control left over what she did. I didn't see it like that to begin with, I was too damned glad she'd made up her mind at last, though I was expecting her to give in again at any moment. But I didn't grasp what she must have been going through all that time. I was an awful fool. I dare say a lot of it's my fault, in fact, I dare say. . . ." With his red-veined eyes narrowed in thought, he sat staring blankly at the wall ahead of him. " I dare say if I hadn't made certain mistakes. . . ." But there that sentence also faded out.

Before he could begin again, Alice started speaking quickly : " Roger, there's something here that doesn't make sense. Roger——" She put her hand on his wrist and shook it, for she did not think he was listening to her. " Roger, if this is true that you've told me, then the case for the prosecution doesn't make sense. If Janet was doing all she could to get away from Ritter, then she can't have killed him because he suddenly decided he wanted to get away from her—besides, according to you, Ritter wasn't trying to get away from her, he was trying to keep her. Don't you see, the way you explain things, you stand the whole case on its head? "

" Oh, no, I don't," he answered listlessly. " She still went out of the sitting-room, didn't she? D'you remember how she looked just before she went, and how excited and strange she was when she came back? And Larg saw her on the stairs, and her fingerprints were on the poker, and she told an impossible story about going out to telephone. That story, you know, it's always seemed to me one of the worst bits of it—it's so stupid. And what's the difference if she killed Ritter for the reasons the police brought up, or simply because he and I between us drove her out of her mind, so that when Ritter tried to hold on to her just once more she couldn't stop herself hitting out at him to get free? What's the difference, what's the difference? Ritter and I between us. . . ." The words sounded like a curse. " Let's move on somewhere else," he said and stood up abruptly.

The darkness outside was less dense for the rain had stopped and now and then a thin white moon appeared through rifts in the heavy cloud. Silvery gleams were reflected by the wet pavement. The puddles in the road made splashes of blackness on a faintly shining surface and might have been of infinite depth.

Alice's cheeks were burning. The damp air touched them with coolness and ought, she felt, to clear her thoughts so that she could answer that question of Roger's: " What's the difference? " For there must be a difference; you can't suddenly turn a person's motives upside down and not find any difference. But the air, instead of clearing her head, seemed only to make it more swimmy and confused.

She was glad of Roger's arm as they walked along. Afterwards she could not remember much about the next pub that they went to, except that for a while they had stopped talking of the murder and had talked in a sad, tired intimacy of themselves. Roger was very tired, tired to complete exhaustion. He told Alice that he had not had a proper night's sleep for weeks, that it was sleep that always played him false the moment anything in his life went wrong. The air-raids had been hell, he said; he had only managed to sleep then if he got blind-drunk, and he didn't like getting blind-drunk, it was a waste and he couldn't work next day. He had wasted all those months of the blitz, he said fretfully, hardly doing a stroke of work that counted. He had wanted to join the navy —it wouldn't have been such a waste of time—but he had not been released. That a capacity to sleep in situations of some strain might be a convenience even in the navy did not seem to have occurred to him.

Later still in the evening they found themselves walking along the Embankment. Out on the river dark shapes moved by, while the sliding ripples caught a little light from the moon. The Thames in the blackness of a wartime night was very beautiful, but in its depth and silence and secrecy rather frightening.

Suddenly Alice remembered that Roger had never actually told her what he considered the worst mistake of his life. She reminded him of it.

He said. " Ah, yes," and stood still, resting an arm on the parapet of the river. " Yes, it was when I first met her, you know, it was in France," he said. " I picked a quarrel with her one day, at least, I tried to because she'd been annoying me by being so friendly in such a detached sort of way and never behaving as if she knew I was in love with her. So I tried to quarrel with her, but she wouldn't let me. She took hold of the railings at the edge of the path with both hands, and held on to them very hard, and said : ' I can't bear to quarrel—I don't know why, but I can't bear it. I always feel that if ever I quarrelled with anyone, the quarrel would have to go on the rest of my life.' So that was when I kissed her, and as soon as I'd done that I realised that she really hadn't understood that I was in love with her, she'd not been able to believe it. Somehow she didn't seem able to believe that anyone could be in love with her. And she clung to me—she clung to me as if she'd never had anything to hold on to in her life. . . ." He paused for a long time. " I was . . . awfully moved. . . . I'm afraid you generally make mistakes when you start feeling protective and trying to think for another person. I thought the right thing was to take things gently, go very carefully—I thought we'd better come straight home. But we oughtn't to have done that—it was a ghastly mistake—we ought to have stayed."

" But the war," said Alice.

" Damn the war," he answered. " We could have got home later. And it would have made all the difference. She'd have belonged to me, I could have fought Ritter off, and then, don't you see, none of this appalling horror would have happened? "

CHAPTER SIX

WELL, if he was right, it had certainly been a big mistake. For days Alice could not decide what she made of what Roger Mace had told her. For the first time she felt that she knew something about Janet Markland, yet there must be something missing from Roger's portrait of her, as there had been from Peter Willing's. Although in the frustration of his love for her, Roger had taken great pains to understand her, he had not succeeded in portraying a character who, driven to an extremity, would really commit murder. That, at least, as she pondered his story, was Alice's feeling. The woman whom he had described, crippled in her capacity to love by an unhappy and abnormal girlhood and then by the attempt to love a man as unstable and dependent as Ritter, yet who had not been able to free herself from a harassing sense of obligation, would surely never have used violence to effect her escape. She might have taken refuge in illness or temporary breakdown or some fascinating and absorbing form of superstition; she might even have found the moral strength at last, as Janet herself claimed that she had, to break with what was destroying her. But she would not have taken to murder. So something must be missing.

Alice tried talking it over with her husband.

"Roger Mace—you remember him, don't you?—he's told me an awful lot about Janet Markland," she said. "Among other things, he absolutely believes the explanation of her relations with Ritter that she gave at the trial. And somehow he's made me believe it."

"But then what motive had she for the murder?" asked Oliver Church.

"Roger believes she killed him to break his hold on her, a sort of parasitic emotional hold."

"He's believing what he wants to believe," said Oliver.

"But he knew her pretty well."

"He doesn't doubt that she killed Ritter, does he?"

"No," said Alice uneasily.

" Well then? "

Hesitantly Alice tried again: " You see, it seems to me—
well, that the most significant part of a crime, or perhaps of
any action, is the motive. Not how it happened, or where or
when, but why. If you build up a story on a basis of rage or
greed or jealousy, and then find that there wasn't any rage
or greed or jealousy, then—well, I think you ought to start all
over again, just as much as if you found out that the poker,
say, which was supposed to have been used for the killing,
hadn't really been used at all. It's a question of—almost of
the actual *person* who's on trial. If by any chance Janet
wasn't Ritter's mistress all that time, and if she wasn't trying
to stop him breaking off with her but was really the one who
was insisting on breaking off, then, don't you see, she's hardly
the same person as the one they had on trial? D'you understand what I mean? I've a feeling it might be awfully
important. All the people who knew Janet agree because of
the evidence that she must have killed Ritter, but none of
them agree on why she did it. To me that seems—that seems
the most fundamental thing in the whole structure."

" But do you mean that *you* think she may not have done
the murder? "

Alice had not yet quite dared to put that question to herself.
At length she said: " Yes."

Oliver looked at her interestedly, waiting for her to go on,
but she did not say any more just then.

A day or two after that she rang up Kitty Roper and asked
her how she could get in touch with Frank Lely. Kitty gave
her a telephone number. Major Lely was stationed at a village
in Hampshire; Alice managed to speak to him and arranged
to meet him at six o'clock the next day.

Frank Lely.

Frank Lely, the man who had seen Aubrey Ritter lying
dead, the man who had seen the room in which Aubrey Ritter
had been murdered, the man who disliked Janet Markland, the
man who had a theory that she had not killed Aubrey Ritter
. . . Alice forced herself to think about it all. She had not
liked Frank Lely, and she did not like thinking about the

scene in that upstairs flat, that flat in the old converted house near Parliament Hill Fields which must have been so different from the expensive modern flat where Ritter had lived with his wife. It was surprising really how little Alice had thought about that scene, how her mind had shrunk from it, how she had managed to avoid visualising it in any but the vaguest of shapes and colours. But now, she felt, she must think about it as hard as she could, she must get over her fear of it and try to imagine it as it must have been.

What did she know about that room?

Nothing at all. It had scarcely been mentioned. And yet. . . .

And yet surely she did know something about it. She found herself feeling about that room as she felt about one which she had allowed to go beyond the normal bounds of untidiness and which had started nagging at her constantly with a claim for her attention. She felt as if she ought to get up into that room and tidy up, put things in their proper places. *Their proper places.* . . . But what did she know then about things not being in their proper places?

It was no good. Like a shape under the surface of dark water which may be a fish or a clump of weed or simply an old boot, some idea, some scrap of half-knowledge, loomed vaguely but would not define itself. She started thinking over what she was going to say to Frank Lely.

She had to cancel some of her C.A.B. work to meet him, but a feeling of urgency had got into her. They had arranged to meet in the lounge of the one hotel in the village near which he was stationed. The train journey took her an hour and a half. The hotel was a pleasant-looking old pub with a square, ruddy frontage, a bowling-green beside it and big trees round it. The village had a triangular green and a small grey church showing behind a thick bank of yews, and was so quiet and traditional that it was very strange to see uniforms and hear transatlantic accents everywhere.

Frank Lely was waiting for her in the lounge. As he unfolded his thin height out of an armchair and came to meet her, Alice wished they had been able to choose a less crowded place for their meeting. The place was full of Canadian

officers. There were also a good many old ladies with their
knitting who had removed themselves from London for the
duration. There was a constant coming and going and a
swishing of swing-doors.

Frank Lely said straight away: " I'm sorry about this
but I'm afraid it's the best we can do. I've got about an hour,
then I'll have to get back. I think if we go over into that
corner we'll be fairly undisturbed. What'll you have to
drink? "

His manner was frigid and his words abrupt. As before,
Alice found his big, pale face with its curiously dull look
and air of unhealthiness distinctly repellent. Probably, she
thought as they settled down in two easy chairs in an alcove,
he did not like her much either.

Fortunately there was so much noise in the lounge that their
voices were lost in it.

" Well, you want to discuss Mrs. Markland, I gather,"
said Frank Lely, glancing at his watch as he said it. " What's
on your mind, Mrs. Church? "

Alice decided to match him in abruptness.

" Did she do the murder? "

" No," he said. Then he leant back, crossing his bony
hands over his stomach. " But why? Aren't you satisfied
with the verdict? "

" No," said Alice.

" Why not? "

" Are you? "

" I have to be. I haven't a single shred of evidence to
upset it."

" Then why did you say, ' No,' when I asked you if Janet
Markland did the murder? "

" You started this," he said. " Suppose you open up
first."

Alice took a breath. She was feeling strangely nervous.
" It'll sound so foolish," she said, " because it's simply a
feeling. At least, I think that's all it is, unless. . . ."

" Unless what? "

" Oh, unless I've heard things—seen things—and not
understood them and only half remembered them. . . ."

" Ah, yes. But let's not bother about that just now. Let's stick to that interesting feeling of yours. What sort of feeling is it?" He sounded satirical, yet suddenly Alice had the idea that he was as nervous and as intent as she was.

That made it easier to go on. " It's a feeling about the kind of person she is," she said. " I've talked to four people who've known her at various times of her life and—well, none of them seems to doubt that she killed Ritter, and yet when I try putting together the four descriptions they've given me, I can't, I simply can't see her as the sort of person who'd actually kill anyone, at any rate for any of the reasons they've managed to think up. And so . . ."

" And so? " He did not mean to help her.

" And so," she said sharply, " I'm beginning to feel ready to back my own judgment, at the risk of looking a fool, that she didn't do the murder and that the evidence, that wonderful, convincing evidence, has something wrong with it somewhere! "

The corners of his small, red mouth twitched slightly.

" Fair enough," he said, " except that the evidence *hasn't* anything wrong with it. Facts, you know, solid facts."

" Facts often aren't so very solid," said Alice, " and not nearly so immutable as people make out."

" And human character is? "

" If one manages to understand it."

" Hmm," he said sardonically. " Well, perhaps I agree with you—perhaps." He reached for his glass. His hands fascinated Alice, they were so thin, almost as if there were nothing there but the pale skin stretched over the dry bones inside. " Suppose you tell me your idea of Janet Markland? Why can't she be a murderess? "

Alice had been dreading the question. As she hesitated, Frank Lely said with sudden good nature: " Don't worry if it sounds silly as you say it—it will, you know. But let's hear it."

" Well then," said Alice, " it goes something like this. Janet Markland's a civilised human being, she's intelligent, educated, self-controlled. She hasn't been particularly fortunate in her life, but all things considered, she's made a tolerable success of it. Perhaps she's rather lacking in warmth and impulsiveness—it sounds like it—but she's got a strong sense of moral obligation, she tries to be understanding and loyal. Well now. . . .'' Alice's feeling was becoming clearer to her as she talked about it. '' Well now, contrary to popular superstition, it isn't the slightly over-civilised, reserved, self-controlled people who commit murders, it's the people of crude and undeveloped passions, it's the vicious or the unbalanced or the downright mentally deficient. Janet Markland wasn't any of those things. Perhaps she was avaricious . . . I'm not sure. It's possible to make out a case that almost all the main actions of her life were dictated by mercenary motives, and if that's so perhaps—perhaps she's more vicious than appears and perhaps she did murder Ritter on account of his money, but if not . . .''

As Alice left the sentence hanging, Frank Lely shook his head.

'' She wasn't mercenary.''

'' She wasn't? ''

'' No.'' His dull brown eyes gazed through the whisky in his glass which he was holding up before him. '' No, she always sent those old aunts of hers money, even when she'd hardly any herself, and she used to send Markland money for two or three years after she'd left him, and once . . . Once I was very hard up and I happened to tell her about it. She simply wrote out a cheque. And she never asked for it back or ever referred to it. Incidentally, I never paid her back either.'' His lips twitched again.

'' But then——? ''

'' Oh, Mrs. Church, haven't you ever heard of repressions? ''

'' Oh, Lord,'' said Alice, '' I knew we'd get to them sooner or later, in fact, I'd have brought them up myself in another minute or two. Yes, of course I've heard of them, and of course Janet *was* rather repressed and repressed people behave very oddly now and then, in fact, they do sometimes go out of their minds and commit murder. But there's been no plea of madness in this case. Yet suppose it was madness, one short flash of madness during which she snatched up that

poker and lashed out with it—yes, suppose it was! Well,
what do you think would have happened afterwards? What
would she actually have done? I'll tell you. She'd have had
a breakdown, she'd have gone ill or insane, *or else she'd have
confessed!* '' Suddenly as she said it, it became completely
clear to her. If Janet Markland had killed Aubrey Ritter,
that was what she would have done. She would have gone
mad or confessed.

'' She did confess,'' said Frank Lely quietly.

That pulled Alice up. She had forgotten that for the
moment. But it was true; she herself had heard it.

'' But she explained that away,'' she said after a moment,
'' and that explanation could easily be true. After all, everyone there thought Ritter had committed suicide, even while
that American boy was shouting murder. If she believed that
it was she who had made him do it, she might easily have said
what she did.''

'' Perhaps,'' said Lely. '' On the whole I agree with you.
I've had a feeling all along that Janet hadn't got it in her to
commit murder. She could never lose her head sufficiently,
she'd always keep some grip on herself. I know it's a truism
to say we're all capable of murder—myself, I don't believe
it. We're all capable of killing—wars show that up—but
that's quite a different order of things. To kill when the whole
social order's behind you, applauding you for it, egging you
on to it, finding means of training you to overcome your
reluctance to do it, is no more like murder than, say, the
homosexuality of the Greeks resembles what you see in
Charlotte Street. It's only in quite a few individuals that the
impulses to perverted actions are so strong that they have to
come out in spite of centuries of social prohibition—and you
can take it from me, Janet Markland isn't one of those people.
She couldn't endure any impulses as strong as that. If they
did master her suddenly, then, as you've just said, she'd
crack up, she'd go mad. As I see it, the chief aim in her life
has always been security. Those mercenary motives you spoke
of, they didn't exist, she wasn't more interested in money
than it's decent to be. But the conditions of her life had been
such that security, material and emotional, had come to seem

to her the only really desirable thing on earth. All women have that in them. Take Kitty Roper; in her it's quite crude, quite simple. She wants to be housed and fed so that she can breed in safety. In Janet it's more complicated and less honest. Probably she never admitted to herself what she was after. I imagine, for instance, that she thought she was in love with Markland when she married him. Several other people had been, which is usually a good enough reason to believe it of oneself. That she was on the rebound from Rit's sudden passion for Kitty and also from her aunt's loss of money, wouldn't, I think, ever have occurred to her. She wanted to be loved and to be looked after. The joke is that she should ever have thought Markland was the person to do it—anyway, when she found he wasn't going to put much work into either job, she left him. She had a shot at being independent but it didn't last long. Soon she got herself a job stage-managing Peter Willing. I dare say his idea of that was that he depended on her, and perhaps he did too, but I think that her angle on the relationship was that she'd got herself a nice bulwark against the threatening world. And then Rit——"

" I was just going to say," Alice interrupted, " what about Ritter? It was you who told us all she'd been Ritter's mistress. Do you still believe that? "

" Why not? "

" How does that square with your theory about her passion for security? She was taking quite a risk, wasn't she? "

" Was she?" He gave another of his little twitching smiles. " There are ways and ways of doing these things, you know. Janet didn't take any risks." His eyes mocked at her. " There's no concealment so effective as leaving things wide open to the light of day. But remember that even so a good deal was concealed from Rosamund, the one person who mattered, and all of us had to co-operate in keeping it concealed from her, because of course poor Rosamund was so jealous and unbalanced that she'd only have misunderstood this beautiful, idealistic friendship and only become more unbalanced than ever—poor, poor Rosamund!" Like a wave of heat surging out when the door of a furnace is opened, savagery burst into his tone.

Alice was startled. She thought how impossible it is to trace all the emotional cross-currents between any group of people. She wondered if Lely had actually been in love with Rosamund Ritter. At any rate it was plain that he had been profoundly stirred by pity for her.

" It was Ritter who told you that Janet was his mistress, was it? " she asked after a moment.

" He told me that he was going away with her to Wales," Lely replied. " I told him he was a fool to get mixed up with her. She'd ruined his work already; she'd spotted the popular element in it and brought that out. Before he let her get her hands on it he'd had something, he'd had a——"

Alice interrupted again: " But that was the only time he spoke of it to you—the *only* time? "

Shrugging his shoulders with a kind of sulkiness, he answered: " I didn't want to be in his confidence about it. The less I had to do with it, the better it suited me. But I couldn't help seeing what was happening."

" I'll tell you something," said Alice, " I'll tell you what *I* believe about it. I don't think she was Ritter's mistress—except for that short time. Roger Mace told me about an occasion when Rosamund thought she was going to have a baby. Ritter wanted to stop her having it, and Janet asked him if he wanted to drive Rosamund right out of her mind. Now I don't believe that if Janet had been his mistress she'd have done that. She wouldn't have wanted another woman to have his child. No, I'm sure of that." It was strange how the unsympathetic company of Frank Lely was making her own thoughts come clear to her. " I'm *sure* now that she told the truth at the trial about her relations with Ritter."

Lely glanced at his watch again. " What difference does it make? " he grunted. " Whatever you and I may feel about Janet, about Rit, about everything, there's still the evidence."

" Yes," said Alice, " the evidence." She sighed. She spoke next at random. " The poker . . ."

Frank Lely waited questioningly.

" The poker had her finger-prints on it, didn't it? " she said.

" Just so," said Lely. " You can't get round that."

" No. . . . Though they might have got there at some other time, mightn't they? "

" She said she'd never been up to the flat at all."

" I know, but . . ." Suddenly Alice found herself sitting bolt upright in the deep padded chair. She felt an immense excitement. " The room," she exclaimed, " you saw the room! That room's been on my mind for days. I *knew* there was something I ought to have realised about it. Please tell me what it was like. It was in a mess, wasn't it? It must have been, he'd only just moved in. It *was* in a mess, wasn't it? "

" Yes," said Lely, surprised, " it was in a mess."

" Things all over the place," she pressed him, " cases of books, crockery, bedding, nothing properly unpacked yet— was it like that? "

He nodded, his thin eyebrows lifted.

" Was there a fire? " she went on.

" Yes, I think so. It was a cold evening."

" A *coal* fire? "

" Yes, I think . . . No! " His long body went taut. Something brightened in his eyes. " No, it wasn't, Mrs. Church, it was a gas fire. And just exactly how did you know that? "

" Well, Ritter'd only just moved in, you see," said Alice, " that's what I'd kept forgetting. Of course the whole place would be in a mess. Well, I've done plenty of moving myself, and I know that if there's gas or electricity one doesn't bother with lighting up a coal fire while one's still struggling with unpacking—particularly nowadays when it sometimes takes weeks to get one's coal delivered. And there was a point for a portable gas fire in Cecily's bedroom where I spent the night, but there wasn't any fire. Obviously Ritter had borrowed it. Yes, I'm sure that's what had happened. So the poker must have been lying around because it just happened to have been unpacked, not because it was in use for poking the fire. And . . . And," she cried, her excitement growing, " Ritter'd just come from an all-electric flat! So you see, it's quite possible that that poker hadn't been handled for literally years —not since the Ritters left Fitzroy Square—and Janet may have been the last person to handle it! "

Lely burst out laughing.

" That's just as pretty as can be," he said. " I wonder if there's any way of testing the age of finger-prints. But anyway, where d'you think it gets you, Mrs. Church? Someone, I suppose you mean, dropped that poker in the pool of blood to incriminate Janet, removing the blunt instrument that had really been used. Well, it could have been like that. But Janet *did* go up to that flat, remember, and that she did snatch up that poker and use it, even if it was only lying around mixed up with the bed-linen and cooking-pots, still seems to me a more likely story than yours."

" All the same," said Alice, " if we could upset the story somewhere else—for instance, if we could find out why she really went upstairs and why she's lied about it ever since, then the fact that the poker had her finger-prints on it needn't worry us any more."

" If," he said, " *if*! I'm sorry, Mrs. Church, I really am, but I don't think you're going to get anywhere along that line."

He was watching Alice now with amusement. She felt very angry with him. She spoke wildly: " Well, it might have been Janet herself who put the poker beside Ritter and hid the real weapon, mightn't it? And she could have put it there without realising that she was putting her own finger-prints on it. She may only have meant to protect the real murderer without incriminating herself. She may have hidden the real weapon—she may have hidden it somewhere in that empty first-floor flat when she dashed in there after passing Ed Larg on the stairs. And she may have lied about going upstairs because, until her finger-prints turned up, she may have thought she could get away with it. And afterwards it may have seemed to her that there wasn't any point in retracting the story because she'd see she'd have no chance of being believed unless she incriminated the other person. Why," Alice exclaimed in surprise at herself, " it's all quite simple really! "

But she knew it was not, and that Frank Lely was not the person to let her go on pretending that it was.

" Thin," he said, " very thin, Mrs. Church." He brought

the tips of his spidery fingers together and looked at her gravely across them. " First of all, who was this ' other person ' ? Who was this ' real murderer ' ? I assure you, that's a question I've gone over a good deal. Somebody else—could it have been somebody else? If by any strange chance it wasn't Janet, then it has to be somebody else. And it has to be somebody else who, as you point out, Janet is protecting. But who is there that Janet Markland would protect right up to the gallows—the *gallows*, Mrs. Church? To whom does she feel such devotion that she'd keep what she knows to herself and take on herself that sentence of death? I think the answer is—nobody."

Unhappily, Alice nodded.

" In fact," Lely went on in his crisp, hard voice, " I'm inclined to think that if Janet knew who'd killed Rit, she'd want to see the law take its course with him. With all my doubts about the value of her influence on him, I don't question that she had a genuine affection for him. If she knew who the murderer was, I think she'd feel much as I did that first evening when I still took for granted that it was Janet herself. And I'll tell you that what I felt was a violent hope that she'd be hanged by the neck until she was dead! " He stirred impatiently. " I'm afraid we aren't getting anywhere."

He was looking at his watch again. Alice guessed that he wanted to bring the interview to a close. Yet she knew he had the same unease as she had. Fumbling for her bag and gloves which had slipped down into a corner of the chair, she started pulling on the gloves. She was feeling bitterly disappointed.

But Lely said sharply: " You aren't going, are you? There's no hurry, surely." All at once he sounded nervous and distraught.

" We aren't getting anywhere," she reminded him.

" Perhaps we haven't tried the right line. Let's think— for the Lord's sake, let's think! " He leant forward, letting his hands hang down between his knees like two bunches of limp asparagus. " I expect Peter Willing told you he'd gone into the history of young Larg to see if there was any conceivable reason why he might have lied about seeing Janet. There wasn't, so that line's no good. Myself, I've been going over all the other people who might have done the murder, people who might have had the motive and the opportunity, and that line's been no good either. Still, I think I'm going to tell you about it in case there's something I've missed that you can put a finger on. I'll take them one by one, and for your benefit I'll begin with myself.'' He drank. When he spoke next his voice had lost the note of anxiety; it had back its normal sound of sardonic detachment.

'' The case against Francis Lely,'' he said. '' Motive? I'll take the possible motives one by one. Financial—none. I hadn't had any financial dealings with Rit, I owed him no money, he owed me none, he didn't leave me anything in his will. Sexual—none. None to speak of. It's true that I liked Rosamund, I liked her a lot. She was lovely and helpless and crazy, and when I found her dead I hated Rit for about two hours, hated him so much perhaps I could almost have killed him. Then I got my senses back and admitted it wasn't his fault—that's to say, I knew he was just about as helpless as she was. Just a simple little inevitable tragedy, Mrs. Church, that's all it was. Other motives—political, blackmail and so on and so on—none. Opportunity? '' He shook his head. '' I could have killed him, of course. I could have gone upstairs provided that door downstairs wasn't properly closed, any time in the day before Cecily's party, killed him and then gone downstairs again and stood on the doorstep and rung the bell to be let in. But then Rit couldn't have answered the telephone when Cecily rang him up to ask when he was coming down. And supposing Rit was dead already then and wasn't the person who answered, I couldn't have been the person either, because I was down there in the room with you all. And for that reason, besides the other more obvious ones, I couldn't have been the brown-haired woman in a black dress seen by Ed Larg on the staircase. And supposing that woman was Janet. . . . Well, Janet Markland certainly wouldn't go to the gallows for *me*, Mrs. Church. Now what about it? ''

'' Not guilty,'' said Alice.

'' Thank you. Now we'll take your case.''

'' Is that necessary since our time is limited? ''

" It's a very limited little case. Motive—none. You'd never met Ritter and probably didn't dislike his plays so intensely that you thought he needed wiping out. Opportunity —precisely the same as mine, no better, no worse. I think we can say not guilty. Whom shall we take next? "

" Kitty Roper."

He gave a quick little grin. " So that's how you feel about her? "

" Well, at least we can find a motive for her," said Alice, " she told me herself of her connection with Ritter."

" To continue then," said Lely drily. " The case against Kitty Roper. Motive—possibly plenty. If Rit's first impulse after Rosamund's death was to break off with Janet, it's likely enough that he thought of breaking off with Kitty too. I can imagine that that would annoy her very much indeed; she'd always prefer to be the one who did the breaking off. Or Rit might have been considering doing something which Kitty thought might give her away to her husband—put the whole story in a play or something. Or she might just have discovered that Rit was trying to marry Janet. We needn't elaborate, we can simply say, motive, yes. Opportunity?" He raised his eyebrows questioningly at Alice.

" She came very late to the party," said Alice.

" But she was in the room with the rest of us when Cecily rang up Rit to ask him when he was coming down and she didn't leave the room again after that. And that goes for all the rest of us except Janet and possibly Cecily herself. So what's the verdict on Kitty? "

" Not guilty, I suppose."

Alice's tone seemed to cause him some amusement.

" Who next then? Cecily? " he suggested.

" All right, Cecily."

" Motive," he said thoughtfully. " To tell the truth, I'm not sure about that. She's a good-natured soul, Cecily, in spite of all her prickles. I've always been rather fond of her. I wouldn't get mixed up with her for a king's ransom, in fact, we've always fought like hell, but there's astonishing kindness and loyalty in her. It's just like her that when Rosamund died and all the rest of us were scared off by the

hate Rit took to the lot of us, Cecily just battered her way
in past it and put him in that flat where she could keep an eye
on him. She was good friends with Rosamund too; she was
always trying to get her to take herself in hand, settle down
to her music, go to a psychiatrist, anything. But what her
real feelings were about Rit, I don't know. She's all tied up
in knots herself, and Rit probably exploited her good nature
as much as he did that of any woman who'd let him. He'd
a great capacity for self-pity, he'd no toughness at all. Perhaps
Cecily was more in love with him than she ever let on; it
wouldn't surprise me. But I don't know. So in her case I
think we'd better say, motive—possibly."

Alice nodded.

"Opportunity, then," he said. "Well, you know, she did
have more opportunity than any of the rest of us. She could
have gone upstairs while she was supposed to be in the kitchen.
That might be important."

"But why should she have gone upstairs?" asked Alice.
"Ritter had just told her on the telephone that he was
coming down."

"She might have decided that he wasn't to be trusted. But
still, how could her bright blue dress and grey hair have
turned into a black dress and brown hair? You see, that's
what one always comes back to, Mrs. Church. Sooner or later
one has to remind oneself young Larg did see Janet on the
staircase. Myself, I'd say the verdict on Cecily's not guilty."

"And that leaves Peter Willing and Roger Mace."

"Peter," said Lely softly, "ah, yes, Peter." He looked
away reflectively over Alice's head. "Peter the kind, the
helpful. Poor old Peter, he couldn't commit a murder if he
tried, it'd give him such indigestion."

"You seem," said Alice acidly, "to have a temperamental
preference for the people whom you think *could* commit
murder."

He smiled.

"I liked Mr. Willing," said Alice.

"Good Lord, so do I," said Lely. "Anyway, let's take
the case against him. Motive—Rit was one of his best-paying
clients, and besides, he really liked those plays of his, thought

they were great stuff, thought posterity would lap 'em up, felt it was a privilege to be on them, as it were. . . . No, there's no motive in that direction. But jealousy, perhaps—jealousy over Janet. I don't know. One never knows, does one? Peter seems to be devoted to his Evelyn and his children, yet perhaps the little man has a capacity for righteous indignation and got it into his head that Rit's way of acting had really murdered Rosamund. How can one tell? Perhaps we'd better say, motive, possibly. And opportunity? It's the same as for you or me again. If Rit was murdered before the party began, then Peter could have done it. But he couldn't have been the voice on the telephone, and he couldn't have been the woman in black. And there you are again, you see. All that applies to Roger too, even if he was the one with the best motive of anyone. And we know that Janet went upstairs, and we know that she's consistently and stupidly lied about it, and that's much more concrete in the way of evidence than anything we can produce against anyone else. Don't you agree?"

Alice sighed. " I'm afraid so."

" Of course, there is just one thing," he said. " I don't know—it might be important. D'you remember, when Janet was being questioned, she referred to the fact that the night was clear and starry and that a warden and policeman were discussing astronomy at the gate? Well, how could she have known that if she hadn't been out to the telephone? She got to the party before I did, and it was still raining when I arrived."

Alice stood up.

" I'm afraid that doesn't mean anything at all, Mr. Lely. Very nearly the first thing I said to Janet when I met her in Cecily's sitting-room was that the sky was full of stars and that a warden and policeman were discussing them. I'm sorry. But thank you very much for giving me your time and going over all these points with me. At least you've eased my mind. You've convinced me that in spite of my private feelings, Mrs. Markland must have done the murder. I'm afraid we can't have taken enough notice of those repressions we talked about—there's something wrong with our psychology somewhere."

She held out her hand.

Frank Lely hauled himself up to his feet and looked down at her frowningly from his astonishing height.

" I don't like having my perceptions defeated by facts," he said. " Facts, I feel, should be ready to yield to manipulation. But unfortunately they're a stubborn lot." He added that he would go with her to the station.

They walked almost the whole way in silence and separated with only a few terse words. It was dusk by the time Alice got into the train and dark before she reached London. The blinds were drawn in the compartment; she saw nothing of the woods and fields, nor of the suburbs with their inappropriate scars of war. The train was a slow one, stopping at each station. The continual halts and the dim lights and the lack of heating in the carriage and her own tiredness fused together into a sense of overpowering depression. She stopped thinking about the murder. She stopped thinking about anything in particular, and huddled in her overcoat, kept her eyes closed and tried to dodge her own sense of failure. It seemed in some way specially connected with seeing Frank Lely, and although she knew how mistaken that kind of impression can be, how discomfort or repulsion can cling to our memories of certain people when they themselves have been nothing but sympathetic and well-meaning, and that it is really some criticism of ourselves that we are trying to turn on to them, she hoped that she would never see him again. She hoped that she would never see any of them again. Her tiredness became an ache that seemed to start in her knees and soon spread all over her. She decided that as soon as she got home she would have a hot bath, go to bed and forget as much as she could.

Yet as soon as she got home she started telling her husband all about her talk with Frank Lely.

Oliver, who was sitting by the fire, eating some supper off a tray, listened with an absent look in his eye. He seemed to be annoyed with Alice for having made herself so tired, and blustered at her about it a certain amount, telling her that he wished to God she'd never taken to this C.A.B. stuff, because until she'd done that she'd known how to mind her own business. Alice went on telling him about her talk with Frank Lely. It was as if she could not stop herself. The words poured out as they often do when one is nervously exhausted, running on of themselves, taking charge of her tongue, making their own points, answering their own arguments.

A worried frown appeared on the forehead of Oliver Church. By degrees the lines deepened. Soon he stopped bothering about his supper and sat with his hands loosely clasped between his knees and his eyes on Alice's face. When at last she stopped talking he stood up and started roaming about the room. He picked up a ruler from the table and put it down again, looked at a diagram on a scrap of paper and tossed it aside, stared hard at a small scratch on the wallpaper and even ran a finger down it as if he were wondering how it had been made.

Suddenly he cleared his throat and said: " Yes . . . well . . . that *is* the important point, of course."

" *What* is?" asked Alice. She knew Oliver's habit of spilling small fragments of what he was thinking about into the conversation and forgetting that by themselves they might be unintelligible.

" Her denial—her senseless denial that she went up to the man's flat," he said, picking up a used match and carefully splitting it with his nail. " You're quite right, that's what it all hangs on."

Alice was not aware that she had said that that was what it all hung on and now she suddenly found herself weary beyond words of the whole subject. She yawned. " Even so, it doesn't help, it doesn't help in the least," she said.

" Because you may not have looked at it in the right way," said Oliver.

" I've looked at it in every way I can think of," she replied.

" But always assuming that it was untrue."

" But it *is* untrue."

" How d'you know? "

She flared up in exasperation: " Oh, you haven't been

listening! She was *seen* coming out of Ritter's flat, she **was** *seen* on the staircase.''

Oliver shook his head. '' I've been listening all right. And your argument is, I gather, that because you believe Janet Markland is a certain kind of person, she can't have murdered Ritter.''

'' Is it? I suppose it is,'' said Alice, yawning again. '' But the facts contradict me.''

'' And if one runs into facts that flatly contradict some pet hypothesis, what does one do? ''

'' Drop the hypothesis.''

'' Certainly not. You assume that the facts may not be what they seem.''

'' Sounds like wangling to me.''

He smiled. '' If I were you,'' he said, '' I'd try saying to myself that if a person insists on a story as palpably false, as obviously foolish and as entirely detrimental to her own interests as the one Janet Markland's stuck to about going out to telephone and not going up to Ritter's flat, then it can be for only one reason, and that's because it's true.''

'' But,'' said Alice, '' Ed Larg *saw* her.''

'' If I were you,'' said Oliver, '' I'd get hold of Ed Larg. Perhaps he didn't actually see what he thought he saw.''

Alice was too tired to think that out and showed it by turning bad-tempered. '' It's no use, I tell you,'' she snapped, '' it's no use whatever.''

Oliver patted her knee and said: '' All right, you go off to bed and we'll talk about it to-morrow.''

'' There's been too much talking about it already,'' said Alice.

'' We'll see in the morning,'' said Oliver. Alice was too sleepy to notice the purposeful look in his eye. The problem had caught his imagination at last, just when hers had grown utterly tired of it.

Alice did not know when her husband came to bed. Next morning while she was still at breakfast, sitting at the table with a cigarette and her second cup of coffee, he came into the room with some sheets of foolscap and a fountain-pen and sat down opposite her.

"Now," he said "tell me the whole thing from the beginning."

"But I've told you the whole thing I don't know how many times," said Alice.

He took no notice. He wrote various headings across a sheet of paper. "Well?" he said impatiently.

"But last night——"

"Last night you told me everything that a lot of people had been saying to you. Very useful too to show the sort of people we're dealing with. But what I want is a careful account of everything that happened on the night of the murder. Every single thing, important or unimportant."

"But I don't know how many times I've told you——"

"It doesn't matter how many times you've told me—this is the time when I happen to want to be told. Now then, what time was it when you got there?"

"Oliver," said Alice, "this thing's been taken into small pieces, and hashed and chewed——"

"Alice, for heaven's sake don't get one of your contrary fits just now," he said. "Just settle down and tell me every single thing you can remember—come on now, don't waste time."

"I don't have contrary fits! And it's going over all this stuff again that'll be the waste of time!"

Oliver simply waited with his pen poised above the paper.

All in all that day, Alice talked for five or six hours. Again and again Oliver made her go over the story of the evening of Cecily's party while he covered page after page of foolscap with his small, swift handwriting. Sometimes, though not very often, he asked questions; they came usually when Alice added some detail that she had forgotten in former versions of the story. For instance, he held her up for some time when, at about the third repetition, she remembered and tried to describe the curious change that had come over Janet Markland just before her momentous absence from the sitting-room.

"You've said nothing about this before," he interrupted her. "How d'you mean, a change came over her?"

"Well, it was her face, the way she was sitting. . . ."

"You're sure it happened? You haven't merely developed

a feeling that a change must have come over her? You've a clear objective memory of it? ''

'' Of course,'' said Alice. '' I'm being extremely clear and objective, so don't try browbeating me. I can remember that while she was sitting there talking to us——''

'' Us? ''

'' Roger Mace, Kitty Roper and me. Suddenly every scrap of colour drained out of her face and she seemed to go absolutely rigid. Then she got up and walked out. I've always thought that that was the moment when she made up her mind to do—whatever she did.''

'' We're assuming, for purpose of argument, that that was to go outside and telephone to Ritter and tell him not to come down; in fact, it was the final break with him. Did anyone else notice this? ''

'' Roger Mace, I think.''

'' Are you sure? ''

'' Yes, he was watching her all the evening. I'd decided already that he was jealous of Ritter.''

'' So anyway it was a great effort to Mrs. Markland to make that decision? ''

'' Yes, it must have been. Oliver, are you sure you're going the right way about this? She can't have gone out to telephone, she must have lied.''

'' We're assuming for purpose of argument, that everything that Janet Markland said in her defence was true.''

'' But I've reminded you, I don't know how often, that Ed Larg saw her on the staircase! ''

'' Ed Larg,'' said Oliver, '' is coming to lunch to-morrow. I arranged that this morning. We'll then go into the question of how it was that he managed to see her on the staircase when in fact she wasn't there. Now go back to this particular change you saw come over Mrs. Markland—go on from there.''

So it continued. They had a short break for lunch, then started again; perhaps they would have gone on all day if Alice had not forced Oliver to release her so that she could get to the shops before they closed. She was slow over the shopping on purpose and sat for a long time over a quiet cup of tea in an Express Dairy.

Sergeant Larg arrived at one o'clock the next day.

As soon as she opened the door to him, Alice found that she had not remembered him at all clearly. For one thing, she had not remembered how young he was; seeing his fresh, pink, boy's face under the khaki cap, she felt a twinge of conscience at having allowed Oliver to draw him back into the horrible atmosphere of murder. But as she greeted him, she told herself not to be too much of a fool. The rear-gunner of a light bomber is not unaccustomed to the nearness of violent death; probably, she thought, it was those of her own generation, who had grown up in what at the time they had taken to be security, who most craved for protection from the mere thought of death and destruction.

Ed Larg turned out, in spite of his quiet manner, to be quite without shyness. He had, in fact, an unusual candour about himself which, while it seemed in a way very naïve, somehow gave him an air of maturity and self-possession. Anyone who does not mind how much of himself he gives away achieves remarkable poise, even if he is only twenty-one. Carefully he explained just exactly how he felt about being in England. He liked it, it suited him, he said, he didn't worry about things being different, why should he worry, it was interesting; he got along all right with the people, he was interested in them—weren't Alice and Oliver interested in people too? He thought maybe they were. He liked talking to people and studying them. He didn't mean psychology and he didn't mean anything literary, he didn't mean characterisation; he just liked getting the feeling of people and trying to understand them, and you could do that anywhere, you didn't have to be at home to do it. No, he wasn't homesick—well, not exactly. Sometimes he got a letter from his mother and carried it around with him for days before he even opened it—could they imagine that? Could they imagine having a letter from their mothers in their pockets and carrying it around for days without even reading it, because everything about it felt so far away and strange and belonging to another existence? Then again he'd get another letter from his mother, or maybe his sister, just telling him of everyday things back home, and he'd feel it was the whole world. But he reckoned everybody

had to grow up sooner or later, only it felt queer in a way
when you kind of noticed it happening to yourself. He
couldn't imagine what it would be like going home again;
he'd have become something which he'd never have been if
there hadn't been a war, which was queer too if you thought
about it.

Oliver asked him what he wanted to do when he got home.

He answered that he'd always thought that maybe the
best life there was was a university professor's, but then again,
there was flying, wasn't there? His eyes suddenly shone. Yes,
there was flying. Had either of them ever seen England from
the air?

Both had to admit that they had not.

He told them earnestly that they must never miss an opportunity to do so. It was more beauitful than anything they
could ever have seen. Sometimes when you went up in the
early morning and saw the whole country falling away, little
and green, below you, kind of set in a ring of gold cloud, it
was more beautiful than. . . . More beautiful than. . . .
He fumbled for words and could not find any to describe the
wonderful thing he had seen. Silent for a moment, he sat
there, apparently pondering deeply on his astounding
privileges. Then he added that France wasn't so interesting,
it seemed to be all little straight strips, besides when you were
over France you were always thinking of flak. But they must
never, he repeated most seriously, never, it would be a crime,
miss an opportunity of seeing England from the air.

And what, Alice asked him, would take the place of flying
for him when the war was over?

He looked startled. Why, nothing, he said, nothing could.

When at length they returned to the subject of the murder,
Oliver apologised for dragging him back to it. But the boy
assured them that was okay, he was interested, he was
interested in the people—like he'd said, he was always interested in people. But still, he didn't see how he could help.

Oliver began to explain.

Ed nodded and looked worried and said he'd sure be glad
to do all he could, but he'd already told the police and the
judge just what he'd seen and that hadn't helped Mrs.
Markland any.

" It's just possible," said Oliver, " that you didn't see what you thought you saw. That's a thing that can happen to any of us."

" You mean," said Ed, " that maybe I'd been drinking. Well, I had, but not enough to start seeing things."

" No," said Oliver, " I didn't mean exactly that."

" Then you mean it was all done by mirrors or something? "

" Well, not necessarily by mirrors. But it might be that you were the victim of some sort of delusion."

" Me, at my age? They won't like that when they hear about it back at camp." Ed grinned. " Well, what do we do next? Visit the scene of the crime? "

" That was the idea," said Oliver.

Ed sighed. " Just between you and me, professor," he said, " I'm getting kinda tired of that district."

CHAPTER SEVEN

IT WAS at about half-past three on an afternoon dark with fog that Oliver, Alice and Ed reached the house near Parliament Hill Fields. They had not warned Cecily of their coming, and Alice wondered what sort of reception she would give them. On the way she had attempted to describe Cecily to Oliver, trying to make him realise that she was a person who required delicate handling, but he had not seemed to pay much attention. In the trolley-bus Alice had tried to guess what idea Oliver could possibly have in his head, if, in fact, he really had any idea and was not simply beating the air. What could he think that Ed Larg might have seen on the stairs if he had not seen Janet?

The more she thought about it, the more Alice began to suspect that Oliver was only playing a trick on her. For of course it had been Janet Markland on the stairs: she was not going to let Oliver take her in with his talk of delusions. She was sure he was as convinced as she was that it had been Janet whom Ed Larg had seen. When they arrived at the house, when they reconstructed the scene on the stairs, he would simply prove to her that no other theory was tenable. And that was what it was all for, she decided; Oliver was determined to make her stop troubling about the case.

When Cecily opened the door she stared at them in blank surprise. But then Alice recognised thankfully that Cecily was in one of her good moods, for almost immediately she smiled and invited them quite warmly to come in. She was wearing a charming dress of coral-red wool and her grey hair was smartly set. Her cheerfulness gave her the life and beauty that her attacks of ill-humour so often ravaged from her.

Looking Oliver up and down, she said with a little odd laugh: "So you're Alice's husband." Then she turned to Ed Larg and with a lift of her eyebrows, said: "Oh, it's you again. You always bring trouble, don't you?" But she said it as if it amused her, and when Ed responded with his pleasant grin, she added: "Come in—I seem unintentionally to be giving a party this afternoon. Lucky I thought of tidying up yesterday; that always makes me feel like seeing people, just while the first splendour lasts." And she led them into her sitting-room.

The room was at its most attractive. The applewood furniture glowed softly from a good polishing, there was a bright fire, and there was a big jar of catkins standing on a low table. With the fog pressing against the windows it would have been dark but for the light from two reading-lamps.

In a corner of the couch, smiling up at the new guests with scarlet lips and great, shining, blue eyes, sat Kitty Roper. Cecily gestured at her, saying with another of her odd laughs: "Kitty's discovered lately that old friendship's a wonderful thing."

"Of course it is, love," said Kitty comfortably. "It feels so safe, somehow, talking to someone you've known all your life. You know it simply doesn't matter what you say, it's never frightful enough to make them think you're any worse than the awful creature they've always thought you."

Cecily made a face. "Old friends, at any rate, have their uses," she said sardonically.

"Uses?" said Kitty.

Cecily gave a guffaw. "What a bloody fool the woman is! You don't really think do you, Kitty, I don't know why you've suddenly taken to coming here so often lately? But it's all right, I don't mind being your alibi if you want one— I won't give you away."

Kitty raised her plump shoulders and let them drop again in a gesture of helplessness. "You're such a funny old thing. You always get such odd ideas in your head. Don't you think so, Mrs. Church? Have you ever known anyone go around with such an extraordinary collection of absolutely unrealistic ideas about other people in her head as our poor old Cecily?" She swung her smile round to Oliver, her warm, kind, inviting smile. "I wonder, Mrs. Church," she observed, "if you've brought your husband along because the trouble and mystery are over—or because they *aren't* over."

" Mystery? " said Cecily. " What mystery? There hasn't been any mystery."

She strolled away to the other end of the room and sat down before her embroidery-frame. There was a piece of coarse canvas stretched in it, which she was embroidering with an intricate design in white silk. She had switched on the bluish daylight-bulb above her work, so that it stood out like something rare and exquisite in an illuminated showcase.

As she stabbed at the canvas with her needle and pulled it through, the silk made a rasping sound against the canvas. " Make yourselves comfortable, everybody," she said, " I'm not going to look after you."

As they found seats around the fire it seemed to Alice that Oliver moved a little faster than was necessary to obtain the place on the couch next to Kitty.

" As a matter of fact, Mrs. Roper," he said, " my wife has a curious idea about what Sergeant Larg really saw on the staircase here, and she's brought us both along to make a demonstration. But I'm afraid Miss Lightwood may be annoyed with us. She must have suffered more than enough already over what's happened here. So I've been trying to persuade Alice to drop the idea. But no doubt you know what it's like, trying to make her drop any idea she's got hold of." He smiled at Kitty with a look which made Alice, who had been married to him for seventeen years, stared at him in astonishment.

Kitty did not fail to smile back. " Well, well," she said, " so we're still detecting, are we?"

" Detecting? " said Cecily sharply. " I don't know what you're talking about. The whole horrible thing's finished with, isn't it? For the Lord's sake, let's keep off the subject for once. Murder isn't the only thing that's ever happened to us." She sounded irritable but less explosive than usual, and there was pathos in the way she added: " I'm in such a good mood to-day—please, please don't spoil it. Alice, come and tell me what you think of this design. It's something rather new for me, I'm not sure what I feel about it. Yesterday I was all excited about it, but to-day. . . ." She drew back a little from the embroidery-frame and cocked her head on one side, frowning uncertainly at her work.

As Alice crossed the room she heard Kitty telling Oliver that she had heard he was a very, very gifted man. To Alice's intense annoyance, he disclaimed it in a boyish, bashful voice and then asked from whom she had heard it. Alice noticed Ed's quick little grin. She felt so angry that as she looked over Cecily's shoulder, she glowered at the embroidery as if it were hideous.

Cecily saw the look and exclaimed: " You don't like it! " Driving the needle viciously into the canvas, she left it sticking there. " Nor do I! I know it now, I don't like it at all! I haven't really liked it all along, I've been kidding myself. The thing's horrible, it's crude, it's obvious——"

" But it's lovely! " Alice said sincerely. " It's really beautiful. I don't know why on earth you should feel doubtful. I like it as much as anything of yours I've ever seen."

" Really? " said Cecily. " Please don't say that just to please me. I value your opinion a great deal, so you must say what you really think."

" But really! "

Kitty was saying to Oliver: " I know it's silly of me, but d'you know, tucked away inside me I've always had a longing to study science? I couldn't, of course; I'm not nearly clever enough. Yet it's always been a sort of dream of mine. I always think it must be so wonderful to have all that knowledge and power. The *power*—just think of it! You're really the most powerful people in the world, aren't you? "

" Well—well, really I don't know," said Oliver, still sounding bashful. " We're quite humdrum people, you know. Most of us are very dull and prosy and very ill-informed about everything outside our own line of work."

" That simply can't be true! " said Kitty.

Alice heard a soft little chuckle from Cecily. " Never misses an opportunity, does she? " She gestured at a chair near her. " Sit down, Alice. You're really sure you like this? You don't think I ought to unpick it? " Reaching for the needle again, she went on: " Now tell me, what *is* all this about detecting, and what's the real reason you all came here this afternoon? Is there something behind it, or is Kitty just fooling? What a woman she is, isn't she? D'you know, she drops in here once or twice every week? And she always arranges that her husband should ring her up while she's here; apparently she's made him believe that I'm on the edge of a mental collapse and that her visits are the only thing that are saving me from an asylum. Then as soon as he's rung up she dashes off to meet Frank, or perhaps it isn't Frank any more. Isn't she ridiculous? People like Kitty always think their lies deceive everybody; they even tell you about the lies they tell other people and still don't think you might start suspecting them yourself. Now, Alice, what *did* bring the three of you along? ''

Alice answered helplessly: '' I don't really know, Cecily. It's Oliver's idea. He knows I've been uneasy about the verdict all along, and I think he's come here to prove to me on the spot that it can't be wrong. I think that's what it must be.''

'' Oh,'' said Cecily thoughtfully, '' so you've been uneasy about the verdict, have you? '' She bent nearer to her work for a moment, so that the light from the bulb above it fell on her face. '' Why? ''

'' Oh, it's just that I've been talking to all the people who knew Janet fairly intimately, and none of them gives her the kind of character that seems to me to fit with a murderesss.''

'' You never came and questioned me about her,'' said Cecily softly.

'' You didn't want to be questioned,'' said Alice.

'' Didn't I? ''

'' You didn't seem to.''

'' But if I'd known what you were thinking. . . .'' Cecily paused. As she drove the needle into her work, the silk rasped harshly through the canvas again. '' Why didn't you come to me, Alice? Did you think I *wanted* Janet to be convicted? ''

'' I think . . .'' Alice began and hesitated.

'' Tell me, tell me,'' said Cecily in a low, fierce undertone. '' Tell me what you really think, Alice. Tell me the truth—

is that what you think about me, that I wanted Janet to be convicted? "

" I think the discovery that Janet had kept an important part of her life secret from you was really, for you, the most horrifying shock in the whole affair," said Alice, " and so— so I think your feelings about her had got so mixed up that you might not have been able to tell me anything useful."

" Ah," said Cecily. After a moment she laughed and reaching out a hand, laid it on Alice's shoulder. " Quite a clever thing, aren't you, Alice? In your quiet way, you know quite a lot about people. Yes, that was the worst part of it for me—worse than Rit's death, even. Not really a very admirable person, am I? I'm jealous and mean. Jealousy— that's a disgusting emotion, isn't it? Why shouldn't Janet have had her private life if she wanted it? I always had mine. I told her about it, of course, but then telling isn't everything; what one tells is generally half make-believe, so, after all, why tell it? But don't think I want Janet hanged, Alice. You shouldn't think that."

Standing up suddenly she planted herself in front of Kitty and Oliver.

" Well, Oliver," she said challengingly, " what about these parlour-games you want to play on the stairs? Suppose we get started now? Then when it's all over we can have tea." She looked animated and gay. Alice could not make out what mood was working up in her and felt apprehensive. " Come along," Cecily added. " The new people in the other flats will be thrilled to the marrow. They're always trying to get me to tell them the gruesome details." She swept out into the hall.

As the others followed her Alice noticed that Ed Larg seemed nervous; he appeared to be enjoying his part in the performance less and less. They went upstairs in silence until they reached the half-landing between the first-floor flat and the flat that had been Ritter's.

" Now," said Oliver, standing still, " if you don't mind, I'd just like to take a look round." But he did not look round. He stood there, staring straight up at the window.

To Alice the whole scene seemed extraordinarily changed.

Even though the daylight was darkened by fog, it was not the same as the lamplight and deep shadow which had been the setting for the crime. It surprised her to see how worn the red stair-carpet was and how cracked the paint on the stairs, also that the long window on the small half-landing, which she remembered as an oblong of dusty black-out curtain, had a hideous panel of stained glass down the middle. The wall-paper was faded and grim. The whole place had a shabby air, nondescript and rather dreary. She wondered what Aubrey Ritter had felt about it when he allowed himself to be rescued by Cecily from the beautiful flat where he had stayed on, alone and desperate, after his wife's death.

Oliver crossed to the window and saying vaguely: " Do you mind? " opened it and looked out.

There was a wide sill on which he knelt with one knee, leaning out so far that Kitty caught him by the arm, saying: " Oh, do be careful! "

" What d'you think you're going to find? " asked Cecily. " The scratches made by the murderer as he climbed up the drain-pipe, or his cigarette-stub in the gutter? "

Drawing his head in again, Oliver replied: " I'm told on the best authority, that's to say, it was a police analyst who told me, that cigarette-stubs are almost useless as evidence. With the exception of one brand—which it is I won't tell you, as it might be thought slanderous—the tobacco in them all is practically indestinguishable. Now, if you don't mind, Miss Lightwood, I'd rather like to draw this curtain and switch on the light, so as to recreate as nearly as possible the conditions under which Sergeant Larg saw Mrs. Markland."

" Go ahead," said Cecily.

Oliver pulled at the black-out curtain. It slid across easily enough, but to adjust it so that it shut out every chink of daylight was not so easy, for the window was very tall, reaching right up to the top-floor ceiling, and the curtain was on the scanty side.

Oliver appeared to take a good deal of interest in the curtain. He felt it between his fingers and frowned in a slightly puzzled way at the amount of light that came through the fabric.

" I take it," he said, " that you can't use a very strong light on this staircase, Miss Lightwood, otherwise it would show through the curtain."

" Say," said Ed Larg, " even if the light wasn't so good, I know I saw what I said I saw!" Coming from the shadows, his voice sounded as if the proceedings were getting on his nerves.

" Well, suppose we have the light now," said Oliver. " Then, Ed, if you don't mind, I'd like you to stand just where you were standing when the woman in black passed you. I'll be the woman in black and you can tell me just where to go and what to do."

While Ed went to stand in a corner of the half-landing, Cecily went downstairs to switch the light on. At the same time two little elderly ladies came out of the top floor flat and demanded excitedly what was going on. From then on the play had an audience. When Oliver went up to the top floor to impersonate the woman in black the two little women fell back in fright, as if he were in fact the murderer.

" Now," he called down to Ed, " which door did the woman in black come out of."

There was a pause while Ed looked around him.

At length he said unhappily : " I—I don't know. Somehow it all seems different now."

" You mean you don't remember which door Mrs. Markland came out of? " asked Oliver sharply.

" Oh, I know that—it was that one." Ed pointed at a door on the left. " But still it—it doesn't feel right, it all feels different."

" Excuse me," said one of the little old ladies, clearing her throat, " excuse me—but perhaps it's that paper shade round the bulb that's the trouble. I put it up myself after my sister and I moved in because the warden was always complaining about light showing from this landing-window. He was such a nuisance about it though I do think one ought to be careful about lights because you never know, do you? And it may not be the person who shows the light who has to suffer, it may be someone a mile away, and you'll find the shade's just put up with pins and it'll come down in a moment, only I'd be most grateful to you if you'd put it up again when you've finished, because I can't quite reach it without standing on a chair, and standing on a chair at my age, well. . . ." She broke off with a self-conscious little giggle.

" Thank you very much for the suggestion," said Oliver gravely. He said, " Thank you," again as Cecily reached up and removed the paper shade. " Now," he said to Ed, " how's that—any better? "

" Yes, that's better," said Ed gloomily, the improvement clearly giving him no pleasure. " There wasn't any shade that night, I remember that. But still, you know it's different. It's not just that it looks different, it kinda *feels* different."

" I wish you could tell us precisely what it is that seems different if it isn't just the light," said Oliver.

" Maybe it *is* just the light, I don't know," said Ed irritably. " But that night, well, I wasn't thinking of anything, I was just walking upstairs and I saw this woman, and she ran past me hiding her face, and I thought she'd been up visiting some guy and didn't want it known, and that was all I thought about it. And now it isn't like that at all, it's—it's just different." He wriggled his slender body uneasily. " Maybe that Scotch I had before I came was stronger than I thought it was," he suggested.

" Most improbable," said Oliver drily. " Well, let's go on, even if things do seem different. Just tell me what this woman did and where she went, then we'll leave it at that."

" Okay," said Ed, and proceeded to describe Janet's movements as he had described them to the police on the night of the murder.

Alice could not see that her husband's investigation was getting him anywhere, and more and more she felt inclined to believe that he himself had no expectation that it would. At last they went downstairs again and Cecily gave them tea.

Alice was not prepared for what happened after tea.

Kitty suddenly said she must rush to catch her train, and immediately, with a display of old-world courtesy most inappropriate to him, Oliver offered to accompany her to the station. Ed, he added casually, would no doubt be glad to see Alice home. Kitty appeared charmingly grateful and

Cecily was openly amused. Alice, with an effort, managed to say nothing.

She went on saying nothing for a considerable time and was still silent when presently she and Ed started walking along together towards the trolley-buses.

"Say," said Ed, "he *is* a professor, isn't he?"

"That," said Alice, tight-lipped, "is one of the words for him."

"And what do *you* think of him—a good kid, huh?"

That remark almost restored Alice's temper.

However, Ed went on: "I'm sorry, that was a very, very personal remark—I hope you didn't mind. Anyway, what's on the professor's mind? What's it all about? Why did he want me? A guy like that doesn't waste his time."

"I'm afraid I don't know any more about it than you do, Ed," said Alice. "I'm inclined to think he just wanted to prove to himself and to me that there couldn't be anything in my suspicions."

"So you've got some suspicions?"

"Well, I've got—worries."

"I see," he said. He thought for a minute or two. "You knew Mrs. Markland pretty well, I guess?" he continued.

"That evening was the first time I'd ever met her."

"Then what are you worrying about?"

"Oh, I don't know. Somehow she just doesn't seem the right sort of woman to be a murderess—yet perhaps, Ed, what I really mean is that I'm not the right sort of woman to have met somebody who's a murderess."

"Ah," he said, "I know what you mean. I get that feeling too. But somebody has to meet these people, don't they?"

"Of course."

"Somebody has to deliver the milk to them, and sell them newspapers, and have been at school with them, and worked in the office with them, and lived next door to them."

"Yes, I know."

"Say, did you ever think that someone must have taught that guy Himmler at school? Sometimes I think about that and it gets me kinda worried—you can't ever tell what's happening all round you. But it doesn't help to worry too much.

I reckon you've been worrying too much over all this, Mrs.
Church, and what you need is something to take your mind
off it. What d'you say to our going to see some show? Think
that'd do you good? "

Unhesitatingly Alice replied that she was sure it would do
her a great deal of good. They bought an evening paper and
studied the possibilities.

It was Ed who decided on something new and stupendous in
technicolour. It turned out to be one of those wonderful films
that have everything, songs, sentiment, villainy, shooting,
hard riding, deserts, drawing-rooms, drink, glowing golden
complexions and tender lips of the same dark, sticky red as
the trickles of blood oozing out of the stabbed breasts and
slit throats of minor characters dying in profusion. Ed, at
least, enjoyed it very much. In a whisper, he explained:
" Everywhere you go it's uniforms, uniforms, but when you
go to a movie you can just sit back and forget about them for
a while." He seemed even to enjoy the un-uniformed gentleman with gleaming oily curls who played the organ. He
played tunes from the last war while the light playing upon
him changed from heliotrope to gold, and from gold to azure,
and from azure to eau-de-nil. It was about ten o'clock when
Alice, still accompanied by Ed, reached home to find Oliver
sitting by the fire, drinking coffee and once more studying
sheets of foolscap.

He looked up only for an instant as they came in.

" There's one thing that sticks out a mile," he said, " but
I still don't see what it means."

Alice went for two more cups and poured out coffee for Ed
and herself.

" I'm so glad you enjoyed the tea-party anyway," she
said. " Kitty Roper's a charming person."

" That's right, she is," said Oliver. He laid down the sheet
of paper he had been holding. " I've been sitting here for
two hours trying to make sense of something," he said, " and
I just can't get it right. By the way,"—he looked up at Ed—
" you had a pleasant evening, I hope."

" Swell," said Ed politely.

" Good," said Oliver absently, thrusting his fingers through

his thinning hair. " It's that black-out curtain! There just
has to be something the matter with it! "

" Why? " asked Alice.

" Because the warden *said* there was something the matter
with it. It's that warden. . . ." He paused. " Listen, Alice,
every time you told me the story of what happened that evening
you mentioned the warden knocking and complaining about
the light, the light on the staircase. But you didn't seem to
attach any importance to it. Nor did anyone else. Yet really
it's a very curious occurrence. Why did a light show there that
night if it had never shown before? Why just that night?
It's the one completely unexplained fact in the whole thing.
I've kept thinking about it. I thought about it most of last
night, and then suddenly it struck me that although Cecily
Lightwood had been living in the house for some time, there
was no one in the middle flat and Ritter had only just moved
into the top one when he was killed. So it was possible, I
thought, that the black-out arrangements were new, the old
curtain or screen or whatever had been used having been
removed by the tenants who had left. If that was the explanation then there might not be any significance in the fact that
a light had shown. However, I examined that curtain to-day
and it's so thick with dirt that I should think it was put up
in nineteen-thirty-nine and hasn't been taken down since.
And that means that the fact that a light showed *is* significant,
is very significant."

" I never touched that curtain," Ed broke in defensively
before he could be questioned on the point. " I said so right
away when Miss Lightwood asked me—I told her I never
touched the curtain."

" Just so," said Oliver, nodding. " You never touched it.
Nobody touched it. Yet a light showed. A light showed where
no light had ever shown before. Something about the arrangement of that curtain was different from its arrangement every
night for about three years, and for that reason a light showed
while murder was being done. Why? I had one idea about it
straight away, rather an obvious one, but it didn't work out.
The top of the window was too high so it couldn't have been
done, besides it would presuppose a rather peculiar state of

mind in the murderer for which I should find myself quite
unable to account, and further——''

'' Suppose,'' Alice interrupted, '' you tell us what the idea
was before explaining any more about what was wrong with
it.''

'' Ah yes,'' said Oliver, '' just so. Well, the idea was that
until that night there had been two thicknesses of black-out
material instead of only one, and that that night one of them
had been taken down. It was an idea that had certain things
to recommend it. You see, we happened to be looking for a
woman dressed in black, or, just conceivably, wrapped in
something black which Ed might have mistaken for a black
dress. But nothing black had been found, no coat, no shawl,
nothing. So what about a black-out curtain? That would give
you, in one, an explanation of how Ed might have seen a
woman in black who was not Janet Markland, and of why a
light had shown where no light had shown before.''

'' Say,'' said Ed excitedly, '' that woman I saw had on a
black dress—a *dress*! That's what I told the cops and that's
what I saw. Maybe the light wasn't very good but it was good
enough for that. She wasn't wearing any black-out curtain,
she was wearing a dress, just an ordinary dress.''

'' And also,'' said Alice, '' what did she do with the curtain
afterwards? The police searched the whole place, and if
there'd been a loose piece of black material lying around,
they'd have found it.''

'' Didn't I tell you the idea was no good? '' said Oliver.
'' I'm simply telling you things in the order I thought of
them. Actually there are more things against that idea than
the ones you've pointed out. I didn't know yet when I thought
of it whether the curtain was a long one or a short one; in
fact the window's very high and the curtain's on hooks on a
runner, and isn't at all the sort of thing that could be snatched
down in a moment. Further, why should the woman think
of disguising herself only when she'd got as far up the stairs
as that? To disguise herself from Ritter? Hardly likely.
Because she'd heard Ed behind her? Not likely either; Ed
was only going up when she was coming down, so he can't
have been as close on her heels as that. The only possibility

is that she heard Janet Markland in the hall when she was
going out to telephone, and thought she was coming upstairs.
But I don't think it happened because of all the mechanical
objections to the idea. And yet. . . . And yet a light showed."

"Maybe the murderer disarranged the curtain for some
reason," Ed suggested.

"What reason?" asked Oliver.

"Maybe he—she—was nervous or something."

"Do you go around disarranging black-out curtains when
you're nervous?"

"N-no, I guess not."

"He probably doesn't go around murdering people either,"
said Alice.

Oliver gave a laugh. "Ed doesn't go around disarranging
black-out curtains when he's nervous, Ed is not a murderer,
therefore murderers do go around disarranging black-out
curtains when they're nervous. As logic I'm afraid it's rather
thin."

"Say," Ed interrupted with a new surge of excitement,
"maybe the murderer hid behind the curtain!"

"That," said Oliver, "is just what I was coming to."

It was about that time that Alice began to have the feeling
that Oliver's investigations might be leading to something, for
it was only then that she began to feel sure that he was working
seriously on the hypothesis that Janet Markland was innocent,
had told nothing but the truth at her trial, had never been
on the staircase, and that Ed Larg, an entirely disinterested
witness, must therefore have seen something quite different
from what he believed he had seen. As she grasped this, Alice
felt suddenly very moved. She sat back, sipping her coffee
and enjoying the sensation produced by her discovery.

"I think," Oliver went on, "we must be on the right lines
now. There has to be something the matter with that curtain,
and it seems to me that there almost certainly has to be someone mixed up in this murder who hasn't appeared in it yet.
The reason for that is that with the exception of Miss Lightwood, who happens to have been dressed in bright blue,
nobody who was known to be in the house could have answered
the telephone when Miss Lightwood rang Ritter up from

downstairs. I gather,"—he looked at Alice—" there's no doubt at all that somebody did answer? It couldn't have been Miss Lightwood conducting an imaginary conversation to provide herself with an alibi? "

" No," said Alice, " I could hear the buzz of a voice in the receiver. Besides, even if it had been fake, it wouldn't have given Cecily an alibi, rather the reverse, in fact, because she's the one person besides Janet who could have gone up later."

" Yes, yes, true," said Oliver. " Well then, that supports what I was saying. There must have been somebody in the house who wasn't known to be there, and that person, at some time during the evening, must have hidden behind the curtain on the staircase. That person may have been the murderer of Ritter or may merely have seen who the murderer was. She may have been hiding there to observe, rather than to act. But it must have been that person whom Ed saw come out of Ritter's flat and run past him down the stairs. She must have managed, as Mrs. Markland did, to get past the warden and policeman, who can't have been nearly as observant as they believed themselves to be, as is common enough with all of us, and got away. That, I think, must be a rough outline of the truth, even though there's a good deal that still needs fiilling in."

" You've still got to fill in who the person was," said Alice, " and why she did it."

" Naturally. And I think that if we investigate we may discover something of this sort. Aubrey Ritter, for whose character I admit I can't manage to feel much admiration, and whose plays I don't know anything about, because I always avoided going to see them out of some sort of prejudice——"

" He's got a prejudice against everything but Wild West films," Alice explained to Ed.

Oliver continued : " Ritter, I was saying, seems to have had the enviable knack of carrying on with a number of women without letting them get to suspect one another's existence, or anyway, their relationship with him. It isn't improbable that there were one or two who believed, when his wife died, that they were now going to be the centre of the picture.

But what actually happened? Ritter goes in for a minor nervous breakdown and then goes openly to live with Cecily Lightwood——''

'' Oliver! '' said Alice, astounded.

He raised his eyebrows at her. '' You know Miss Lightwood better than I do, so I'm ready to take your explanation of their relationship. But think how the set-up at Parliament Hill Fields would look to a woman suffering from jealousy.''

'' But—but—— '' Alice felt that there was something quite wrong somewhere. She looked at Ed, hoping that he could see the flaw in the argument. But he was nodding his head and looking deeply interested. '' But how could she—this woman—have known where Ritter was? '' Alice burst out. '' Nobody but Cecily knew where he'd gone to. Nobody but Cecily—— '' Then she pulled herself up. She noticed a quickening of her heartbeat. '' No,'' she said softly, '' that isn't quite true. Somebody else did know where Ritter was.''

Oliver asked sharply: '' Who? '' and grabbed at his notes as if he ought to be able to find the answer there.

'' Kitty Roper,'' said Alice.

'' Kitty? ''

'' Yes, Kitty. She came sailing into the room saying, ' Where's Rit? You promised me Rit! ' ''

'' You're sure of this? ''

'' Absolutely.''

'' It may be very important.'' Oliver ruffled through his notes. '' But unfortunately, Alice, Kitty Roper was in the room with the rest of you when Miss Lightwood did her telephoning.''

'' Yes, but—— ''

Alice's thoughts groped wildly with the problem. She felt there had to be an answer. She had to put her coffee-cup down, her hands were shaking so much. As she did so, the answer came to her.

'' But,'' she cried, '' *Dr. Roper has a black overcoat!* ''

There was a strangely long silence after that.

At length Oliver said quietly: '' Well, I'm inclined to think that between us we've put the whole thing together—or nearly the whole thing. Let's go over it from the start.'' He took

no notice of the beginnings of a burbling interruption from
Ed. " Kitty Roper and Ritter knew each other when they
were quite young. Presumably they had a love-affair, Kitty
having succeeded in taking him away from Janet Markland.
Then Kitty married and forgot about Ritter for a number of
years. Eventually they met by chance in Paris and the love-
affair started once more, and seems to have continued inter-
mittently until Ritter's death. When Ritter's wife died Kitty
may have thought that this was a good time for a divorce from
her husband, though I don't think on the whole that that's
very probable; if her husband had divorced her she'd have
lost her children, who appear to be the real passion of her life.
No, I imagine she intended things to go on as they were.
Hearing from Cecily that Ritter had moved into the new flat,
Kitty thought she would visit him and actually arrived at the
house much earlier than she admitted afterwards. Hence, of
course, Ritter's lateness at the party. What she didn't know
was that she'd roused her husband's suspicions and that he'd
also arrived at the house and hidden himself behind the
curtain on the staircase. From there he saw her come down,
then he went upstairs himself."
" And found Ritter dead? "
" I rather think not. Remember, Ritter wasn't actually
dead even when Ed found him. Yet if Dr. Roper went
upstairs as soon as Kitty left, and if he didn't leave until just
before Ed's arrival, he must have spent quite a time in Ritter's
flat. Kitty, after all, had to go downstairs and out into the
street, then turn up on the doorstep and ring and be admitted
by Cecily, and from your account she'd been at the party some
time before you heard Ed shouting: ' Murder! ' So Dr.
Roper would have taken a grave and very strange risk if he'd
remained in the flat all that time with Ritter dying in front
of his eyes. No, I think that when Dr. Roper came out of
his hiding-place and went upstairs, he found Ritter very much
alive and quite pleased with himself. It was Dr. Roper who
did the murder. I'm beginning to feel it's stared us in the
face from the start. Who, after all, had a better motive? "
" And the poker with Janet's fingerprints?"
" As you suggested yourself, the fingerprints were probably

old ones. Roper may have been wearing gloves and used the poker, though in that case I should think there'd be signs of smudging, or he may have used some other weapon which he took away with him, throwing the poker down on the floor to make it look as if it were the weapon that had been used. I dare say the real weapon was a hammer. There were packing-cases about, weren't there? If so, there was probably a hammer.''

'' But say,''—Ed Larg bounced forward in his chair again, staring at Oliver in consternation—'' but say, this woman I saw—this woman in black——''

'' Was, I'm afraid, Dr. Roper,'' said Oliver.

'' Now wait—now wait a minute, will you! '' Ed exploded. '' Wait till I tell you something! I may be pretty young to begin with, and maybe I don't look my age at that, and maybe I seem to you pretty dumb, but still I'm not so young and so dumb I don't know the facts of life—and I *can* tell a man from a woman! ''

Alice took his cup away from him and filled it again. She said nothing for a moment, trying to visualise Dr. Roper in his neat, double-breasted black overcoat, with his watchful, suspicious eyes on his wife.

'' He's a smallish man, you know, Ed,'' she said as she returned Ed his cup, '' and he's quite slight, and his hair's brown——''

'' Listen,'' said Ed, '' it was a woman I saw. She was— she had—hell, she was the *shape* of a woman! ''

'' You'd swear to that? '' asked Oliver, watching him curiously.

'' Sure I'd swear to it!''

'' Even remembering how bad the light was? ''

'' It was a woman.''

Oliver gave a sigh. '' Well, that's that, then. It was a nice theory while it lasted.''

Later, when she thought it over, Alice was a little puzzled at the readiness with which Oliver had abandoned the theory. His own theories were usually very precious to him; he prized them and defended them with what could be very exasperating tenacity. When they were going to bed that evening she asked him why he had given up this particular one with so little of a struggle.

" Because," he replied, " it was a rotten one."

" But I thought you were pleased with it," said Alice.

" So I was, just at first."

" It seemed to me pretty promising," she said. " Think how many doctors have been murderers. Dr. Crippen, Dr. Ruxton, Dr. Palmer. . . . What was the matter with it? "

" Something quite obvious—the curtain."

" But the whole thing was built on the curtain."

" And that's why the whole thing collapsed as soon as I saw that something had gone wrong with the curtain."

" But what went wrong? "

Oliver sat down on the edge of the bed, yawning. " Didn't the two old women, the new tenants, have to put a shade up over the lamp because the warden was always complaining of light showing from that window? So whatever had gone wrong with the curtain on the night of the murder had stayed wrong with it, hadn't it? And that wouldn't have happened simply through someone hiding behind the curtain, would it? No, we've not got it yet, Alice. The curtain's the clue, but we haven't got what it means yet. We'll have to go on thinking."

Unfortunately for herself, Alice found that she had to go on thinking most of the night. She could not stop it. But it was a useless kind of thinking. The thoughts and images pursued her into drowsiness; too sleepy to deal with them, order them, make sense of them, she had to let them flicker across her mind like a disturbing, meaningless cinema show. She often suffered from these half-waking, half-sleeping dreams when she was worried. The show was always in technicolour, the greens, the violets, the sunset hues, the magenta shadows having a lurid unreality which seemed to possess some meaning of its own. Sometimes it seemed very important to discover the sense of the kaleidoscope.

That night the story of Janet Markland was all confused in her mind with the film she had seen with Ed Larg. Across a background of wild improbability and hectic colouring moved Janet's slender figure, always in black. The black, of course, meant death; that was easy. But those brilliant, transparent hues behind and around her, what ought they to have conveyed? Through it all Alice had an aching sense of strain and urgency. What did it mean, for instance, when Janet Markland, playing " Three Blind Mice " on the cinema-organ, rose suddenly, turned and bowed, her face a deathly pale green in the light playing upon her, then went silently away, mounting a long, steep staircase and disappearing into a blood-red cloud? Why a blood-red cloud? Suddenly Alice realised that she had been asleep, for now she had certainly just been awakened by Oliver gripping her shoulder and hissing excitedly into her ear: " The Browns! Alice, wake up —we've got to get hold of the Browns! "

" Who on earth are the Browns? " asked Alice sleepily.

" Those friends of Ed's. We've got to get in touch with them first thing to-mororw."

" Their name's Smith."

" Smith, Brown, we've got to find them."

" Good heavens, why? "

" It's too complicated to explain now, but I've got it."

" Got what? "

" The explanation."

" What explanation? "

Oliver gave a grunt. " All right, go back to sleep again, it'll keep till morning."

" But what'll keep? "

" The truth, Alice dear. The truth will nearly always keep. But just tell me one thing. . . ."

" I can't see what the Smiths have got to do with the truth."

Oliver chuckled softly. " No, all right. But just tell me this, was there a light missing anywhere? "

" Why a light? "

" Oh, Lord. . . . A light, Alice, on the night of the murder, in that house at Parliament Hill Fields. Was there a light missing from any passage or room? "

" I don't think so." Then she remembered. " Yes, there was. There wasn't any light in the bathroom. I had a bath in there by the light of my electric torch next morning."

" Good, then that's everything. I've got it all."

" Got what? "

" Go back to sleep," said Oliver again. " Just don't worry and go back to sleep." Alice heard him chuckle once more. " But how simple," he was muttering to himself as he rolled over, " how incredibly simple."

By the time that Alice had properly grasped that Oliver had just been telling her that he had solved the problem of the murder, he himself was sound asleep.

But every trace of drowsiness was now cleared from Alice's mind. She lay there wide awake, wondering and waiting for the morning. A light, she kept thinking, a light missing from the bathroom, what had that to do with it? A light missing, and a curtain showing a light that had never been there before, and Janet mounting a staircase she had never been on and disappearing into a blood-red cloud. . . .

A blood-red cloud! No, it was not drowsiness this time. Suddenly Alice had seen it too. Suddenly she knew the answer to the whole problem, and Oliver was right, it was simple, incredibly simple. And the Smiths, of course, would be able to corroborate it.

But then came the question, what to do about it, and that was not so simple.

By about seven o'clock Alice could not bear lying in bed any longer and got up, dressed and made some coffee. She had not consciously decided what she was going to do, and yet she knew ... she had a sense of complete uncertainty and yet at the same time felt no hesitation whatever as to what her next action should be, whether it was putting the kettle to boil, or putting on her coat, or going softly to the telephone. But still, as she left the house, walked along the street, waited for the trolley-bus, she went on torturing herself because she could not decide what she ought to do, what she ought to say. It was only later, when she was standing at the door of the house near Parliament Hill Fields, ringing Cecily's bell, that she recognised that all this indecision was a piece of self-deception and that at the point when she had lifted the telephone and had spoken into it to Cecily, the only decision of any importance had already been made.

Cecily came to the door so quickly that Alice knew she must

have been waiting for her impatiently. Saying nothing, but gripping Alice by the arm, she hustled her into the sitting-room. Though the morning darkness had almost gone, the curtains were still drawn. A new fire was burning with noisy cracklings in the fireplace. Cecily was wearing her green velvet dressing-gown with the long panels of embroidery which Alice remembered having admired on the morning after the murder. Her grey hair was carefully dressed and her face had a more elaborate make-up than usual. She seemed tense, yet had a slight, sardonic smile on her lips, and in her restlessness and suppressed excitement looked at her most vivid, elegant and arresting.

Going to the fireplace, still saying nothing, she leant one elbow on the mantelpiece and looked down into the fire. The sight gave Alice a curious shock; for an instant the pose was almost the same as that which Janet Markland had been holding at the moment when Alice had entered this room for the first time. But then Cecily turned. Still leaning on one elbow, she gestured carelessly at a chair, then groped unseeingly for a cigarette and matches.

" The war," she said suddenly, " d'you know, I keep thinking about the war this morning, and when it'll end, and how it'll all turn out afterwards. I've often thought when I've heard of a person dying recently : ' But then they'll never know how it's all going to turn out! ' And I've felt that that was something that simply couldn't be allowed because it was too unfair. I mean ordinary people who just die; for some reason I don't feel like that about the ones who are killed fighting or in air-raids. Their deaths have something to do with what's going on, they're part of the pattern of things. But when people like you or me die—people who really, when all's said, are living almost their normal lives except for a bit of extra anxiety and strain and monotony—I feel it's awfully unfair that they should never know what's going to happen. It's—it's something horribly hard to leave behind, that hope of knowing about the peace. You probably don't know what I'm talking about."

" Cecily——" Alice began.

Cecily's forehead contracted, as if she could not bear being interrupted. " The war's never been anything like I thought it was going to be," she went on rapidly. " I used to think about it a lot before it came. I was terrified of it, I thought it would be unbearable, literally unbearable. I couldn't imagine how anyone could sit through such a thing as an air-raid. Of course I knew it was coming sometime or other, as we all did, though inside me I always had the feeling that really and truly it couldn't—so when it did come I felt a fool, and that made me feel very angry. I never feel the right things, you know; I've always known that if people knew what I really felt about anything, they'd all hate and despise me. For instance, there was a time when I *wanted* the war to come—can you believe that? I don't mean for respectable reasons, like it's being better then than later, or feeling a duty to put an end to dictatorship or anything like that, but simply because I *wanted* it—I wanted a cataclysm, I wanted a disaster so enormous and overpowering and impersonal that my own personal feelings and troubles and problems and miseries would disappear in all the crashing and banging! They don't, of course—so I was a fool there too, wasn't I? Things get worse, they get much worse, because conditions are more difficult. They get so much worse that they get utterly unbearable and things like air-raids turn out to be quite easy to stand. I'm supposed to have a very good nerve in air-raids, you know—in fact, to tell you something more that'll make you despise me, they rather excite me, exhilarate me. . . . Isn't that horrible? Isn't it disgusting? I don't know why I'm trying to tell you all this, now of all times; I suppose it's just my damned habit again of doing everything all wrong, *feeling* everything all wrong. . . . Here, you said you liked this——" With an abrupt gesture she picked up the piece of embroidery at which Alice had seen her working the day before and tossed it into Alice's lap. " If you do really like it, keep it. In case you've got doubts about accepting it in the circumstances, you can think of it as a sensational souvenir. Everyone's allowed to take souvenirs from the enemy. But if you don't like it,"—she advanced a threatening step towards Alice—" burn it, d'you hear? Put the damn thing in the fire.

And you *don't* really like it, do you? You don't, I can see it—here, give it back to me! ''

If Alice had not held on tightly to the piece of embroidery, Cecily would have snatched it away from her and thrown it on to the fire. Smoothing it out over her knee, Alice said. low-voiced: '' It's beautiful, Cecily—it's really beautiful. I'm very glad to have it.''

Cecily laughed contemptuously. '' You'd better burn it. You will when I'm not there.''

'' I certainly shan't.''

'' You'd better. You won't want to be reminded of me.''

'' Cecily, I——'' The words caught as Alice looked up into Cecily's lined yet curiously youthful face, the face of someone who had aged through the deepest unhappiness and inner conflict yet never achieved the normal process of growing up. '' Cecily, I came this morning to say——''

'' Don't, don't, don't say anything! '' She turned away, putting both elbows on the mantelpiece and her head between her hands. '' Suppose we say that you came to ask me all that I know about Janet, as you've been asking all the others —Peter and Roger and Kitty and Frank. You asked all of them and you never asked me. You avoided asking me on purpose, didn't you, Alice? You must have known that I could have told you far more than anyone else, but you avoided asking me. . . .'' She gave a deep sigh, then turned once more and faced the room. '' I'll tell you about Janet,'' she said, '' I'll tell you everything about her.''

This time, when she paused, Alice did not try to speak. Leaning back in her chair, with the square of embroidery spread out over her knee, she waited for Cecily to go in.

'' I've loved Janet all my life,'' Cecily began. '' She always seemed to me everything I wasn't. She was reasonable and reliable and sensible and self-controlled, and very honest too, at least I thought so. I see now she wasn't, can't have been. Those reserved people, perhaps they never are, except superficially. I mean, I see now she never let anyone know what she was thinking or feeling. But the way she acted always seemed so simple and straightforward that one took for granted her feelings corresponded. And that wasn't so. At

school she was always down on me because I had crushes on
the mistresses, and I used to think even then that there was
something really wonderful about the way she never cared
very much for anybody. Somehow it made her seem so strong.
She was rather stern too, and I used to feel that was very good
for me. At home I always had everything I wanted—we were
fearfully rich in those days, and my mother was an emotional,
excitable creature with a passion or clothes and for me and
for men and for luxury—I always rather despised her, and the
touch of austerity there always was about Janet seemed to me
marvellous. I loved it when she scolded me. I loved it when
she told me I was a fool, and when she sort of pursed her lips
at me when she found out I was using lipstick. I used
only to put it on and rub it off again and feel fearfully wicked,
and the best part of the feeling wicked was the knowing that
Janet was going to tell me she didn't like it, because that
meant we could have a scene and I could end up by telling
her that she was absolutely right and that I was a miserable
worm. . . . Hell, I didn't mean to go into all that, I just meant
to tell you about her and Rit.'' She paused, then noticed
that Alice was glancing about the room. `` What is it? '' she
asked sharply. `` What are you looking for? ''

`` A clock,'' said Alice. `` I was wondering about the time.
You see, Cecily, really I want to warn you——''

`` It doesn't matter, it doesn't matter what the time is! ''
said Cecily. `` I've attended to everything. But it takes a bit
of time, you know. . . . Let me go on telling you about Janet
and Rit. I want to tell you all about it while I can. You
know we were all at college together, of course—that's to say,
I was at the Slade and the other two were doing English
literature at University College. I wanted to be a portrait-
painter in those days, and I could have been, I should have
been if I hadn't had to start making money almost at once.
I'd quarrelled with my family, you see—my mother and my
stepfather. I don't mean they wouldn't have given me the
money if I'd asked for it; they would have; my stepfather was
always humiliatingly generous to me—it was loathsome. He
seemed to think he could buy my affection like that. So I'd
told him what I thought of him and cleared out, and that

meant, you see, that I had to start earning money straight
away, and so I started doing things for women's magazines
and so on, and got on to embroidery designs for them, and
then for my own amusement started working some of the
designs myself. . . . But I'm wandering again. Janet and
Rit—that's what I'm talking about, isn't it? That's what you
want to know about.''

She moved away from the fireplace and with her head bent
and her arms folded, started walking up and down the room.

'' You must have been told so much about Janet and Rit
by now,'' she said, '' but I wonder if you've ever stopped to
think about Rit and me, Alice. D'you know that in those
early days I always took for granted that Rit was in love with
me. It just didn't occur to me that anyone could fall in
love with Janet while I was around. Men fell in love with
me quite often, and never seemed to take much notice of
Janet. I used to be furious with them because they didn't
appreciate her; I used to tell them so, and try to explain her
to them. I used to explain her to Rit, and Rit always agreed
about what an unusual person she was and how much he liked
her, but that was all. It was me he seemed to be in love with
—until Kitty turned up. Kitty changed everything, because
until then we'd all been quite innocent, you see, but Kitty was
a natural little whore, and she just stuck her claws into Rit
and seduced him. And that changed everything. Suddenly
Janet went and married Ian Markland, and Rit came to me
and wept, actually wept about it, and said what a fool he'd
been and now he'd lost her. And I . . .'' The flow of words
stopped though Cecily did not pause in her quick pacing
up and down the room. '' I remember,'' she went on, '' I
remember looking for a long time at a poker lying in the hearth
and thinking how easy it would be while he sat there with his
head in his hands to bring it down on the back of his head.
There wasn't any emotion in the way I thought it, it was just
a sort of picture in front of my eyes, something removed from
me with no particular meaning in it. But I always remembered
it, as one does remember a lot of queer things that don't seem
to mean anything, just as a picture, a rather flat sort of picture.
Anyway, I didn't see Rit or Janet for a long time after that

because I got ill just about then and had to go home to be looked after. When I next saw Rit it was years later and he had Rosamund with him."

At that point the pacing stopped abruptly and she returned to the fireplace.

" I liked Rosamund," she said. " I admired her and I always tried to do what I could for her, and I didn't think I cared about Rit any more. I wasn't the innocent then that I'd been before, and I'd come to the conclusion that I didn't really care for men a great deal. Not that I was sensible about it. I was always getting myself in a mess with them. And that's another thing that I used to admire about Janet— after the rotten business with Markland she took hold of her life so competently and kept herself clear of emotional entanglement. That's something I've always envied more than anything else, being able to keep all that emotional nonsense out of one's life. I've always tried to do it and never succeeded. Anyway, I became great friends with Rosamund, and that meant I saw a lot of Rit, and he took to telling me about his difficulties with her and asking for my advice—and taking it too. He used to see a lot of Janet, of course; I knew that. But he always said what a queer, cold creature she was, and that she always had the effect on him of making him feel that his collar must be dirty. He never made love to me —he knew I'd have been loyal to Rosamund—but after a bit, well, I could feel it there, you know. One always feels these things. At least. . . ." She hesitated and a look of confusion and desperation appeared on her face. " I thought—I thought I felt it! I always thought one always felt these things. . . . And Rit used to tell me how Janet didn't really understand his difficulties and how she was too narrow and hard and unfeeling to understand what he was going through, and I used to tell him that he was all wrong and that Janet was the gentlest and most considerate person in the world but that she just wasn't demonstrative like other people. I always believed that except—except once. There was a terrible time when Rosamund thought she was going to have a baby; it was all moonshine, but she believed it and dashed around telling everyone. Well, you can imagine what that would have meant to Rit; it would have been the last straw, it would absolutely have finished him. I simply couldn't bear the thought. I've always loathed children, anyway. So I was absolutely frank with him, I told him exactly what I felt about it. I told him he'd have to make Rosamund have an abortion, it was the only thing for him. But then Janet—I've never been as disappointed in her as I was then—Janet went all moral and indignant at the idea of an abortion; she simply refused to see that someone like Rit wasn't made for domestic ties and that Rosamund was already too much for him. She got as angry as I've ever seen her and we had a real quarrel. I'd never have believed that she'd be as commonplace and conventional about it as she was. Anyway, there wasn't any child, luckily. And then Rosamund committed suicide. . . ."

A long silence followed.

It had seemed to Alice during the last few minutes that Cecily's voice had been altering. Many of the words had slurred into one another and there had been a sound of intolerable heaviness in them. Cecily turned now and dropped into a chair. Alice thought for an instant that she saw a look of terror on her face, but as Cecily closed her eyes the look changed to one of mere exhaustion.

After a moment she opened her eyes again and fixed them with a painful effort on Alice's face.

" Actually you know all the rest, I suppose," she said, " how Rit nearly went out of his mind and wouldn't see anybody and how I was the only one with enough strength of mind to force my way past all that and make him pack up and come here. If he'd been left any longer to himself I don't know what would have happened—something terrible. Anyway, I got him here, and when I saw how he simply sat all day with his head in his hands, I decided to give that party for him. He didn't want to come to it at first, but then he promised he would. He never asked who was coming and I didn't tell him because I wanted to surprise him with Kitty; I thought she'd do him good. And then, you remember, he didn't come down. So I rang him up and he told me he'd decided not to come down, he couldn't face it. And that made me furious, *furious*, after all I'd done for him! But I couldn't show it because that would have made me look a fool in front of you all, so I told you all he'd said he was coming, and I made up my mind that I'd make him come down whether he wanted to or not, and I went out to the kitchen and then I went straight upstairs. He was simply sitting there as usual with his head in his hands. I started to tell him what I thought of him—and then the telephone rang. Of course, that was Janet.''

The words were more slurred than ever now and it seemed to be with increasing difficulty that she kept her mind on what she was trying to say. Her face, in spite of the make-up, had a greyish tinge, her breathing was growing laboured.

'' Janet,'' she repeated hoarsely, '' it was Janet—he said Janet, so I knew who it was. And she was telling him not to come to the party because she didn't want to see him, because she'd made up her mind to marry Roger and didn't want Rit spoiling it any more. He told me what she'd said. I couldn't understand it. I couldn't understand why Janet should care whether or not he came to the party, but—but I was still furious with him for being like that after all I'd done for him— I'd done *everything* for him! He sat down and started to weep. I couldn't understand, but I picked up the poker—no, it wasn't the poker, it was a jemmy, a case-opener thing, that was lying there on the packing case, but it felt as if it ought to have been a poker, so afterwards I hit him again with the poker and threw it down beside him and took the jemmy away with me. The American boy didn't see it when I passed him, and I ran straight into the empty flat and hid it in a gutter outside one of the windows. The police didn't find it because they didn't look for it; they thought of course it was the poker that had been used. Of course I didn't think of Janet's fingerprints being on it. I wrapped my hand up so that my own shouldn't be on it, but I didn't know about Janet's. I wasn't thinking of Janet either when I changed the light——''

Alice rose quickly and went to her.

Her head had suddenly sunk forward on her chest and her breath was coming with a loud, rasping sound through her open mouth. '' It's all right, Cecily,'' Alice said softly, laying a hand on her shoulder. " It was the red light you changed, wasn't it? " But she was not sure if Cecily heard her. " What have you taken, Cecily?" she asked her urgently.

" Sleeping pills," Cecily muttered thickly. " Whole bottle —should do the trick. Thank you for the warning, Alice. You're a little like Janet yourself, you know—like she might have been—if everything had been different from the beginning. That's why you understood—knew it couldn't have been her—all along. I wouldn't have let her hang, you know. I liked her to suffer—it seemed right—somehow—but I wouldn't have let her hang. But I still don't understand how you knew about the red light. Of course there always used to be a red light on the landing, and the red light made my dress look black and my hair look brown. And when I passed the American boy I realised he'd think—he'd think it was a black dress and brown hair. I think a lot about colours, you know—some people mightn't have thought of it, but it's my job, so naturally I thought of it. And I realised that if I could change the bulbs it'd all look different. He kept saying it all looked different, didn't he? So it did, all the colours were different, you see. So I risked changing the lights—I took the bulb from the bathroom, and hid the red one, and I was in time, he didn't come out until after I'd finished. But the bathroom bulb was much stronger than the other one, of course, so it showed through the curtain, and the warden came bothering. I hadn't thought of that, but nobody seemed to notice. So there you are Alice—now you know the whole thing. Now you know all about Janet Markland, don't you? . . . All about her. . . ."

Those were the last words that Cecily spoke, though she did not die until about four hours later.

THE END